SOLIS

L.B. Dunbar writing as

elda lore

SOLIS
elda lore
L.B. Dunbar writing as

All rights reserved. No part of this book may be reproduced or transmitted without written permission from the publisher, except in the case of a reviewer, who may quote brief passages embodied in critical articles or in a review.

This is a work of fiction. Names, characters, businesses, places, events and incidents are either the products of the author's imagination or used in a fictitious manner. Any resemblance to actual persons, living or dead, or actual events is purely coincidental.

© 2017 Laura M. Dunbar

Cover Design – Amy Queau, QDesigns
Edit – Kiezha Ferrell, Librum Artis Editorial Services

Other Work by elda lore

Hades: Modern Descendants
Solis: Modern Descendants 2
Heph: Modern Descendants 3 (2017)
Triton: Modern Descendants 4 (2017)

See the descending sun,
Scatt'ring his beams about him as he sinks,
And gilding heaven above, and seas beneath,
With paint no mortal pencil can express.
- G. M. Hopkins

VEVA

"It's so hot."

"*He's* hot." My best friend's voice dragged as her eyes focused on the opposite side of the pool. Persephone Fields may have a broken heart, but her eyes still worked, and I lowered my sunglasses down the bridge of my nose to take in the view.

"Mm…mmm…mm…" I muttered, observing the Greek god of a man lounging in the lifeguard chair. Blond, chin-length hair and tan, washboard abs dressed him along with a bright orange swimsuit. An impressive radiating sun tattoo covered his shoulder.

"Veva, I think he's looking at you," Persephone teased, and I instantly covered my eyes. Slouched in the seat, all six feet plus of casualness, he had player written all over him, and I wasn't interested. I did the playing, and I'd recently been burned. I scanned the pool area to make it appear as if I looked for someone.

Zeke Cronus owned a sprawling estate in the heart of California's Central Valley, a place hotter than hell and still as a statue. As an olive grower, his company, Olympic Olive Oil, made him billions, and the wealth of his estate proved it. The Olympic-size pool filled a large portion of his immediate backyard. The striking tile and extreme length reminded me of a Roman bath I'd read about in World History 101. The water was the bluest blue I'd ever seen and the temperature was a slice of heaven compared to the heat.

More resort feeling than private home, Zeke had many visitors. He wasn't officially my uncle, but he was practically family, the best friend to my mother, Hera, and Persephone's mother, Demi. *His queens,* he called us ladies back in Nebraska, but secretly, or not so secretly, Zeke had a plethora of women, and a multitude of children to prove it. It was the one reason Zeke and my mother never hooked up. As a child, I made up stories that Zeke was my father, but the sibling-like friendship between Zeke and my mother just made the thought creepy.

My head rotated back in the direction of the lifeguard stand. Ostentatious, the pool was so large it needed a lifeguard. My eyes roamed upward, and despite the shield of my aviators, I was pinned. His gaze froze mine and I shivered in spite of the over one-hundred-degree heat. Quickly turning away, I heard Persephone laugh beside me in her lounge chair.

"Don't make it so obvious," she teased. "Be subtle."

Subtle was something I'd never done. While my fun-loving friend had simmered a little after losing her boyfriend Harris Black, she was the epitome of cool. Blonde hair, deep brown eyes, lanky and lean— her appearance would inspire poetry. I, on the other hand, was a hothead. My dull brown hair and curvy figure forced me to have an attitude. *Lively*, Persephone called me. *Short-tempered*, my mother corrected. My mother spoke closer to the truth. In anger, I got the vibrant tattoo that wrapped around my thigh and down to my ankle. Varying shades of blue and rich, thick versions of green nearly covered one leg, decorating it with the glorious bird.

My body was a temple, and I was willing to share, as long as I got satisfaction from those who worshipped at it. That lifeguard looked like a player, and while I knew how to play, I wasn't tempted. *Men like him only know how to break hearts*, my mother would warn. She hated men.

"You're staring, again," Persephone laughed while she leaned back and soaked up the blistering Californian sun.

"I am not," I snipped. Her head rolled in my direction and I snapped mine toward her. She laughed again. "Okay, fine. It doesn't hurt to look."

"Nope, doesn't hurt." Her voice faded. She'd lost someone she loved, and my heart pinched for two reasons: to love someone, to lose someone. I'd never known either emotion, but I didn't plan to, either. While I was a lover, I didn't love, so I couldn't lose. It was that simple.

"Blue devil?" A deep, rich voice startled me, and I turned to face a tray with two glasses, each filled with a pale, blue-colored liquid.

"What?" Persephone choked, and I spun back in her direction. Her wide eyes looked as if she'd seen a ghost. Suddenly, her tan face was devoid of color.

"Persephone?" I swung my legs off the lounger to sit upward and face her. My hand reached for her arm. The man serving drinks dragged a low table closer to us and set down the tray. Helping himself to a seat at the end of my chair, he spoke in that deep tenor again.

"What did I say?"

I turned to face him, and *lightning strike me*, it was the lifeguard.

"Nothing." Persephone's weak voice tried to assure both of us. Her head nodded toward the drink. "What's that?"

"It's called a Blue Devil. It's basically a fruity drink with overpriced rum." His laughter followed, booming like someone playing a drum. My chair vibrated with the jolt of his body chuckling.

"And who are you?" I sneered, wondering how the help was comfortable sitting down with a guest. Zeke had so many servants, and typically I didn't look down my nose at any of them, but something about the nearness of this one made my skin prickle. The air around him crackled.

"Did you say *Persephone?*" Ignoring me, his brows rose and honey-colored eyes opened wide. Mesmerized by the color, I stared. It was the strangest color I'd ever seen. I blinked when he caught me and quickly turned away.

"Yes, Persephone Fields." My oldest friend held out her hand and the lifeguard started at the presentation.

"He'd kill me," he muttered, and Persephone and my eyes met. *Cuckoo*, I signaled by swirling my finger around my left ear. Turning back in his direction, he caught me, and I slipped my finger into my hair, twirling it tightly around my index. A fake smile pinched my face. A large one graced his.

"And you are?" He addressed me, and my tongue froze. I hadn't even sipped the tempting drink, but my mouth grew cold, like I'd sucked a popsicle and brain freeze numbed me.

"Veva," Persephone replied, introducing me. "Veva Matron."

"Ah, you two are Hera and Demi's daughters. I've heard so much about you." His face brightened further, and he winked at me. I turned away again. My eyes focused on the magazine under Persephone's chair.

elda lore

Test your ability to tempt a guy, the headline read. His presence tested me, and anger roiled inside me. There was something about him putting me on edge. The urge to punch him grew under my skin.

"So, Veva." He let my name roll over his tongue, emphasizing the Vs in an exaggerated accent. Boys had done this before, but the way he said it vibrated between my legs. I clamped my thighs together by crossing them. I sat up straighter and rested to the side on one hand, peering at him behind my glasses.

"Veva, meaning 'life'?" *Brilliant. He wasn't only blond, he was a genius*, I mocked internally, but those intense eyes left my tongue icy. My only response was a nod.

"Can't you speak?" His smile grew like I was a simpleton and the thought shocked me out of my frozen state.

"Yes, I can speak, and who are you anyway?" My tone was bitter, sharp and stabbing, although I don't know why. I was so riled by his nearness, and the arm supporting me shook.

"Solis. Solis Cronus."

SOLIS

The blonde gasped while the brunette dragged down her sunglasses. Eyes of green and blue swirled in my direction as she glared at me. The world went quiet for an instant then roared back to life with a splash in the pool, a scream in reaction to the water, and the chatter of people lounging around the patio. *My father and his extravagance for visitors and house guests*, my head rumbled with the thought. He had so many people in his life, and yet never time to give to anyone.

"Solis." My name whispered off the rosy lips of the blonde vision before me. My cousin had been right. She was beautiful, and I'd transverse life and death to be with her. But she had been my cousin's girl, a fact I wasn't ready to reveal to her. Her softened eyes expressed she recognized my name, but I didn't wish to discuss my cousin in the presence of mixed company. I didn't know if I could trust either of them, especially the girl pinning me with those gorgeous eyes.

"Solis Cronus, Zeke's son?" Each time I heard it, it was like ripping off a fresh Band-Aid.

"Yes, in more ways than one." I caught the sarcasm and swallowed hard. The first time I admitted I was his son, the shock was so great, I thought the woman questioning me at the time would crumble. Her heart crushed as she learned that Zeke Cronus had another child. He only legitimately acknowledged a few, and I was told to be grateful he allowed me to live at his home. *His palace*, I called this place. It was more than we, my mother and I, ever had before. *Before*. I shook my head of negative memories and returned the glare of those green-blue eyes with a forced smile on my face. *Quit looking at me*, I wanted to thunder.

"He has so many," Veva muttered, driving home a point I was already too aware of, but her tone softened with the words, and after the sharp snap of her previous snark, a warmth flowed over my skin. The heat of the day burned, as it always did in the Valley, but this warmth soothed me, like a bath after a hard day of training. Velvety soft, it caressed me, careening down my skin, and sparking a jolt of life to an area that needed to stay down in a swimsuit. Arousal in the thin material was never a good thing, unless I pressed up against the barely-there covering of a girl's bikini. The thought drove me harder and my eyes slipped down to the apex of Veva's crossed legs.

"That's an impressive tattoo." I spanned the shapely length, struggling to distinguish the design at first. Hundreds of shapes, almost like eyes, stared up at me. The shade of each center, a rich royal blue with a turquoise rim nearly matched her eyes while feathery swirls of dark green and hints of purple feathered down the span of her leg. She slowly uncrossed her thighs; the movement so sensual, I grew harder, if that were even possible. I leaned forward to rest my elbows on my thighs while she stretched out her leg to place her foot on her friend's chair. Fully exposed, I could see the elaborate details, including those unusual eyes which were actually feathers. An intricate head of bright, royal blue lay on the top of her thigh, emphasizing this was a bird.

"It's a pea*cock*," she stated, her tongue clucking over the second syllable and moisture escaped my straining length. Instantly, my mind wondered what gifts that clicking tongue could offer. Suddenly jealous of a tattoo, my mouth watered at the position of its beak pointing to covered treasure.

"So, Solis, you live here?" My head jolted upward at the question from Persephone. I'd forgotten again we were not alone. Before I could answer, Veva interjected.

"Damn, we thought you were the help." Her voice returned to its previous bite. She sat back on the lounger and swung her legs to cross at the ankles behind me. Her foot brushed my lower back while she adjusted herself, and returned to the casual beauty I'd noticed from across the pool. A spark prickled up my spine at the contact.

"Lifeguard, right?" I chuckled. "Nah, I just like to sit in the chair. Closer to the sun." My smile pinched and my face hardened, like it would crack from the pressure. Something had shifted between the girls and their initial star-struck impression of me. I was good-looking, and I knew it, and I didn't mind using that to my advantage. One of the traits of dear old dad I inherited and appreciated was the fact women were attracted to me, but the novelty of my appearance wore off with these two, while most girls continued to blindly stare with eager anticipation that I might grace them with my presence between their thighs and in their hearts.

Veva lounged back, returning her glasses to her eyes. Her body language shut me out. I touched her ankle, ready to massage up her shin, but she flinched and kicked out to remove my hand. Despite the kick, a surge of electric energy singed my hand and my reaction was to retreat. *What the fuck was that?* An unsettling sense that I somehow knew her zipped through me, as if I was familiar with her. *Did we have history?* I questioned her, but her eyes hid behind the shaded lenses. Her facial expression remained non-responsive, as if she hadn't felt a thing.

"Do you work here?" Persephone asked. I noted, despite Veva's disinterest, she listened.

"Does anyone work here?" I chuckled, referencing the luxury of my father's home. An olive oil mogul in America, he lived a life of leisure. He disappeared for long stretches of time which I eventually learned involved two women in Nebraska, a place I'd never been. I hadn't been anywhere but the slum of our original home and this estate of ecstasy. My father didn't travel with his multiple children. He simply built a haven to house us.

"We're guests as well," Persephone offered, running slender fingers through her long, blonde hair. I watched the motion and felt the weight of Veva's eyes on me. *I'm not a guest, I'm his son*, I wanted to retort, but the words choked me. I was his son. The concept often seemed foreign to me, even after all this time.

I faced Veva and her head rolled away. The side of her face said: *Disinterested, this conversation bores me,* but when her hand lazily stroked up her thigh, my body thought differently. My eyes trained on the trail she blazed as her fingers tickled the length of those feathers painting her skin. Her index finger curled and swirled around the head of the bird as if he were real, as if the peacock lay against her leg. My lower region ached. I looked up to find she was taunting me on purpose.

She'd lowered her glasses and narrowed eyes glared at me. Sarcasm dripped from her piercing look: *Want to pet the bird? Too bad.*

I reached forward and offered each girl one of my specialty drinks. A Blue Devil would cool them off in this heat. I needed to cool down too and I instantly thought Letty from the kitchen would offer some quick release. After each girl took their glass with a brief word of gratitude, I stood, dragging the serving tray with me to use as a shield to hide the straining Velcro of my swim shorts.

"Ladies, it was a pleasure meeting you in person. I'm certain I'll be seeing you around." Persephone smiled politely and sat back while she sipped her drink, rosy lips wrapped around her straw. My eyes quickly snapped away and I caught Veva watching me again. She rolled her tongue around the tip of her straw, latched her lips over it and sucked deep, her cheeks caved inward to draw in the sweet liquid. I might have groaned aloud. Her lids lowered, hiding her amusement at my expense. I let the tray slap at my thighs as I shuffled away, my dick so hard it hurt.

VEVA

A bath house near the pool was the closest place to rinse and change from a day in the sun. It was also ripe with gossip about Zeke's lifestyle and those within his home. Persephone and I had only been here a few days. Spring semester at Central Valley ended, and Persephone begged not to return home for the summer. *Too many reminders of Harris Black*, she told me. *Too many painful memories*, she told her mother. We were caught between just turning twenty-two and finishing college. As I waited for Persephone behind a bank of lockers, I heard a group of girls.

"Can you believe he slept with Ionia? She's such a cow." A shrill voice scraped down my skin like sharp claws.

"He's also been with Letty." This point driven home with conviction in the tone of a second girl.

"He's really making the rounds," the first added. "He's such a player."

"Well, when you look like sunshine and sin, you can get away with it." A third voice boomed louder than the other two and a titter of giggles followed. I stopped dressing and stood at attention.

"And you say this from experience?" The clawing tone returned. The silence that followed confirmed the answer.

"You didn't?" screeched the second girl, a hint of awe to her voice. I listened harder, leaning forward in the direction of their chatter.

"Callie, how could you?" The first girl questioned but there was something more to her tone. "You know how I feel about him." Hurt. Pain filled her words as she admonished her friend.

"You two were over," the deeper voice of said Callie spoke. "Besides, we were drunk."

My head snapped back at this admission: worst reason ever to be with a guy. Silence hung in the air and my heart softened for the misunderstanding among friends. Thankfully, Persephone and I had never had these issues. When she learned I made-out with Tripper Grant last summer, she wasn't upset with me. She worried. She didn't want me to get hurt. I sensed each girl's emotion for this mystery man. *Sunshine and sin?* They could only be discussing one guy.

"Solis just has that damaged goods thing about him." Screeching girl attempted to smooth the waters between the three. "I heard he killed his father."

My eyes opened wide and I stared upward to notice I could see all three girls in the reflection of the mirror. The entire glass spanned three banks of lockers, and two sets down, another girl stood listening intently, her forehead pressed against the closed locker door.

"I heard that's not true. It was his stepfather, anyhow. Zeke's his biological father."

"Zeke?" Claw-girl snorted. "Well, that explains a lot. Like father, like son." She huffed air as she closed the wooden door to the locker near her head.

"Mel, why do you care? You said you were over him." Callie asked.

"I am," she said in an exaggerated tone. "I just hate that he's such a player."

"You hate that you got burned by how hot he is," screechy girl admonished.

"Di, that's so not true. I told you. *I* used *him*." Claw-girl-Mel looked up and met my eyes in the mirror. She flipped her brown hair over one shoulder and exited the area.

"We both know she's lying," screech girl Di said. "Was he good?" The screeching sound softened. "I heard he's really patient and loving." Callie was a larger girl, and I sensed from the fall of her shoulders that she didn't know how to respond to her friend.

"Yeah, he was gentle. A bit sloppy, as a drunk, but he was decent enough." Callie's voice matched her previous friend. There was something in her tone combining pain and pleasure. She may have hoped he'd choose her as his next lover instead of another conquest.

"He hasn't really been interested in me," Di offered, brushing her long red hair.

"Di, you don't ever want it to be like that anyway. One night stands aren't bragging rights. You want it to be special to a guy. Special for you."

My shoulders slumped. Callie spoke wisely. One night stands weren't worth the emotional defeat the next day. My eyes searched out the girl two locker banks over. She leaned on her shoulder, her head facing the mirror. She had raven-black hair and pale skin for someone living under sunshine. Tears streaked down her face, and I knew with certainty she'd been another conquest of the infamous Solis Cronus.

There was no denying Solis was a fine specimen of the male gender: gorgeous, chisel-faced, and sculpted perfection, but I'd noticed his back held a nasty-looking scar. It zig-zagged over his spine, fiery and raised, in the shape of a poorly drawn lightning bolt. My heart softened—though I'd never let on to him—for the pain inflicted to cause such a scar on his glorious skin. Nor would I admit the strange sense of loss when he left us earlier at the pool. Immediately, I disregarded it as relief, as his nearness unnerved me. It made no sense to me.

"Hi, Ionia," Persephone said out of nowhere, and the cheerful tone carried through the bath house. Crying girl swiftly swiped her cheeks and turned in the direction of Persephone, who continued past the middle bank of lockers. The two gossip girls straightened and stared at one another. I took a second peek at Ionia. She didn't look like a cow to me. She was pale with dark hair, thin and delicately hourglass in shape. She looked sweet, with big eyes, and like someone who might be a friend to me, if I didn't instantly hate her for having slept with Solis. Jealousy, that's what I felt when I realized what she'd done. Of course, Solis Cronus, *sunshine and sin*, would pick on a girl so innocent. She gave in to him, with heart, soul, *and* body. I had the need to scorn her for stupidity and hug her for the inability to recognize that sunshine blinds and sin burns. Solis Cronus was a force to be reckoned with. Thank goodness my heart was safe from such a storm.

elda lore

SOLIS

I wished Letty had been enough for me, but attempting to bury myself in her didn't bring the relief I needed. Closing my eyes brought visions of turquoise-ringed, dark blue orbs, surrounded by green, and I couldn't get Veva out of my head long enough to enjoy Letty against me. After a weak orgasm on her part, I withdrew from her, feeling incomplete and incapacitated. Taking matters into my own hands, I took a shower before dinner.

The weekly feast was a mandatory meal my father prepared to honor his guests and display his wealth. So many women and their daughters filled his palace, particularly on the weekends. My own mother had once been here, and I swallowed the thought each time I entered the glorious dining room. Zeke wasn't the father I knew when I was a child, nor was this place my original home. My inheritance was still new, compared to those of my siblings.

A set of fraternal twins sat split to the right and left of our father. His treasured daughter, Athena, graced the opposite end of the table as if she were the queen. Interspersed among the guests sat Hermes, Dionysius and Heph. These other guys were more like me, sons of random women whom came to live with the mysterious sperm provider after their mothers disappeared, died, or demanded Zeke take responsibility for his children. We weren't his only ones, but the seven of us made up the older portion of his children. Perpetually appearing in our twenties, our true age remained irrelevant among the mass number of his offspring.

"May I sit here?" Despite asking, I took the empty seat next to Persephone anyway. Veva sat on the other side of her, engaged in a discussion with War, a military hero. He attracted women despite his temper, and I didn't care for him. A strange clenching at my chest struck me at his interest in Veva. I could only hope the truth of his numerous relationships would be revealed before Veva could be tempted by him. *Oh, the irony.*

"What brings you girls to the estate?" I asked as I passed the salad to Persephone. Invitation was the only way for mortals to enter the gates.

"Summer break from Central Valley. Taking the summer off to figure out what to do, I guess." Central Valley was a university about an hour away. Persephone's sad tone hinted at being lost.

"What do you study there?"

"Horticulture. I love beautiful plants. Silly major, right?" She admired the large floral arrangements set intermittently along the long table. My father was nothing short of over-the-top with decoration. Flowers of bright yellows and deep oranges highlighted the golden color of the dining room.

"If you like flowers, that's cool." I kicked myself under the table, sounding ridiculous in my response. While one ear listened to Persephone, the other caught the laughter of Veva. The sound bubbled around her, and then tenderly popped, like soap bubbles.

"And what about Veva?" My head nodded in her direction and I noticed her sit a little straighter in her seat. She faced War, and with her acorn-colored hair piled on her head, I noticed the soft, downy wisps on the back of her neck. Swallowing hard at the desire to run my nose over that space, I noticed Veva's back prickled and her head tilted just enough to emphasize one ear listened in our direction.

"She's studying to be a midwife and getting a second degree in counseling."

One brow shot up at the combination.

"She wants to help migrant workers with health care and women's rights, especially in marriage."

Both eyes opened wide in reaction.

"That's so…noble."

Veva visibly bristled behind Persephone. Turning to face her cousin, she pointed at a carafe of olive oil on the table.

"Excuse me, could you pass that, Pea?" Persephone handed the dispenser to her cousin without addressing her.

"So," Persephone swallowed hard, side glancing left to right. "Don't you have a cousin named Hades?" For a moment, the world stilled around me. It's as if those most immediate heard her, and she'd said a dirty world. Conversation resumed with a whirl and chatter rose quickly. Sucking in a deep breath, I willed the conversation not to happen.

"I do." I stuffed my mouth with too many greens and chewed hastily, hoping to give her time to pass on the conversation.

"Have you seen him lately?" Her voice softened to tinkling bells, and the soothing sound thumped at my heart. I shrugged. Defining lately was difficult. When you live centuries, time becomes irrelevant.

"I wanted to thank you." Her voice barely above a whisper, I leaned in to hear her better. To others, our position appeared as if we shared a secret. Her eyes scanned the close surroundings. My brow rose in question, as if I didn't know what she referenced.

"For giving him light. And letting him visit me." She swallowed hard and liquid filled her eyes. *Don't cry*, I begged. It would break me. I'd confess everything, if tears fell. They weakened me.

"I don't know what you're talking about," I lied. My father didn't know what I'd done last summer to help my cousin. Hades' father knew when he returned home to the underworld. The distant relationship between the elder brothers prevented any fear on my part that Uncle Hades would tell dear old dad. Persephone wiped briskly at her cheek. She turned and smiled weakly at me.

"Of course, you don't." She kept my secret, and I held hers. The pained expression showed she loved someone forbidden to her, and the broken heart still lingered. She paused for a long moment, chewing slowly, and silence grew between us. That popping-bubble laughter rose over Veva's head, surrounding her and War. My annoyance grew that he provoked such a sound. *Mine.* My lips clamped tight as the desire to yell threatened to escape. War wasn't a funny guy. Spiteful in nature, I couldn't imagine what he said that would make Veva laugh like that.

A gentle tap on my shoulder turned my attention and I came face to face with Mel. *Shit.*

"Hello, darling." Her terse tone nipped at me. She'd forced her body between myself and the guest to my right. I hadn't properly introduced myself to our other guest as Persephone drew my attention and Veva lassoed it to my left.

"Hello, Mel." My jaw clenched. *Please, don't make a scene*, I begged. Mel Selgos was the daughter of another conquest of my father. Thankfully, she wasn't his daughter. Difficult to distinguish at times, I had to confirm my female encounters were not siblings of mine. The thought made me shiver. Mel's breath on my neck did as well, and not in a pleasing manner.

"I've heard you slept with that cow, Ionia, and Callie told me you seduced her when you were drunk." Her teeth snapped just below my ear.

"Perhaps we should step into the hall," I offered, placing my napkin to the side of my plate and pushing back my chair. The extra wide smile of this once-tempting brunette beamed at me. She'd gotten what she came for: my attention. Leaving the dining room with her made a statement to the others in the room, particularly any females. I'd been played by a cunning girl. She held out her hand for mine, but I shook my head. My eyes fell first to Persephone.

"Please excuse me." I dipped my head and Persephone responded, "Of course."

Next, my eyes drew to Veva. She'd been watching the interaction with this girl, but when my eyes drifted to hers, hardened blades of royal blue met me. She immediately twisted away, exposing that subtle neck of hers. My fingers twitched to touch the curls loosely escaping at the base of her neck. Her back remained rigid, though. Her posture informed me she wasn't interested in any petty lover's quarrel.

Fortunately, Mel and I were no longer lovers. That was last summer. Mel's return reawakened her desires, but I had long since moved on. Several times over. She was a silly girl, looking to nab a rich man, but she could not bait me. I wasn't a rich man. Slippery, I refused to be hooked by her. Once in the hall, I rounded on her and a repetitious argument began. *How could I sleep with her friends? Why didn't I call her? Why was I avoiding her?* I wasn't interested in Mel, and after my attempt to have Letty earlier, I realized I wasn't interested in any of my previous lovers. I only had eyes for one, and she sat with a bristled back to me, shutting me out of her bubbly laughter and mesmerizing eyes. My body began to tremble with subtle jealousy. I was never jealous. I didn't have to be. I didn't know what was happening to me, and a shaky hand wiped my forehead as my thoughts drifted off while Mel reprimanded me.

VEVA

Oh my God, I screamed inside my head. I couldn't believe he left with that selfish girl. All buxom brunette and nails-on-a-chalkboard sounding, her presence grated on my tender nerves. My blood surged within me. I'd already been on edge as he spoke intimately with Persephone throughout the salad course. Their heads bent to whisper with her sweet smile and his bright one returning it. The conversation seemed intense and when Pea wiped a tear, I noticed the pained expression on Solis' face. Tears were his weakness. If that bumbling brunette let the waterworks fall, she'd be under him in the hall. My heart jackknifed in my chest.

"What's wrong?" Persephone reached for my hand under the table.

"Nothing," I snipped, retracting my own. I loved Persephone. *Loved her*, like a sister. We'd grown up down the country road from one another, raised by single mothers on a bustling farm, where we were nearly female soulmates. I didn't want to be jealous of her, but my heart raced with envy that Solis confided in her. He could have been telling her a grocery list for all I knew, but I couldn't take Solis falling for Pea. Everyone loved her. *Why wouldn't they?* She was blonde and beautiful, sweet and sensual, but I hated that guys fell for her first. Tripper loved her first. Harris Black appeared on the farm, and instantly they were a couple. She had magnetism, while I repelled men after they got what they wanted from me.

My mother, Hera, hated men. She believed they were evil and her bitterness rubbed off on me at times. Her feelings came from jilted love. My father left her, but it was more than that. I saw it in her eyes. She wanted Zeke Cronus at one time, and deep down, I think he had loved her, but he couldn't keep it in his pants. He'd flirt with Demi, Pea's mom, as well, but Demi had no interest. It was all flirtatious fun, and I understood that nature, but not for my mother. I could see the pinch each time he touched Demi. The clenched fist. The hurt heart. While I

elda lore

fantasized of Zeke being my father, I worried about it, too. My mother assured me he wasn't mine or Persephone's. He had enough children of his own, she retorted, adding insult to the injury of her broken heart. I wasn't upset with Persephone. In my heart, I knew she'd done nothing wrong. In fact, I blamed Solis instead. He wanted to seduce her. I could read it in his expression each time he looked at her. That look of comfort he wanted to bestow on her. Without knowing she'd lost the love of her life, he wanted to wrap her in his arms and give her sympathy. *Well, I'd sympathize him*, I cursed in my head. I stood abruptly.

"I'm no longer hungry," I said to Pea.

"I'll come with you," she offered, pushing back her chair.

"No." The word said too loudly, lingered in the air, and War looked up at me. He smiled at the aggressiveness of my tone. "I just need air," I said to neither of them. I spun away from the table and headed toward the hall.

+ + +

Zeke's home was a sprawling, ranch-style estate, roughly appearing as if it was built in the 1970s, but inside contained top of the line amenities. Many hallways were lined on both sides with floor to ceiling windows. The main entrance housed a grand door, gilded with gold, and two side panels of glass that balanced with panels on the opposite wall, allowing one to view the back patio from the front stoop. A massive, mosaic-tiled sun filled the circular space of the floor. The foyer marked the division between the main wing and the guest wing, where Persephone and I stayed. It was here that I found Solis and his friend, Mel, in a deep argument.

"How could you touch her?" The clawing voice retorted.

"I'm not having this conversation with you." His gruff voice surprised me, but I had no sympathy for the whining nature of the girl before him. I just wanted to get past them.

"Excuse me," I snarled, briskly passing over the marble tile with the click-clack of my heels echoing off the walls. My arms pumped at my side as I hurried down the guest hall. Turning left for the adjacent wing of the room I shared, thick fingers grasped my upper arm and I was yanked backward to face my assailant.

"Where are you going?" Solis demanded, breathing fire in my face. His warm breath assaulted me, blurring my senses as the electric touch of his heated skin wrapped around mine. I was shocked to stillness. I'd felt this current before, when he rubbed my ankle. Sparks of energy shot up my leg straight to my core; the intensity made me pulse with instant need. I'd squeezed my thighs to stop the beat, but the rhythm increased and I ached for relief. The sensation attacked me again.

"To my room," I snipped in reply. I had a problem that needed tending to. The mention of my room lit up his honey eyes.

"Why?"

"I was no longer hungry." With the mention of hunger, his eyes scanned my lips. My tongue snuck out and licked the dryness. His eyes widened, and that strange honey color shifted to deep, caramel brown. Warm and gooey, I could get lost in that glare. Blinking rapidly to rid the thought, I stared at him.

"Why do I sense that you don't care for me?"

"Because I don't. I hate that you're blindingly beautiful." *Shit, shit, shit*. The words tumbled out of my mouth, as if he drew them from me. He blinked and smiled slowly.

"You think I'm beautiful?" The arrogant curve of his lip, detonating a dimple, pissed me off more. My mouth watered and I cursed again.

"Forget I said that," I growled. "You're so arrogant. So…smug."

"I think you're beautiful, too." His tone softened, rolling seductively low, while his eyes roamed over my face and down the length of my neck. His fingers slipped around the curve of my throat and he gently tugged at the fine hairs on the nape of my neck. His pinky finger stroked upward over the sensitive skin, and my body responded with a shiver. The dimple cut deeper, his eyes focused on my hair. "Your hair is this beautiful acorn color, with streaks of gold." My concentration snapped.

"Don't think I'm beautiful. I'm not one of your conquests." I straightened, damning myself for liking the warmth of his hands on my skin. Using my hand to deflect his grasp, I continually received pricks of shock, sparking each time our skin collided. It was as if I'd purposely swiped a carpeted floor and grabbed a metal doorknob, looking for the electric current it would conduct. Glutton for punishment, I cursed myself and forced his touch away from me with a sharp push on his chest.

"My conquests?" He snorted.

"Yes. Let's see Ionia, Mel, Letty, Callie." My fingers ticked off the girls I'd heard speaking earlier in the day. "Oh, and let's not forget Di, who thinks you'll be all sweet and romantically gentle with her virginity." My voice boomed in frustration and my nostrils flared as I breathed deep.

"You're adorable when you're jealous," he taunted me. His fingers reached for my hair again but I swatted them away.

"That's all you have to say?" I barked, my tone coarse. He attempted to touch my hair one more time and my hands swirled between us like I swished at an attack of angry bees. Flapping fingers and swatting palms, I slapped the air. "And don't think for one second I'd let you near my Persephone."

Instantly, my breasts crashed his chest. His hands gripped firmly around my upper arms, holding me pressed against him. Both our breaths hitched exaggeratedly, forcing the sharp tips of erect nipples to drag over the hard form of his upper chest.

"Don't," he jiggled me, increasing the brush of sensative nipples against the warmth of him. "Don't you ever say I've gone after Persephone." His flirtatious tenor changed. Heat charged the air. Gooey caramel melted to fireballs of anger. "I'd never touch her," the booming sound of his voice warned me.

"What's wrong with her?" I snipped. *What's wrong me with me?* I thought, as I was suddenly defending the honor of my best friend with encouragement of their union.

"She's beautiful and sweet." His fingers dug into the skin at the back of my arm and he jostled me to emphasize the words. "But she isn't mine, and I don't want her to be."

"Why not?" The sharp snap to my speech surprised me. Again, I cursed myself. I didn't want him to desire Persephone, and yet suddenly I seemed to promote it.

"Because all I can see when I look at another woman is peacock eyes." His smile grew and his eyes lit. The fire smoldered and returned to warm embers. Our mouths were separated by mere inches. Mine opened slightly, drawing his eyes to my lips. I breathed in his hot breath, and the heated oxygen traveled down my throat, warming my insides to volcanic desire. Admitting he looked at other women, however, only pissed me off more. My palms, bracing his shoulder, pushed against him.

"I despise you," I muttered through clenched teeth.

"I loathe you," he retorted and reached for the back of my neck again, dragging me to him. Our mouths drew even closer, the touch of his lips millimeters away from connecting with mine. His parted for the capture.

"Solis?" Nails-on-a-chalkboard clawed the air, smothering the moment like cold rain. Solis' head came forward to rest on mine, but I untangled myself from the close call of kissing sunshine.

SOLIS

I'd lost Veva after Mel's voice ripped the connection to shreds. She escaped my grasp and raced down the guest hall, leaving me to face another round of Mel's pleas for us to be a couple. It wasn't going to happen. I didn't commit. I was more like my father than I thought, but I didn't want to be. I'd never admit that to just anyone. I didn't want the solitary life of flitting from one bed to another, but that's the life I led. I'd already lived the chase of moving from one place to another, continually searching for safety, denying I needed it. I wanted one place to remain stable: one bed to be solid, one woman to finally be mine, but I didn't allow hope to haunt me.

Conquests, she called them. Veva would be my next one, because that girl had me so riled, and I needed to tame that storm. Put out the thunder and move on. The lightning between us ignited the closer we drew to one another. She felt it, too. It's why she kicked me off of her ankle. It's why she swatted my hands away. That quick current of energy flickered between us when we touched, and the thought of that live wire Veva being plugged in turned me on.

But Mel droned on and on in my ear. My irritation grew and her tears fell. Normally a sucker for the salty liquid streaming from a female eye, tonight the sight agitated me. The weather matched my mood. It had turned stormy as dark clouds tumbled over the estate. The rain fell sweetly, momentarily cooling the parched land and refreshing the olives, but as Mel continued yapping, my annoyance flared. Lightning struck somewhere nearby. Mel flinched, but I held my ground.

"I think it's best if you retire," I suggested, knowing if the storm raged too fiercely, the transmitter would snap and the lights would extinguish. I actually liked an evening in the cool flames of candlelight, but tonight was not such a night. Tonight, I wanted Mel to shut up. Thunder clapped. Lightning snapped. Taking Mel's arm, I escorted her to her room. Somewhere down this stretch of guest rooms, Veva and

Persephone shared a bedroom. At the end of the hallway was a common space filled with oversized chairs and low tables. Much like the grand foyer, the area had floor to ceiling windows on either side, allowing for natural light to flood the space.

Standing outside Mel's door, she reached for me. Catching me off guard, our lips collided and I returned the kiss, briefly. I sensed someone watching me, and my lids opened to find Veva standing in the middle of the common room, glaring down the hall at me. My lips continued the numb connection with Mel as I watched Veva observe us. My hands slipped around Mel's lower back and I drew upward, willing Veva to take in the performance. She pissed me off, and I wanted her to see what she missed out on by rejecting me.

Mel moaned in this exaggerated way she had, more dramatic than endearing. In fact, it distracted me and turned me off. Instantly, I pulled back from her, never losing eye contact with Veva.

"See," Mel's screechy voice exclaimed, "I knew we belonged together. You missed me, admit it!"

My attention snapped to Mel.

"Mel, I'm sorry. That was a mistake." I wiggled my arms to loosen her hands from my biceps. When I looked up, Veva was missing from the common space. I didn't see her retreating down the opposite hall, certain her room would be among those nearby. My father liked to keep the younger girls together; it kept their mothers separate for his entertainment. *By gods above, what had I done?* It hit me like the lightning bolts raging outside—I had acted like my father, pitting one woman against another. In my attempt to make Veva jealous, I'd used Mel. As I kissed Mel, I upset Veva. I shook my head, disgusted with myself, and stepped away from my forever ex-lover.

"Good night, Mel." I bowed, continuing down the hall in the direction I'd seen Veva.

Standing amid the common area, the lightning crackled, illuminating the dark sky. The rain subsided some and thunder snapped in the distance. The glow of low lights lit the comfortable space, but Veva was not present. One of the exterior glass doors stood slightly ajar, and my eyes scanned the patio. Surely Veva couldn't have been so foolish as to venture out into a storm? Sliding the door open, I stepped outside and let the soft drizzle wash over me. I'd been a fool tonight.

+ + +

Needing an escape, I made my own path to an outer house, a separate home on the property, once considered the in-law residence. As my father had no wife after my mother, no in-laws existed to fill the space. My father's parents were long dead, and the story of their demise was an old tale. The run-down house had been gifted to me when I arrived, and Heph helped me convert the place. Wet underbrush swiped at my ankles, dampening the hem of my pants. As I neared the hut, I noticed the front door askew..

I didn't bring girls here. I had two rooms in the main house, but I preferred to keep this space as private as I could. Careful to never be followed, this was my sanctuary. I slowed as I listened for the intruder to my personal residency. Hesitantly, I pushed the door open wider. My senses alert, I smelled her before I saw her: summer rain mixed with warm skin. Her acorn hair soaked to deep oak, droplets dripped to dampen the back of her dress. The peacock tattoo prominently displayed, wrapped around her leg as she stood with her back to the entrance, her arms crossed and her hip cocked as she stared at the canvas before her. On the large sheet was the beginning of a painting, in swirls of turquoise, bright blue and dark greens.

"What is it?" she asked without turning to me. Ignoring her question, I asked my own.

"What are you doing in my studio?"

VEVA

I stared at the mixture of color that matched the pattern on my leg. He had faintly sketched the intricate outline of a peacock, and started the laborious task of filling in each feather with minute detail. My eyes glazed as I wondered, *Why?* Why was he painting that bird, those colors? And why was he a painter? His body was that of an athlete, all rippled abs and bulging biceps, and yet he had incredible skill. Attention to fine details like texture brought life to the start of this image. My fingers itched to touch the silky feathers, as if they were real.

"Veva?" He'd asked me a question, but I hadn't heard him. My heart had raced as I stormed from the common room in the main residence, but staring at the image before me calmed me. My arms wrapped tightly around my middle in an attempt to hold myself together. My fingers were bruising my skin, they pressed so firmly against my upper arms. I didn't respond to him, only nodded in acknowledgement. I wouldn't let him know I was impressed with his ability.

"An artist, huh?" The words huffed forth, and I sensed his presence behind me. My eyes closed as the energy coming off him reached out for me, like electrical currents drawn to one another. Electrons and protons attracted to their opposite by magnetism beyond their control.

"I like to paint." His response caressed my ear, tickled my lobe, and wrapped seductively around my neck. He remained silent, but I could feel him breathing me in.

"Mad at me?" A wicked smile curved his lips and skipped out of his mouth. I didn't have to see the smile; I heard it, felt it, and the skin on my shoulders prickled.

"I hate you," I muttered, with no conviction. He'd just kissed another girl in front of me, and I despised him, but I lost my ire staring at the image before me. He stepped around me and unpinned the sheet dangling from clips attached to the wall.

"Let's try something, okay?" I hadn't moved, but my eyes followed him as his fingers unclamped the clips and he carefully draped the large canvas over the back of a couch. He returned with a new sheet and pinned it with clips to hold it upright. He set several cans of paint near my feet before he stood and held out three brushes.

"I can't paint." My eyebrows furrowed deep and my eyes glared at him at the insult. I wasn't creative, unless you counted stick figures with uneven limbs and large heads as art.

"You don't need to. Take a brush," he demanded. I yanked one from his grasp. He stepped back and tugged his linen shirt over his head with one hand. My mouth fell open. *Did he wish for me to paint him?* He was already a work of art. Stepping aside, he faced the canvas. I looked back at the blank sheet.

"Tell me something you hate?"

"What?" My head spun in his direction, and I noticed he casually propped himself against an island cabinet. Behind him was a small galley kitchen open to the larger room. The very square space consisted of nothing more than the kitchenette, a couch and empty floor space before the large wall for painting.

"Come on, Veva, what's something you strongly dislike?" His deep voice prompted me.

"Millipedes."

His shoulders quivering, he laughed heartily but low.

"Okay, dip the brush in a color and whip it at the sheet, saying what you hate."

"What?" My entire face scrunched up at the instruction. He pushed off the island and stalked two steps toward me. Taking my hand like I was a child, he pointed the brush toward an open can of paint. The gray color matched my mood. His other hand on my hip, he forced me to bend forward. With the wrapped hand pointing downward, I dipped the brush in the paint. Standing us both upright, he spoke deliberately, directly to my ear.

"Now, fling the paint at the sheet, saying what you hate." He stepped back and I looked over my shoulder at him. He tipped his head toward the sheet letting his eyes lead me there.

"I hate millipedes," I said without conviction and flicked my wrist. Paint spiraled off the brush in an arc of droplets, but hardly made it to the edge of the canvas.

"Veva, that was pathetic," he sighed.

"Well, I'm not an artist," I snapped.

"There's my girl." He winked, and my blood popped those first bubbles, hinting at a boil rising soon. I hated that he called me *his*. "Say that again like that, and whip the paint at the canvas." He flung his arm forward to imitate what I should do.

"I'm not an artist, and I'm not your girl," I snipped out, using more force behind the paint brush, snapping my wrist sharply as I whipped paint at the sheet. The sound of the droplets, like the first kiss of rain on a standing body of water, satisfied me.

"Where's my Veva, the girl of life? Do it again. Pick something else." His voice sounded removed, as if he stepped away, allowing me space. He'd called me *his* again, and I shuddered at the thought.

"I hate small things on four legs, like shrews and rats." I shivered as I flipped the brush, covered in a darker shade of gray, at the canvas.

"Again," he barked, and the sound cracked like the whip driving a horse. It irritated me, and I repeated the motion.

"I hate small flying things like moths and flies."

Pause.

"I hate clowns." I heard him laugh and the humor at my fear spurred me onward.

"I hate cottage cheese." I gagged at the thought and threw more paint.

"Tell me more fears." His voice coached me.

"I hate darkness." Splatter.

"And thunder." A clap resounded outside the hut. Splat went more paint. The sporadic image grew.

"I hate cheaters." My teeth clenched while I snarled and my heart galloped in my chest. "And liars." The paint hit the target harder, but I already bent to reapply more color. The white sheet slowly transformed to a crazy succession of dots and stripes in black, gray, charcoal and ash.

"I hate players." My arm launched backward and I let the paint fly as I rotated my shoulder forward like I intended to throw a ball.

"I hate mothers who are bitter. And fathers who disappear." My hand crisscrossed two slashes to form an X. "I hate secrets."

"And all that's unaware in my life." I growled.

"And heights." I continued.

"And sunshine tattoos." Without realizing it, I'd dipped the brush in bright yellow. The strike of color resembled a lightning bolt as it jagged against my angry, dark creation. My heart raced and sweat moistened my hairline. Upset that the brilliant color leapt from the muted darkness, I dropped the brush to the floor and bent to retrieve a whole can of gray. I'd wash the brightness away. Righting myself, Solis' hands covered mine around the tin container.

"Whoa, whoa, whoa. Slow down." His voice attempted to soothe. My chest rose and fell with the exhilarating effort of releasing all my hates and fears. I jerked the can toward me, but Solis was stronger. He refused to let it go. I gulped for air and looked up into concerned caramel eyes. He held mine captive as he inhaled deeply and then exhaled. His chin tipped, encouraging me to follow his lead and let my breath dance with his. Inhale deep. Exhale slow. Inhale again. Exhale one more time. Calm washed over me and exhaustion hit. I released the paint container, thankful for Solis' quick recovery. He caught it as it fell from my clutches.

"I'm so tired," I mumbled. A bead of sweat rolled down my temple. As he squatted to replace the can on the ground, my knees gave out and I folded downward, sitting with a thud on the wooden floor. I stared in wonder at my weak attempt at a masterpiece. Solis followed my gaze.

"Not bad." The smile returned to his voice, but I sensed he mocked me. I no longer had the fight in me. *Must sleep*, I thought. My hair, still damp from the rain, and my face, sweaty from the effort to expel my hatred, caused my head to weigh too heavy on my shoulders.

"Peacock?" His loud tenor softened, but still boomed, wrapping around me. His arms came next and I felt myself fall back against his chest.

"So tired, Sunshine." My lids felt too heavy and the pull to close them great. One more blink of the lightning bolt over the thunderous sky, and the world faded to black.

SOLIS

I awoke as I expected, stiff from the wood floor beneath me and stiff from the wood protruding from my lower region. What I didn't expect was to wake alone. Holding Veva when she nearly passed out felt better than I imagined. In her sleep, she stroked my forearm, cooing my name, while I inhaled the rain scent of her hair. She'd lulled me to sleep, and for the first time in a long time, I had no dreams. *Nothing*, like Veva. Vanished. I listened for running water from the small bathroom, but a quick scan of the square space proved her absence.

Damn it.

Rolling slowly to my side before pressing upward, I sat. My body creaked, and I twisted at the waist to crack my back. Pressing my chin with my palm, I rotated my head side to side and it cracked as well. My chest was bare, but my linen pants were splattered with paint. She had a wicked arm on her, and if she ever threw a punch, I had better be prepared. I stared at the sheet, covered in an angry array of dark tones, with one bright slash of yellow. I scrambled for my camera and took a picture. I'd have to send it to her. Or better yet, I had an idea. The paint would need time to settle, and it gave me time to devise a plan.

Afraid of heights. I'd break that fear. I loved to climb.

+ + +

"I'd like to show you girls the valley," Heph said, slowly spitting out each word like we'd practiced. I'd recruited him for the plan to rid Veva of one fear. For a huge man, he was incredibly shy. The rumor was that he was dropped as a child, abandoned like me. My father didn't wish to explain, other than that Heph was a half-brother to me. An ugly scar marked his forehead, his nose disjointed, and a prosthetic leg left him with a limp, but he was definitely not weak. A master at metal work, the strength he possessed frightened me, and I was no small person, either.

An artisan like me, I'd learned several techniques from him. He, in turn, had things to learn from me, like how to catch a girl. Not an easy task for a large man with a small vocabulary.

"Where do you wish to take us?" Persephone sweetly asked during breakfast. Heph looked at me, as I told him it would be a surprise for the girls: an adventure. His eyes opened wide in fear, and when Persephone's delicate hand touched his wrist for his attention, he tilted his head. *Help me*, his eyes cried, and I didn't intend to torture the poor chump.

"Actually, I thought the four of us could go?" My eyes easily avoided Veva, who ignored me with expertise borne from experience. I addressed Persephone instead, with a too-chipper tone.

"No." Veva's hand slapped the table, and my attention fell to her face. Her head shook.

"I think it sounds like fun," Persephone responded, narrowing her eyes at her friend. "We haven't explored the valley much since we've been here."

"Persephone," Veva hissed through her teeth. Her eyes strained to convey her displeasure.

"Let us surprise you," I offered, still addressing Persephone. I tipped my head to Heph and he took the hint, nodding too exaggeratedly. My finger sliced across my throat for Heph to stop. Eyes shifting sideways, Veva caught my motion, and my hand dropped. She stood abruptly and stalked from the breakfast room. My head followed her retreat.

"I don't think she likes you." The words softly tumbled forth from Heph, his head lowered to his plate.

"She'll be fine." Persephone touched Heph's wrist, and he flinched from the affection.

I shook my head in dismay. Poor Heph, he had so much to learn. I told Persephone how to dress and where to meet Heph and me. An hour later, Veva stood next to Persephone in short shorts, exposing the full length of the peacock tattoo, a tank top enhancing her curves, and ratty gym shoes. Sexy, but not overstated, she looked less fierce in the more casual clothing. Her hair was pulled up in a ponytail; she fidgeted with the ends. I parked the Jeep and hopped out to help each girl climb in. Veva refused the support of my hand but when her foot slipped, I grabbed her hips and lifted her to the backseat.

"Did he just throw me in the backseat?" she complained to Persephone as I walked around the back of the vehicle.

"No, I think he lifted you like a paperweight and set you back here." Persephone laughed, and the beam of Veva's eyes bored into the back of my head as I slipped into the driver seat. Taking off with a jolt, we headed for the edge of the valley where a national treasure existed, including large rock formations for climbing. The variety of levels offered a great challenge, but as I assumed Veva and Persephone were novices, I figured a lower difficulty climb might be the best start.

"So where's the surprise?" Veva snipped, placing her hands on her hips, eying the gravel parking space and the jagged rock formations around it.

"There." I pointed to the top of one jutting structure. Her mouth fell open.

"Rock climbing?" Veva snorted. "I'm not rock climbing." She crossed her arms over her curvy breasts and turned her head like a spoiled child. She looked off in the opposite direction and squinted in the bright sunshine.

"Yes, you *are*." Persephone pinched the under arm of her friend, who flicked her elbow out to ward off her friend.

"Are you torturing me?" Veva glared at me. "You know I'm afraid of heights." That feisty tone, mixed with a touch of fear, reminded me of her admission from the night before. My hands twitched between dragging her to me to comfort her, and shaking her for her stubbornness.

"Time to face your fears, Peacock." I stalked away from her, anticipating the climb.

"Don't call me that." Her voice called after me. The pile before us was an easy incline, and I paused to allow Persephone to step in front of me. Turning back, I noticed Veva still standing by the Jeep.

"You can stay behind if you'd like. Lots of millipedes around the rocks and other creepy, crawly things." I wiggled my fingers for emphasis and turned away from her. Eventually, I heard the rustle of gravel behind me and the crunch of determined feet as she neared. I slowed, and she purposely bumped into me.

"I hate you," she muttered, brushing past me. I watched her sweet ass sway before me and shook my head. Within moments, we fell into companionable silence. Heph led the way, coaching Persephone where to place her feet, leading by example. For a man with an artificial leg from the knee down, he was surprisingly agile. I stayed in the rear to support Veva. When her foot slipped, I was there to right her body. She may have flinched, but I used any excuse to touch her. The heat of the day was nothing compared to the electric sparks nipping at me when our skin connected.

The incline grew steeper, but Heph persevered. This climb was a Sunday stroll for him and me. At one point near the top, Veva stopped moving.

"I can't do it," she whimpered. Both hands outstretched and legs spread to support her climb, she appeared like a giant X against the rock wall. Her head tilted down. "Oh, God, it's so high."

"You can do this," I countered. I'd been staring at her ass for the last hour, my body fighting its own struggle for control. Finally, I slid up against hers. "You can do this, Veva." My hand covered hers and I pointed with our collective fingers where to place her hand next. Stretching, her fingers gripped the natural ledge and with my hand braced on her hip, she slid to the side. We climbed in unison for a short stretch until Heph found the plateau and reached down to hoist Veva upward. I maneuvered to the top on my own and sucked in a breath at the amazing view.

The space wasn't really large enough for four, so we stood close to one another. I teetered toward the edge, my toes aligned with rock and nothingness. I flung out my arms.

"I'm a god of the universe!" I yelled. Veva stood close behind me, and the flip of my outward arm startled her. She stepped to the side, arms flailing through the air as she lost her balance. Instantly, I encircled her with one arm and pulled her against my side. Her breaths came in ragged pulls, her fear palpable.

"Did you push me?" she shrieked, struggling against my grasp. My arm tightened around her. "I could have fallen to my death." The exaggeration extreme, I held her against me and stepped back from the edge. My mouth rested below her ear, inhaling the combination of exertion and rain scent on her.

"I'd never let you fall," I whispered against the skin that I imagined tasted salty and sweet. "I'd never let anything hurt you, not even me." I held her flush against me; both arms secured her back to my chest. My chin rested on her shoulder. "Look at the view."

Her gasp confirmed what I saw. For miles, the uninhibited world stretched before us. Rock formations and tufts of green landscaped the scenery. I wished for my camera. I'd not only capture the glory before me, but the beauty of Veva. She looked radiant, her face relaxed, as she observed nature before her.

"You did it, Vee." Holding her, I tried to reassure her, despite the fact she shook against me, trembling from the exertion of the climb and her fear of heights. My eyes drifted to the pebbly rocks at our feet, where something caught my attention. I bent to the side, not releasing Veva, but taking her down with me while I squatted. She screamed and her hands gripped the sides of my shorts. Righting us, I presented her with the gift.

"A hidden heart." The heart-shaped pebble rested in the palm of my hand. "My mother called them that: hidden treasures in nature. A sign of good things."

Her fist clamped around the rock, removing it from me. "You scared the crap out of me for a stupid rock." Her arm reached back, preparing to fling the treasure out into the great open space, but I gripped her wrist.

"Never mind," I muttered, embarrassed at mentioning my mother. I released Veva. My heart sank, like I anticipated the heart-shaped rock would once Veva hurled it. I stepped back. I couldn't watch her throw away my gift. Thoughts of my mother were rare, and I'd just shared one with Veva. Her hand came forward and I turned away. Heph went down the wall first, and I guided Persephone to follow his lead. Spinning back to Veva, I found her staring off at the vast display of nature, her fist clutched to her chest, her other hand covering it to hold it in place. She briefly closed her eyes, then lowered her hand and opened her palm. To my surprise, she still held the rock. I watched as she pocketed it before turning toward me. The intensity of her turquoise gaze washed over me, a cool bath cascading down my body in the powerful heat. My mouth grew dry, and I wondered if kissing her would quench me. My heart hammered inside my chest. Reaching out a hand, I nodded toward the rocky descent. It was time to return home before I did anything foolish, like suck those peachy lips and drink in the dewy mist of those eyes.

VEVA

We returned to solid earth, but Heph stopped and began to pile rocks in decreasing size. I noticed several other similar piles around me.

"What's that?" Persephone asked.

"A cairn. You stack rocks in a way to make a display of largest to smallest. Some artists try to balance mismatched shapes to make a statement. Other people form the pile as a marker or a memory. Something that says, I was here. Romantics say the marker meant someone was thinking of you." Solis explained and waggled his eyebrows at Persephone. My heart dropped. He was really into her. I turned away to approach a pile. I took in the varying shapes and the flat rocks. I should have made a cairn on the plateau we climbed. I wanted to make a statement like that on the world, to mark a spot to say, *I was here*. The idea of a lover making such a statement to me seemed absurd. I didn't have romance in my life; I had meaningless flings, like Tripper Grant last summer, or any of the nameless souls from the past year at college. I ached when I thought of the love I'd witnessed between Persephone and Harris Black. The edge of mystery about who he was and where he came from enhanced my curiosity of their insta-love. The intensity of their love was a quandary in and of itself, as I didn't understand such deep emotion.

My hand returned to the rock in my pocket. I don't know why I even contemplated throwing something so precious out into the abyss. It really was amazing how nature formed this one pebble into a jagged yet distinct heart, and it lay on top of that plateau waiting for someone to discover it. Equally curious, was the fact Solis found it and gave it to me. It was sweet. My teeth clamped at the thought, but then my jaw relaxed and my cheeks softened. A smile fought to curve my lips, but I couldn't fight the strength of my pleasure.

Taking it out of my pocket one more time to look at it, Heph startled me.

"I could make you something to hold that, so you could wear it as a necklace." His voice was rough, but gentle. I turned to face him, prepared to tell him I wasn't interested, but the tender look of his huge brown eyes stopped me. My anger disintegrated in the presence of the man who stood before me. My eyes took in the scar across his forehead, the bump on his nose, possibly broken a time or two. My head dipped, and I noticed, not for the first time, the metal contraption making up the lower half of his left leg. He hadn't complained once while we climbed, while I muttered under my breath and cursed in my head the entire time. Without realizing it, I'd cupped the rock in my fist, holding it against my chest as I had done after I almost threw it away. Unclear why I made this motion, I lowered my coupled hands and held out the rock for Heph to view.

"How would you do that?"

"I could make a wire support and attach it to a clip. You could slip it on a leather cord or a silver chain." His big eyes peered at mine, hopeful. I remembered hearing he worked with metal, and the delicate way his large hands twisted in explanation of how the wire would attach to my precious rock endeared him to me. I stared at him a little too long, but there was something familiar about his eyes. My brow pinched as I fought to recognize him, but the sound of Persephone's laughter behind me scattered my thoughts.

"I'd like that, Heph. Thank you." I spun to face my friend, and found Solis chuckling. Despite the four of us spending this day together, I suddenly felt like a third wheel. Solis made Pea laugh in response, which had been so rare over the last year. Her sadness followed her like a shadow, despite her smiles and general cheer. Inside, she told me, her heart was black, and ached for Harris, and while I didn't doubt she loved him, her life was too young to never love again. The images of Solis and Persephone together hardened my insides like the stones surrounding us. Lava bubbled where my heart should be, at the thought of Solis kissing Persephone. I recalled the night before, when I caught him in the hall, his mouth engaged with Mel's, his eyes watching me while he devoured her. My breath rushed out of me in a whoosh, and I gasped.

"Veva, what's wrong?" Persephone rushed to me. Heph spun me to face him.

"She's gone sheet white. I think she's dehydrated." Instantly, I was off my feet and in Solis' arms. He carried me like the pebble in my pocket.

"I'm fine. I'm fine. Just spun too fast or something," I lied. It wasn't the heat getting to me, or rather it was the heat. Each time Solis touched me I felt those sparks, growing all too familiar and way too comfortable with the prickle at my skin. The more he touched me, the more I craved the shocking sensation, and I cursed myself for enjoying it. I didn't want to cave in to the warming energy. But I did want in, and my head warred with my body. He was a player, I reminded myself, and I didn't wish to be played, but his god-like body sang out to mine, and I wanted to be strummed. I shook my head to rid the thought, causing silver dots to float before my eyes. Maybe I was dehydrated after all. Maybe I needed to quench the unending thirst for Solis.

"Feeling any better?" His voice rushed over me like a trickling stream. I was in a cold sweat despite the heat. My skin tingled and chilled at the thought that his mouth on my skin might produce the same sensation. My lips dried, and I couldn't speak. I merely nodded, letting my hands rub up and down my gooseflesh arms. He had carried me to a spot shaded in shadows by the mighty rocks.

"Cooling down a little bit, now that we're in the shade?" he asked, his voice still too close, his body too near. I shivered when his chest brushed my back and his firm hands took over mine, rubbing my chilling arms, a contradiction to the heat. He pulled me tight to him, like he tugged me to him on the rock plateau. He was strong, and I wanted his strength. Needing to push him back when I wanted to draw him close, I didn't trust him. Only a moment before he was flirting with Persephone.

I spun to face him, ready to tell him the opposite of my thoughts. Twisting in his arms, I stood too much in his space, and my eyes locked with his. Caramel smoothness twinkled in the filtered sunlight. He smiled slowly, and coolness continued to cascade over me, traipsing over the hills of my breasts and the valley of my sides to hike the curves of my hips and settle between my thighs. My core beat like increasing rapids against jagged rocks in a river. My breath hitched at the sensual experience occurring from one intense gaze from his eyes. He leaned toward me, and I licked my lips. His hand almost to my face, he tilted his head, and I was mesmerized, as if struck by lightning, my body electrified, stood petrified, anticipating the current about to fill me.

"I'm starving," Heph's rough tenor boomed among the trees. "Let's eat."

Solis stepped back slowly, his eyes questioning what almost occurred. My heart contracted in disappointment and relief. He couldn't kiss me. He'd just been flirting with Persephone, and yet, my mouth instantly missed his without ever having met.

SOLIS

Stupid Heph.

"Just give us another minute."

My mouth had been so close to tasting the sweet nectar of those lips, her blue eyes blinding all thought to us being mere feet away from her best friend and my half-brother. It wasn't the way I anticipated a first kiss with Veva. In fact, the more she pissed me off, the less I envisioned a kiss happening between us ever. When I thought she threw the heart shaped rock away, I vowed to not think of her again. When she looked like she would pass out from the heat and Heph touched her in concern, jealousy reared its ugly head. I'd never been jealous before. I didn't have to be, at least not of other guys. I didn't keep a woman around long enough to be upset if another guy took interest. I actually hoped some guy would come along to distract whomever I'd taken my pleasure from, but with Veva, it was different. I didn't want another man to think of her, let alone touch her. If I didn't know Heph was harmless, I would have flattened him on the spot and made a cairn of him.

But Heph's interruption was a good thing, because once my mouth met Veva's there would be no taming the storm of desire that raged inside me. I'd been erect on and off all day, and my body hummed with suppressed tension. My lips would not just taste hers, I'd devour her. Lips and breasts. Heart and soul. I intended to blind her with my passion, and she'd rain down on me like no other. I hastily swiped a hand through my unruly, chin length hair. I should have brought a hair tie to hold it back. Holding it collected at the nape of my neck, I sighed in relief. That call had been too close. Images of taking Veva lingered and I looked away.

I noticed Persephone staring at the cairn. She missed him. Harris Black, he'd called himself on earth. Hades, my cousin, was his real name. I'd catch her in moments of deep thought, and I imagined her mind wandered to him. I'd given him my gift, but only for a little while. Time cut too short, I worried the after effects would run long. A year later and I stood correct in my concern.

"Can't you bring him back?" she'd asked me. *"Give him solar strength again. I know you did it the first time."*

I couldn't deny the truth, especially since I sensed she held back from speaking during dinner. In the openness of the rocks, there was no one to overhear her plea.

"I can't. I'm sorry." I didn't have the heart to tell her Hades didn't want to go through the pain again. He didn't want to prolong the hurt he or she would feel each time he visited. I told him to keep her for himself, but he refused. He didn't want to trap her in the darkness of his world. I didn't understand how love that strong couldn't bind them together in some way. Then again, I thought of my own mother, and Zeke. Their love destroyed them both. I didn't want to be like that. Love would not claim me.

"She's very beautiful." I'd been staring at nothing, but in the general direction of Persephone, and Veva's softened tone surprised me. Her typical bite gone, something sweet and painful filled her comment.

"She is," I sighed. "But she's not my type."

"Why?" Last night we'd argued this point, as if Veva wanted me to take Persephone. Today, her question asked out of curiosity. I couldn't be certain Veva knew the full truth. Hades had been a god among men, literally. I couldn't die either, but he would *kill* me if I went after his love.

"She belonged to another, and I don't want to be second to someone." The response seemed truthful enough and Veva's eyes opened wide. Her head nodded once. *Did she understand?* My brows pinched at the thought. *Had she loved someone before?*

"Did you know Had...Harris Black?" I corrected myself, almost giving away his identity.

"Not really." She shook her head, surprised that I knew his name. "He appeared out of nowhere, and then disappeared as fast as he'd arrived. Assumed dead, the investigators never found a body, but there was no way to survive what he'd been through."

I nodded slowly as if I understood, but I knew the truth.

"She loved him. I've never seen anything like that. I watched love blossom before my eyes." Veva's hands cupped and then opened, her fingers exploding forth like an unfolding flower. "It's like love was a living thing." She chuckled. "Sounds stupid, doesn't it?" She lowered her head and slipped her hands into the back pockets of her shorts.

"I think…it sounds different." I looked over at Persephone. "Like something special. I'm certain Had…Harris and Persephone were very lucky. Something like that only happens once in a lifetime." I sighed at the thought. A human lifetime, at least. The life I'd lived, I didn't anticipate love. I seemed to be following in my father's footsteps—casual sex with multiple women because I couldn't narrow my interests down to one. Heph asked me once if I thought it was because I hadn't found the right one. He wanted a one and only. I didn't believe in such fate, at least for me. It would take someone extraordinary to be the only one for me.

"Feeling better?" I asked, hoping to change the subject.

"Yeah, we can go."

VEVA

Solis helped me into the back of the Jeep. The top removed, we rode with the wind in our hair on the way to our destination. I anticipated the return trip to be just as windy. Solis stripped off his T-shirt and dropped into the driver seat. As I sat behind him, I stared at the giant scar down the middle of his back: a jagged ripple of puckered skin. My eyes narrowed as I took in the raised flesh and the white line against tan skin. *How painful had whatever been to cause such a scar?* The line cut over his spine like a jolt of lightning electrifying his skin. Actually, the very mark looked like it. A bolt of lightning, wild and striking across the expanse of his back, like a night sky.

I turned to Persephone. She noticed the same thing as me and our eyes touched briefly before each returned to stare. For some reason, I envisioned Solis as an angel who'd had his wings ripped from his back. My heart pinched and I covered my chest with my hand, rubbing over warm skin. Solis' eyes caught mine in the rearview mirror. He watched the motion of my palm massaging the space above my left breast. As I let my hand slowly fall over my large curve, gliding down to my stomach, the Jeep swerved. Persephone and I tumbled side to side in the backseat, and I was reminded of riding in the bed of pick-up trucks on the farm.

"Shit," Solis hissed as he righted the vehicle. Heph held the roll bar to the side of his head and stared at his brother. Combing a hand through his blond locks, Solis' eyes met mine in the mirror one more time. He winked at me.

Shit, I cursed myself. I shouldn't be teasing him. That near kiss was too much for me and I looked away, out at the open land of rocky hills and barren dirt. It amazed me olives grew in this heat and soil. Unlike the dark, rich earth of Nebraska, the valley's land lay brown and dry. Yet Zeke definitely ran a successful business. His estate spanned miles upon miles, and we returned quickly to his property.

Solis pulled up to the front door of the house, and hopped out to help me down from the back of the Jeep. Heph aided Persephone. I was about to thank Solis when the booming sound of Zeke's agitated voice startled all of us.

"Solis, I'd like to see you after you park, please." He nodded once to his son and then spun for the main door. Heph arched a brow at his brother and Solis shook his lowering head. I suddenly worried Solis might be in trouble for taking Persephone and I off the main property. Zeke and Demi became highly protective of Persephone after she'd been missing for months a year ago. When she returned, cognizant of where she'd been and unharmed, the protectiveness remained. As I once told her, I thought she'd had a great adventure, and I hoped when she was ready she'd explain it to me. That day hadn't come and it had been over a year.

Zeke offered Pea and me the place to stay for the summer as a means of vacation. For me, grad school was on the calendar after I graduated, as I wanted to earn my counseling degree. For Persephone, she hadn't decided what to do next.

Persephone and I headed to our room. I needed a shower after the steamy day and Zeke liked people dressed for dinner.

"I think Solis likes you." I stood inside our room, removing the heart shaped rock from my pocket. My thumb ran over the sharp edges and the heat warmed the pad of my finger.

"Veva," she laughed. "It's so obvious he's into you. Besides, he's not my type." I looked up at her. Irony rang through my ears as she used the same phrase as Solis. I understood better what Persephone meant. She'd fallen for a tall, lanky man, with jet black hair, hanging in his face and down to his neck. Solis couldn't be more opposite with his wild blond hair and honey eyes, not to mention the buff, tan body.

"Are you ever going to tell me about him?" I sat on my bed across from hers. She flopped back on hers and stared at the ceiling. Taking a deep breath, she began.

"Remember when I disappeared? I was with Har…Harris Black," she said, swallowing hard. "His real name is Hades." Her head rolled in my direction. "Veva, it's hard for me to even explain where I was or how I got there, but it was otherworldly, literally. The story is long, but the short version is, I couldn't stay and Hades didn't want to keep me." A tear trickled down her cheek.

"Harris Black was named Hades. That's a scary name, no wonder he changed it." I laughed, shivering exaggeratedly, ignoring my friend's tears. She didn't want me to draw attention to them and she hated when I tried to sympathize with her loss.

Persephone stared at me, willing me to understand something I couldn't read in her eyes.

"His father is named Hades as well. In fact, Hades Senior and Zeke are brothers."

I held up a hand, shaking my head. We hardly knew much of Zeke's family history. Yes, he had brothers, but I couldn't recall ever hearing their names. It was hard enough keeping up with his children. The absurdity of the relation proved Pea had lost her mind. Some post-traumatic stress disorder or something, since Harris Black's death.

"Persephone, you don't have to tell me anything you aren't ready for, but I'm your best friend. I can handle the truth."

"Veva, this is the truth. Hades is the son of Hades, Zeke's brother. They're both...gods." She blinked at me as if disbelieving her own words. She took a deep breath. "God, it feels good to tell someone," she muttered. I continued to stare at my delusional friend.

"Hades took the form of Harris Black to see me, but he couldn't stay. And I couldn't follow him."

"But you'd already been there before?" I nodded, as if I understood, but I didn't. "Why didn't he stay with you?" I knew that answer, too. Obviously, Persephone still suffered from the violent trauma of his death. She stared at me, another tear slipping from her eye. My heart sank to my belly. My poor, beautiful Persephone, she had gone crazy, I decided. Poor Pea, but a thought struck me.

"If Hades and Zeke are brothers, then his son, Hades, is Zeke's nephew, which means Solis is..." my voice trailed off.

"Hades' cousin." Persephone finished the thought for me. I stood from the bed and twisted a piece of hair around my finger. My counseling books encouraged to either play along with the story or try to recapture the truth. I paced the length of each bed.

"So if Hades is a god," I glanced over at her as I paced, "And Zeke is a god? You're saying Hades' son is a god, so Zeke's son must be..." I couldn't bring my mouth to form the incredulous word.

"A god."

I smiled weakly at my dearest friend, caught between the sympathy she deserved and the meds she needed.

"Honey, there's only one God."

"You think I'm crazy, right?"

"No, Pea. Just...I just think you're sad and you miss him, and that's okay. Making stuff up is a little freaky, but I love you still, and I'm sure Zeke has a brother, named Hades, who had a son, who is cousins with Solis. That all makes sense. Harris was a god, I'll give you that. He was Grecian-statue-come-to-life in all his sexy glory," I teased and my friend smiled weakly in response. In fact, it would make sense that Solis was a relation, as his physique rivaled those of the historic statues. Persephone's head shook at my comments but her eyes haunted me. She wanted me to believe her.

SOLIS

While the south wing housed our guests, the north wing was home to the relatives. Zeke had his own wing off the main structure, facing east and his fields of success. I found him there, in his office. He stood staring out at the olive groves, but he also had a direct view of the pool area. I couldn't be certain he wasn't ogling a female body sunbathing on the patio.

"Zeke." I didn't address him as my father. I'd had another man I called father, and Zeke and that man did not equate as equals.

"Solis." He turned to face me, sipping from a coffee mug. "Did you have a good day, son?" The title made me bristle. He liked to remind me I was his, as if my body didn't already bear the mark.

"Yes, we did." There was no point disguising who I had been with, he saw me drop off the girls.

"I'm pleased that you're social, welcoming our guests." He paused. "But you are aware that Veva and Persephone are special to me. They are more than visitors. They are practically family." I did know these things. Zeke couldn't decide between Hera Matron and Demi Fields, although the gossip said Zeke's heart lay with Hera more. I only had confirmation that Zeke ever consummated his love with one woman, once. The rumors questioned if either girl was his daughter. He'd already assured me they were not his children, but he loved them as such.

"Both girls are quite beautiful." The comment made my back straighten, family or not, the fact remained they were not of our bloodline and that made them fair game to Zeke. I hadn't seen him take interest in ones so young, but it was something I would not put past him.

"I'm curious if you've taken an interest in either girl?" He stared at me over the rim of his mug as he took another short sip of the coffee within. My mouth fell open and then snapped shut, continuing my silence. I didn't know if I'd taken an interest, either. Intrigued, definitely. Veva ignited something in me I hadn't felt before, and yet strangely felt familiar to me when she was near me. Her hatred fueled a storm. Her touch sparked lightning. I suddenly feared admitting these things to my father.

He nodded once before continuing. "I'd like to warn you that getting involved with either girl would be…complicated. Their mothers are strongly favored by me, and rumbling under the sheets with either girl could result in a family feud I do not wish to partake in." His eyes narrowed. "Not to mention the stunt you pulled last summer makes Persephone beholden still to Hades." I was well aware of the commitment between Hades and Persephone, as well as the result of their love affair. I'd done what I did because Hades asked me, and other than Heph, he was one of the few true friends I had in this so-called family.

"On that note, as you know, I go to the Fields' Farm each summer to help Titus and his daughters with whatever they need. Since they both agreed I should remain here and supervise their girls, I've decided to send you. This also prevents a risk of repeating what you did last summer for Hades." His eyes narrowed at me and an electric current ran up my back, shocked at his knowledge.

"So I'm being punished for taking the girls out rock climbing?" The anger in my tone struggled to remain suppressed. My fists clenched at my sides. This was the biggest bullshit he'd pulled in a long time.

"It's not punishment, it's a privilege. I'm giving you responsibility to help Hera and Demi."

"You're banishing me for entertaining their daughters."

Zeke's eyebrow rose. "And how exactly did you entertain them?"

Bile rose in my stomach. I wasn't the lowlife he was, taking two women at once. "Not like you'd think, Zeke. We went rock climbing. Heph was with us. He can confirm everything remained legit."

"Speaking of Heph, maybe you'd consider the Fields farm as support for him."

Fuck, I wanted to scream. I hated how my father used Heph against me. He knew I'd do anything for him. Knowing the truth of Heph's heritage slayed me. It had never been a burden until now.

"And how long will I be gone?"

"All summer, of course." Zeke triumphed at my defeat, a trait not uncommon to my father. He ruled supreme over his gaggle of children. Despite the illegitimacy of most of us, I remained one of his true children by a failed marriage. He once feared me, but I let him keep the upper hand. One day, he'd push me too far, like his own father pushed him. Wrath filled my veins.

"This isn't exactly fair." He hated when I pulled the fairness card. *You'd make a good lawyer*, he laughed. If I was his true son, and he recognized me, he'd be forced to treat me fairly. It wasn't appropriate that he treated us unequally, but no one promised all children would be loved the same. I stormed from his office. The skies matched my anger. A dark cloud covered the estate and thunder rumbled under the surface like the tension rolling under my skin. I fumed as I stalked the hallway leading to a familial common space. I burst out the door as the thunder clapped louder and stomped around the pool. Every time I headed to my studio I took a different path, determined no females would follow me. Lost in my anger, I trampled new ground to the hut. Lightning cracked the dry sky. I clapped my hand and rain tumbled like a sharp shower head, spraying the hot earth with refreshing drops. I ripped down the canvas Veva made and hung a new sheet. Stretching on my toes, I stroked the first burst of darkness and continued in my anger to paint a stormy landscape.

+ + +

The next morning, I found Veva in the family library. Seated at a table amongst several old books, she flipped frantically from page to page.

"Those are heirlooms," I teased, as one piece of parchment threatened to rip in her haste. Her eyes dropped to the yellowed paper and she smoothed her hand down the crease of the binding. She looked up at me, wide eyed and curious.

"Is that true?" The tone of her voice made the hairs on the back of my neck rise.

"Is what true?"

"You killed your father?" Her question floored me. My fists clenched instantly at images which brushed away sleep and caused me years of uncertainty.

"Where did you hear that?" I remained stuck in place, but Veva stood slowly, her brow pinching at my poised stance. Every muscle in my body tightened. She stepped toward me, but I shook my head in warning. We weren't at a point to share secrets.

"Locker room talk," she stated, tilting her head still noting my tense stance.

"Always believe what you hear in there?" My false smile and clenched teeth pulled a slow curve to her lips. Her adamant "Yes," relaxed me as she teased.

"That's unfortunate," I replied, letting my momentary irritation release slowly. My hands unclenched and I leaned against the door jamb.

"I heard you were an amazing lover from there, too."

I laughed in response, relaxing completely. Surely, she jested, and I was quick to retort. "Want to test out that rumor, and see if it's true?"

"Not on your father's life." Her tipped head proved she'd circled back to being mean.

"You don't have to be cruel. A simple no would do." Preparing to press off the jamb and leave her to her hasty studies, the softened tone in her next question stopped me.

"Persephone told me." She paused. "Is it true?"

I pressed off the doorjamb and walked into the room. I stood at the end of the table.

"Is what true?" The false smile returned to my face and threatened to crack.

"Don't lie to me. I hate liars." She slapped the book and then crossed her arms. Her face turned to the window at her side.

"What do you know?" My head lowered and I stared at the open page. Greek mythology. My eyes closed. "You can't always believe all that you read, either. History omits."

Her head swung back to me and she glared at me.

"I'm Solis Cronus. My father is Zeke. My mother was named Meta. They had a true marriage."

She shook her head in disbelief. What I rattled off were facts she knew.

"How are you related to Hades?"

I flinched at the direct use of his name. Persephone had told her.

"He's my cousin."

"So it's true. You're a god."

A genuine smile crossed my face, seeing an out to this conversation. "Well, I have been told that on occasion."

Her eyes rolled. "This is funny to you, isn't it?" She walked to the window, her back to me. The day blossomed to a sunny blue sky after a night of violent lightning storms.

"Veva," my tone warned.

"Is this a joke? Are you and Persephone in on this together? Let's try to fool Veva to disguise our feelings for one another."

"What feelings?" I asked, stepping closer to her. My hands twitched to swipe her hair to the side, exposing the nape of her neck and those fine hairs I desired to stroke.

"The ones you have for Persephone." Her hand swiped at her cheek.

"Are you crying?" I stepped to the side of her, attempting to peek at her face.

"No," she snapped, briskly wiping the other cheek.

"I don't have feelings for Persephone, Veva. I told you that." I emphasized the last words, softening my tone.

"How am I to believe you? How can I believe anything? So many lies."

"What lies, Veva?" I stood directly beside her, my hands itching to reach for her. The vibe radiating off her skin told me if I did, she'd shatter.

"Zeke. Hades. Who are these people? Who are you?"

"It doesn't matter, Vee." Her incredulous stare told me I better start talking, though, or that heavy book could be a weapon launched at me. Her white knuckles at her elbows confirmed her slow boil.

"My mother married my father, but a prophecy predicted a son of their union would kill him. When she found out she was having a son, she ran away. She found solace in another man. When Zeke found her, he was angered that she'd disappeared and hid me. He forced her to return to him. She gave him a daughter instead. He claimed the girl as his one true heir." Athena. Athena was my sister from my father's first marriage.

She turned to look at me, hearing something in my voice. My jaw clenched. Liquid filled her eyes.

"This is all so strange. A prophecy?" Her tone turned serious. "That's a little sketchy. Why not say your horoscope predicted it? I mean, let's poke fun at Veva, was that a prophecy, too?"

"You think this is a joke. I just shared my life with you." I pressed off the window and paced a few steps away. The full truth swirled behind my teeth and then stormed through my throat for release. I wanted to tell her everything, but her attitude prevented my trust. I didn't need her to laugh at me.

"Girl, what has gotten into you?" I chuckled bitterly, attempting to crack the tension myself as I stalked back her. I could see Veva simmering, ready to explode. While I wanted to take that boiling energy to a new level, her anger was not what I had in mind. I shook my head.

"Veva," I said, reaching out to cover her shoulders.

"Don't touch me," she growled. My hands retreated upward in surrender as she spun to face me.

"Veva, slow down. What do you want to know?"

"Does Zeke have special powers, oh-wa-ha-ha…" Her voice drifted off in eerie mockery, while her fingers wiggled in my direction. "What about his brother, Hades? Or this Harris-Black-Hades fabrication Persephone developed?" Her voice rose with each question and the irony of truth in her asking prevented me for answering.

"Veva, I can't tell you."

She brushed past me to the open book at the table. "Can't or won't?"

My pause answered her. Their stories were not mine to tell.

"You're just like the rest." She shook her head. "So many untold truths. It's all a joke."

My frustration festered that she would lump me with the rest of them. My father. My uncle. Even my cousin.

"Well, I guess you won't have to worry about me for much longer, because I'm being sent away. Zeke is sending me to your family farm, since you and Persephone are here."

Her forehead crinkled. "Because of us?"

"Yes, for some reason he doesn't want me around either of you because I took you *rock climbing*." My mouth spat the last two words, the frustration rising to boil inside me.

"That's stupid." She turned completely to face me. Her arms crossed again as her hip rested against the table.

"That's what I told Zeke." Her eyebrows rose. "I mean, what kind of threat am I to either one of you? You hate me, and Persephone still loves Hades."

"Exactly." Her hands dropped and smacked her thighs, but her eyes squinted at me.

"And there's no way I could hook up with either of you." I stepped closer to her and she repositioned herself to rest her sweet behind against the table. My feet straddled her outstretched ones.

"I mean, you never like it when I touch you." My hand brushed a wayward hair cascading over her shoulder and traced up her neck that called out for my lips. Her back straightened. Her shoulders set.

"And you can't even talk to me without barking at me." My finger dragged along her jaw, drawing down her chin.

"And the thought of kissing me repulses you." My finger jumped to trace her lips, the pout of the lower flesh and the tempting bow of the upper curve. Her throat rolled as she swallowed, and I leaned toward her.

"And if we can't kiss, we'd never, ever, engage in sex, and you'd never learn if locker room talk was true." I breathed over her slightly open mouth as my voice lowered, the deep tone almost strangling me, while my lips hovered so closer to hers. She sucked in that breath and then closed her lips, holding my words inside the warmth of her mouth.

My hand came up to her neck and slipped under her hair. She gently pressed back, the fight apparent in her, but her body screamed for mine. My Veva wanted to struggle. My mouth prepped for the fight.

"Solis, I've been looking for you." Mel's voice crawled over my skin, scraping deep gouges down my already scarred back. My eyes closed. *Damn it.*

"Better not keep your lady waiting," Veva snipped. "Especially one who will have sex with you, according to the locker room."

VEVA

Solis left the room and rage flew out of me. He'd almost had me—his tempting words, his electric nearness, the sad expression at the mention of his father. I swept the table clear of books, and I pushed over a chair to clatter on the floor. I fell amidst the mess I made, and cried hot tears of frustration. He played me.

"Veva." Heph found me as a heaving mess on the tile, sobbing over my own foolishness. The rough tone didn't startle me, and I looked up at those deep, dark eyes. Heph settled on the floor next to me and I curled into him. His awkward embrace and clumsy pat on my back expressed his confusion. I couldn't explain it either, but I wanted to be close to someone.

"What happened here?"

"I…" How could I explain that I lost control? These types of tantrums had happened many times before. Constricted. It was the best word to describe me. Wound so tight I felt I couldn't breathe until I let the energy out of me. I took out my frustration on the books and the chair until my own sobs brought me down to the floor.

"The books?" I looked up at Heph. "I ruined the heirlooms." A shaky hand covered my mouth. Forgetting their precious value, I reacted with my heart, not my head. *You've always been like this*, my mother said. She was the cause.

"These dusty old things. Nah, don't worry about it." His arm was still wrapped around my shoulder, my head resting on his. "What did he do?"

"What did who do?" But instantly, I thought of Solis.

"Whoever made you so mad you turned the library into a training ring?"

I giggled. The place was a mess. I aggressively swiped at my cheeks, my makeup undoubtedly smeared down my face.

"It's silly girl things." I waved dismissively, not certain I could explain my frustration with Solis to his brother.

"Oh." He nodded like he understood. "I don't understand." He looked down at me, and I pressed on his thick chest to sit upright.

"I don't think I understand either, Heph. Sometimes, I just lose it. It's like energy bottled up inside me and I just explode."

"Like soda in a can?"

"Like soda in a can, exactly. Working on the farm, I burned the energy by day, let off steam at night." I decided to stop the explanation there; it wasn't necessary to share the details with Heph. "At school, it wasn't as easy, but I worked out and it helped. Here, I've been too lazy. I need to run or walk or do something to let the negative energy go." I lifted my arms out straight and shook them back and forth. "Solis had me paint the other night and that helped."

Heph's head swung to look at me. "He did? He never takes girls to his studio."

"He doesn't?" It was my turn to wonder.

"Says it's his sanctuary. He doesn't bring the girls there." He nodded to emphasize the statement.

But I was there, I thought, and he didn't make me leave. He didn't try to take advantage of me, either. He made me paint and then he held me. All night he cradled me against him on the hard floor, comforting me by smoothing back my hair. I thought of his breath against my neck when he finally slept, his warmth surrounding me, keeping me calm.

"He likes a lot of girls, doesn't he?" I taunted Heph with my question.

"He does, but he's looking for the one. Tells me all the time, the one is out there." Heph's eyes glazed over, dreamy, and still. His gaze fell to his metal leg. My brows pinched, and I looked at the scar on his forehead.

"What happened to you?"

"I fell climbing the rocks one day, and that took my leg." He paused a beat. "My father kicked me out once, and this is what happened." A thick finger circled his face.

60

"Zeke kicked you out?" While Zeke had too many children to keep track of, the idea that he banished a child surprised me. But then I thought of Solis, and the idea he was being sent away because he took Pea and I rock climbing…Could he have thrown Heph out as well?

"It was such a long time ago. I went in search of my mother, but she didn't want me. She thought I was slow or something." He looked off toward the stacks of books, his large feet rolling back and forth against the tile floor.

"I can't imagine a mother never wanting a child." My voice rose a little with my surprise.

"Mine didn't. Well, at least not me." His lips twisted. "Anyhow, Zeke took me back. He said I was ugly but he loved me, and not to piss him off again. I didn't need to search for her to find love. I had it here." He pointed at the floor, representing this estate. "And here." He tapped his chest. "I don't think he was right, but I haven't left again." Heph's rough voice grew sad. My hand covered his thick wrist, measuring the size of a small tree trunk. He was strong, despite the injury to his leg or his face. He didn't seem smart, but he was wise.

"My father didn't want me either. Whoever he was, he didn't want me."

"How do you know that?" His big eyes questioned me.

"My mother. She's always hinting that the reason he left was because he didn't want a child." I shrugged. I hardened my heart to those words. My psychology courses taught me I used men to replace the emptiness I felt at being abandoned by my father. I called bullshit on that diagnosis. I was fine without a man. They only served one purpose for me.

Heph looked at me. He eyed my hair and my face. He looked down at my hand on his wrist. Then narrowed his eyes when he looked into mine.

"You look so much like her," he muttered. "Except for the eyes. Those must be his."

"Who?"

"Your father," he said. I blinked.

"Do you know who he is?" The question surprised me. Of course, he wouldn't know. Heph hardly knew me.

"Nope. I've met your mother, though. And you could be her twin." I'd heard that so many times. My mother often blushed, but I hated the comparison. I didn't want to be like her. She was a bitter woman because my father left her. She held hatred like no one I'd ever known. She despised men and she tried to instill that legacy in me. Men were evil. They would leave, especially if I gave myself to one. They led to heartache. She cursed all men, even Zeke, though she smiled demurely at him and got that pained expression in her eyes each time she saw him.

"When did you met Hera?"

Heph's head shot away from mine, and he bit his lip. "Um, while I wandered, I came across her." He pressed off the floor and stood effortlessly. A little hobble and he straightened his poor leg. He reached a hand down to me and hoisted me upward like a small child. Releasing my hand instantly, he offered to help me clean up. I stared at him. He didn't wait for my acceptance; he just righted the chair and picked up books. He glanced up at me while I watched him, and a familiarity hit me again. His eyes. There was something about them. I'd seen them before, and the eerie sensation of recognition hovered in my mind. Heph handed me a book, and the thought disappeared. The book of mythology recaptured my attention.

SOLIS

The news Mel told me rocked me to the core. While I didn't see how it couldn't wait until after I kissed Veva, it certainly was shocking information, and Mel knew how to surprise me. She'd interrupted my attempts twice now, and I started to wonder if she had a sixth sense about my attraction to Veva. Impossible, though, as Mel was not a goddess, but a royal princess here on earth. She'd asked for my help, and I recommended a priestess familiar with Athena. Zeke would freak if he knew Mel was involved in this scandal. Her mother was one of his many lovers.

For days, I kept my distance from Veva, trying to prove to my father that I had no particular interest in her or Persephone. The rock climbing excursion was merely a friendly adventure with our newest guests. Heph came to my defense, and it had been a week of waiting for Zeke's banishment. The warning clear, if I crossed a line with either girl, there would be severe consequences. His temper could flare at a moment's notice, and I rested on the edge of a precipice, awaiting the summons to leave.

Now that Veva knew the truth, or at least questioned some things, I was certain she would have no interest in me. A god. It was true. As Zeke's oldest son, despite his favored daughter, I was the secret heir to all his wealth. The thirteenth Olympic Oil trustee. The one not mentioned in history. I would inherit his plantation on earth and his powers within the heavens. I'd already received some control. The weather often mimicked my mood, especially lately. My anger with Zeke increased my ability to alter things. My trainer was impressed daily with the strength and control I exhibited. I bore the scar that gave me that power, but I suppressed the control so as not to overrule my father, as the prophecy foretold. I did not wish to follow in his path, and fulfill a destiny set because of his own actions.

I unexpectedly found Veva in the guest common room one afternoon painting with water colors.

"Whatcha doing?" I asked over her shoulder, startling her. A paint brush stood out of a cup filled with murky water. She snapped the simple case closed and stood to face me, attempting to block the low table from my view. I stepped left; she followed. I stepped right; she blocked me again. With my best right-left fake, I reached forward and tugged her against me, and then spun to place her behind me.

"Hey," she complained, banging on my chest. I peered over my shoulder down at the work. A multitude of gray clouds in varying shades filled the paper. A bright yellow lightning bolt highlighted the center of the page. A second paper sat off to the side, drying. A lightly-tanned back marked by a dark scar centered the page. Golden wings at each side emphasized the body in the middle. My face shot back to hers. One hand circled both of her wrists to halt the beating on my chest.

"Veva, what's this?" My voice snapped harsher than I intended, but panic rose inside me.

"I'm just…" Her tone softened. Her eyes sheepish. "I'm just painting."

I towered over her two samples on the low table. "Those are both good. Tell me about them."

She struggled in my hold, but I refused to release her. I wanted to know why she painted a replica of the image she made in my room and the picture of a broken angel.

"I liked the one I made in your studio. I wanted another one to…" She shrugged, diverting her eyes to the floor.

"Tell me," I demanded, again my voice rough.

"I wanted to make another one to remind me to remain calm," she snapped in annoyance. I lowered our joined hands. Still imprisoning her wrists like a handcuff, I nodded in the direction of the second one.

"And the other one?"

Her eyes shot up to mine and then looked away instantly. "Are you Icarus?" The question asked so low I wasn't certain I heard her.

"Icarus?" My brows pinched.

"The angel who flew too close to the sun. Did your wings rip out? Did you fall to the ground? Did you hit your head and devise this craziness that you're a god?" Each question brought a higher octave, and deeper sarcasm, as she struggled within my hold. I released her and sat sharply in the comfy chair she previously occupied. I picked up the picture with a shaky hand.

"You think I'm an angel?" I stared at the image. It wasn't perfect, but a strange sentiment washed over me at the thought.

"I don't know how to explain what I think, but you have that strange scar…" Her voice trailed off.

"I was struck by lightning." My response was matter-of-fact, the concept old, the experience a long time ago. It was her turn to sit in the chair next to mine with a thud. Her mouth fell open as shaky fingers loosely covered her lips.

"Struck by lightning? My God, that must have hurt."

"It did." Blunt and true, my answer weighed between us. She waited for more. "I lived with my stepfather, a man unkind when my mother disappeared. One night he discovered she was with Zeke and had a daughter with him. He raged out of control. His vengeance focused on me." I closed my eyes at the memory of repeated strikes against my younger body. "That night there was a horrible lightning storm. Thunder boomed. Lightning blazed. The rain was torrential. My anger paralleled it. I couldn't take another beating in her name, and I turned on him. Lightning struck me and I struck him." Memories flooded me. Energy crackled the space around me and the power of my stepfather, a man not really my father in any form. Electricity pitched from the earth and crept up my skin. I screamed in torture, but took the force and struck out at him.

I dropped the paper back on the table, releasing it from my shaky fingers. I stood and ran a hand through my hair. I couldn't finish my story. I didn't want Veva to know the evil I endured, the evil I could produce, the strength within me.

"What happened to him?" The question was inevitable, but I didn't wish to repel Veva more than I already had. What happened next would remain in me. A vision of my stepfather floated before me, and then crystallized into the air, particles washed away in the rain, just like he had been that night. Such power thrilled and frightened me. I'd keep the secret, even though Zeke explained what happened once he found me. If Veva had trouble believing I was a god, she'd never accept the rest of the story. She'd think I was a monster.

"I gotta go," I lied. I stepped around the table. To my surprise, Veva stood, reached out for me, and gripped my wrist. The electric prickles tingling up my arm caused me to pause. I spun to face her. Veva represented something I didn't ever expect to find, but I wasn't ready to get lost in those eyes questioning me. I shook my arm to release her hold.

"I'm no angel, Veva."

VEVA

Later that night, when I entered my room, the original canvas sheet of my stormy night painting covered my bed. A note on the nightstand read:

To calm your fears and surround you in peace.

A lightning bolt scribbled next to the words marked the paper. My lips twisted, fighting a grin. Next to the note, I also found my heart-shaped rock surrounded with a delicate metal holder and dangling from a leather strap. The strap hung long and the charm fell between my breasts. The warmth of the rock surprised me and my fingers fumbled over the solid earth momentarily. I brought the charm to my lips and brushed it lightly over the sensitive skin. The rock nearly singed them with its heat. Dropping the heart, it fell with a soft thud back in place between my breasts. My hand covered the new jewelry and I realized I liked the tickling warmth more than I should.

The next morning, I found Zeke alone in the breakfast room. I hesitated a moment, stepping back from his line of sight, or so I had hoped.

"Good morning, Veva," he spoke over a large newspaper spread near his cup of coffee. My shoulders sank, and I took a giant step forward to enter the room.

"Good morning, Zeke." I loved Zeke, in my own special way, but a certain level of discomfort also wrestled inside me. I wasn't afraid of him. On the contrary, my unease came from the desire to talk to him. I wanted to ask him questions, like: *Why would a man leave a child?* These thoughts haunted me when I pondered the disappearance of my own father, and my mother's accusation of my blame. Zeke clearly loved his children. He surrounded himself with them like badges of honor. On the other hand, another question rankled in my head: *Why don't you love one woman?* Because despite his numerous offspring, evidently, he never settled on one woman and I worried no man would ever settle on me. Too restless of spirit, I worried I wouldn't decide on one man either. I couldn't trust one. I had the track record to prove it. On top of those concerns rested the confounding questions of Solis' origin and the mystery behind people I loved, but now questioned.

"You know, there are easier ways to get the news than an old-fashioned paper," I offered, strolling to the breakfast bar heaped with muffins, bagels and fruit.

"I know," he chuckled. "But I love how antiquated it is. It brings me comfort to scroll paper instead of a computer." He smiled warmly as he brought his coffee mug to his lips and swallowed. He sat powerfully in his chair at the end of his breakfast table. A man clearly comfortable in his own skin, I could see how Solis inherited the confidence.

"Did you enjoy yourself the other day?" He questioned, folding the paper to give me his attention.

"I did, actually," I answered as I gathered some fresh fruit on a small plate and walked to the table to sit near Zeke. "I'm actually afraid of heights, but Solis and Heph were excellent guides."

"I see," Zeke replied, as if I'd said something profound. He paused momentarily and then spoke again, his attention to the coffee mug. "And how exactly did they guide you?"

I stopped, a strawberry stabbed by my fork, mid-air to my mouth, frozen in motion. Innuendo rode in the undertone of his question.

"Excuse me?" I blinked. Zeke rose his mighty head and shook it gently, like brushing off a thought. His snow-white hair didn't move with the motion, and he curled his large lips surrounded with white scruff.

"I meant, how did they help you climb?"

I sensed a greater implication to Zeke's question. I wasn't certain what he fished for, but I wasn't about to hand Solis and Heph over like the daily catch. They took us rock climbing, not to an orgy.

"Solis is very encouraging. He knew I was frightened and motivated me to keep going. Heph is incredibly strong, but very agile, and he told me where to place my feet and hands to support myself." My hands sweated a little at the thought. In the moment, I hadn't been able to question what I was told to do, I just went with it. But thinking of the climb in hindsight, the reality of slipping and falling, made me shiver.

"Well, my boys are turning into good men," he chuckled. His laughter broke the tension, and I braved the moment to speak candidly.

"I hear you're sending Solis away for the rest of the summer." I continued to raise the stationary strawberry to my lips and bit delicately into the sweet fruit. The taste reminded me of the farm, and a small pang of homesickness pricked me.

"Yes, well, I'm assuming your mother and her sister could use some support, since I'm staying here this summer." He smiled, but the twinkle to his eyes was absent. Zeke strangely liked working on our farm, although he had his own elaborate estate. For a second, our summer stay seemed like a punishment to him, denying him where he'd rather be spending his time.

"You know, you could always go and leave Solis in charge here instead." I don't know where the suggestion came from, or why I offered the possibility. "I'm sure he's a competent leader." I actually didn't know that. I'd heard rumors that Solis had only recently joined the estate and was slowly learning his father's business, but the arrogance Solis exuded procured my opinion. Somehow, I just sensed he'd be the ruler of this estate one day.

"I'm not ready for Solis to lead yet," Zeke bit out harshly, and the deep tenor surprised me. My fork fumbled at the force of his voice and a strange flip-and-catch distracted us both. He chuckled again to soften the strength of his words. "In his own time, he'll rule, but not yet. I'm not that old." He laughed and the twinkle to his eyes returned, as if he'd shared a joke with himself.

"Of course not, I just thought, being new to the estate, he might benefit from staying here instead of being sent away." *Stop it*, I scolded myself. *Away* was exactly where I wanted him to be, and yet I continued to reinforce his staying.

"Oh, did Solis mention he had newly moved here?" An eyebrow twitched upward and then fell as he picked up his coffee mug to disguise the question.

"Rumors," I laughed. He joined me with another weak chuckle.

"Well, you definitely shouldn't believe everything you hear. Especially on this estate." He winked at me, his words haunting me. I suddenly thought of what I'd learned from Persephone and what Solis played off in the library. My insecurity took hold and I briefly believed Zeke was in on the fool's game Solis and Persephone played with me; his wink a warning. I excused myself in need of fresh air.

+ + +

I found Heph near the stables. I hadn't ridden a horse in over a year. I didn't encounter many in California, and I missed my chestnut beauty, Spitfire, back home. She was a feisty filly like me, Zeke said, when I named her. She'd race like the wind, and my worries went with her as we crossed the large fields of our farm. Homesickness struck for the second time in the day, but the feeling passed the moment I saw Heph. He was a gentle giant, and his slow, awkward smile put me at ease.

"Thank you," I said, holding out the pendant from my chest. His smile grew, but he ducked his head to avoid mine.

"You like it?" He shyly asked as he addressed the horse he brushed.

"It's perfect. Very pretty." My smile emphasized the truth of my words. He hadn't polished the stone and the subtle silver wrap, serving as its holster, didn't detract from the rough rock. The leather strap made for a more natural necklace than a silver chain, and I loved the uniqueness of such a piece of jewelry.

"Pretty necklace for a pretty girl," Heph muttered, and the heat rose on my cheeks. It was sweet, not in a flirtatious way, but tender, and I blushed all the same at the compliment. I was used to being called *hot*, but not pretty. Never pretty.

"Who you calling pretty?" The deep voice behind me forced the hairs at my neck to stand at attention. My eyes didn't move from Heph, but Solis' presence surrounded me. His warmth seeped into my skin, but I remembered his joke at my expense and I refused to answer him. His breath tickled my neck as he breathed heavily behind while he waited for an answer.

"Veva is pretty." Heph stilled the brushing motion and turned to face Solis. His big, dark eyes narrowed, and he glared at Solis over my shoulder. Words exchanged in that stare, and Solis finally replied.

"Veva is very pretty, Heph. In fact, she's…" *hot*, the word rang through my head, so I blinked, startled, when Solis said, "stunning."

Heph's eyes opened wide, and I spun to face the mockery I sensed in his tone, but his expression held firm. His eyes fixed on mine and I melted under the heat inside them.

"Did you sleep well?" Solis reached up to sweep back a wayward hair from my ponytail. I shrugged in response.

"What's this?" He reached out for the pendant I toyed with in my fingers. Seeing the necklace, he stopped my motion and slipped a hand under the stone to bring it closer.

"Heph made it for me." I smiled over at Heph who looked away. His large shoulders set square, he returned to brushing the horse before him. My grin faded, and I glanced back at Solis, who continued to hold the necklace in his palm.

"It's my rock," he mumbled, his tone thoughtful and low, his eyes not leaving the stone. When he gazed up at me, the honey heat turned to swirling caramel. His brow pinched, but a smile grew.

"Want to take a ride?" He nodded at the horse. "He's mine. Thunder." My hand rose to pet the steed before me.

"He's so beautiful." My knuckles stroked the solid flanks of the gray stallion. Solis gave Heph some instructions, and another horse was brought to me.

"This is Chariot. She'll treat you well." Solis lifted me with ease into the saddle on the coal-black filly. We cantered out of the stable grounds, but as soon as we cleared the first fence, Solis called over his shoulder, "Race!"

It wasn't a question, and he took off at a full gallop, sprinting down the lane beside the olive grove. I kicked my horse into a gallop and we charged behind Solis. I curled into Chariot and we cleared the hunches

elda lore

of Solis' stallion, Thunder. Our horses pressed forth, neck and neck. Solis pushed Thunder harder, but I kept the pace.

"To that line," Solis called out over his shoulder, the wind catching his words and lacing them back to me. He nodded in the direction of a broken fence. Behind the fallen, wooden structure stood a briar of low bushes marking the end of the property. Even further in the distance appeared a cliff, like the world ended and fell into nothingness. I leaned further into Chariot, determined to win, my heart matching the beating hooves beneath me as we pressed onward. I hadn't felt this free in forever, I realized, and the rhythm of the horse spurred me on, taking with it any questions and doubts, along with my strange attraction to someone I was determined to despise. We drew closer to the fence and I sensed Solis prepared to claim victory. Not letting up on Chariot, I encouraged her to race for the fence and prepped her to jump.

"Veva." The cry came too late as Chariot cleared the wooden structure and the prickly bushes in a graceful leap. Briefly, I had a sense of flying, as if Chariot wished to continue racing in the air. The space between the briar and the end of the cliff was shorter than it appeared from a distance. The edge of the world grew closer and I sat up, tugging back on the reins once we landed on solid ground.

"Whoa, Chariot. Whoa, girl," I cried out, but Chariot seemed to have a mind of her own. A strange premonition of her leaping off the cliff before filled me with fear. Impossible, I argued internally. She'd be dead if she leapt from this height, but she barreled forward like she knew what she was doing and where she was going. Clamoring at high speed toward the edge of the cliff, I screamed for her to halt. Paying attention to nothing else but the impending edge, a hand suddenly reached over mine and Solis' stallion forced Chariot to shift away from the cliff. Rocks skittered under Thunder's hooves as he scrambled at the sharp edge, his footing hovering over nothing for moment, before we fully turned away from our demise. Solis pulled tight on the reins and Chariot cantered to a stop.

The instant the horses were in the clear and back toward the briar of bushes, Solis slipped off Thunder, dragging me off Chariot at the same

72

time. We stood walled between the two heaving steeds, our own breaths falling rapidly between us. My heart raced so quickly my whole body vibrated like the thump of a parade drum. With hands on my shoulders, Solis shook me.

"Do you have a fucking death wish?" His fingers slipped to my upper arms and his breath covered my face, hot and angry. My body trembled with the fear of flying over a cliff on a horse and the adrenaline of racing Chariot. I didn't have time to answer before Solis' mouth crashed over mine. Hard and powerful, his lips burned. The force so sudden, I gave in to the instant pressure, thrilling at the weight and strength as his mouth controlled mine. One hand slid into my ponytailed hair, tilting my head. The other cupped the back of my neck, drawing in more of me, as if his life depended on my air to breathe. That's when it occurred to me that Solis' mouth was on mine. With strength I didn't know I possessed, I forced him backward with a sharp press to his chest. His distance wasn't far, as the horses still stood on either side of us.

Both of us breathing heavily, I gaped at him.

"Just what do you think you were doing?" My hands fell to my knees as I tried to catch my breath and calm my heart, which was racing faster than Chariot had been. The rock necklace dangled from my neck, swinging heavily to and fro in rhythm with my heaving chest. My lips tingled in that way any part of me did when Solis touched me. A prickly heat covered my skin, and a pulse beat between my thighs, matching my heartrate. I ached in a way I'd never felt before. I wanted Solis to touch me, and I cursed myself for the thought. My hands begged to reach out for him, but I forced my fingers to dig into my kneecaps and hold steady. I would not throw myself at him.

"You scared the crap out of me," he yelled, his booming voice startling me. I didn't trust myself to stand, so I peeked at him over my shoulder. His hand slipped into his dirty blond hair and held back the chin-length locks. His head tilted toward Thunder as he stared up at the sky.

"I thought I'd lost you." His eyes closed and his tone softened. I had to look away. The pained expression on his face tore at my insides. I couldn't have scared him, could I? He couldn't be afraid of losing me, could he? He didn't have me. He didn't own me.

"Come on, Veva, admit it felt good. Admit you've been wanting me to do that to you." His smug tone extinguished any passion boiling inside me, and my sympathy for his concern dissipated. Thoughts of him thinking of me as his released, like words falling over the cliff, anger taking its place. I would admit to no such desire for him.

"Get over yourself," I exhaled, righting myself. My hands rested on my hips. "I didn't want you to kiss me." My eyes pinched in disgust while my heart continued to leap. My insides vibrated with a need to feel his lips on mine in a less aggressive manner. I'd been with too many boys who wanted it hard and fast. Just once, I wanted it slow and sweet, and the chemistry with Solis would be nothing less than full-speed-ahead. I spun away from him.

"Veva." He growled immediately behind me. I kept walking, minus my horse. He'd apologize, I realized. And I'd hate him. I didn't want him to be sorry he kissed me. *I didn't want him to be anything*, I lied to myself. I just wanted to get away from him.

"Take your horse," he snapped, and I turned back, refusing to look at him. I hitched up Chariot and turned her away from the ledge. Her head pulled back on the reins, not able to tear her large animal eyes from the open space off that cliff.

"Chariot," Solis barked. "No." As if the horse understood Solis' command, she swung her mighty head and pranced toward a seam between the bushes. Her head thrashed as if she longed for control of something, as if she couldn't forget the freedom of falling off a cliff. Understanding that constricted sensation, I kicked at her haunches and leaned forward muttering, "Yes." Chariot bolted for the stable, leaving Solis in our dust.

SOLIS

I so fucked this up, I cursed in my head as my hand briskly painted over the canvas. Large, swishing strokes released the anger that welled inside me at my stupidity. However, Veva nearly killed herself racing for the ledge, and just the thought of it sent my heart beating faster than my galloping horse. The relief that she wasn't hurt had overcome me, and I needed her air to be mine, to reassure me she was safe.

"Stupid girl," I muttered, as my hand stroked feverishly across the canvas. The blues blended, and the purples pulsed, forcing the forest green to gyrate to the forefront. The painting matched one eye from the multitude spread over her leg and thigh.

"Damn it," I cursed aloud. Veva had gotten under my skin, furrowing there with her touch, sweltering below the surface with nips and sparks of desire. That kiss wasn't enough, not even close to being enough of a jolt. Her lips were the sharp prick of a first flame from a lighter, and I wanted the whole bonfire to roar against me, to consume me.

I finished painting and stepped back, never feeling satisfied with my work. The eye stared at me, taunting me, like Veva. Her mouth teased me, but her eyes—there was something haunting about them. A hesitation. A sadness. She'd mentioned a disappearing father and a bitter mother. If only she understood the depth of my tale. Unwanted son, abandoned by mother. Unexplainable power. Yet, somehow I felt like Veva did understand me. Our mouths melding together, hot and fierce, sealed the familiarity I sensed between us. I knew those lips, if only from a dream. The desire to feel such passion haunted me. The feel of them was reminiscent of something I couldn't bring to the forefront of my mind, but recalled like a distant memory. *Had I tasted her before?* I'd remember from all my pasts, and yet the refreshing flavor of her juicy lips told me I'd only thirst for her from this day forward. Each drink would be to recall the memory, to savor it, and never forget again who she was to me.

+ + +

June sweltered into the heat of July, which was my father's month. King of the zodiac signs, Leo the lion was ruled by the sun, and my father roared his power each July by hosting a large celebration for his birthday at the end of the month, lasting an entire week. While we didn't actually celebrate the passing of another year, it was the perfect excuse to throw a party, and a mandatory call to all his relatives to rejoin him at his estate. We didn't have as many extra outside guests—especially mortals—for the joyful occasion, as Zeke liked to think his special week should be about family. To my surprise, he allowed Persephone and Veva to remain on the estate. I'd heard their mothers had been invited, but each refused to attend the grand party.

"Let the celebration begin." At midnight, Zeke raised his glass to the attendees as he stood on the top step of his tiered patio. The pool was filled with floating candles, glittering in reflection to the dark sky overhead. The Olympian pool deck was covered with centuries of family and descendants who lifted their glasses in appreciation and drank to the longevity of our lives. In response, I downed my glass of champagne. I didn't feel like celebrating.

Veva had been ignoring me for a week.

Mel hadn't gone to the priestess I recommended.

Letty was in trouble.

I didn't understand women. When the waitress, dressed in a toga style uniform and a laurel wreath crown, drew near with a tray of champagne, I grabbed two, downing one as I walked through the crowd. As usual, my sister stood near my father, acting as hostess, despite her role as daughter. Her status as the favorite was confirmed each year at these gatherings. I continued to wander, but not mingle. Even though this was family, I felt out of place. I was still newly recognized as Zeke's son: the prophesized son, board member number thirteen, not part of the original twelve. The old adage of "keep your family close, your enemies closer," rang true to me.

Scanning the expanse of the pool deck, searching out only one person among the crowd, two exaggeratedly shadowed turquoise eyes found me. The ultra-sheer material of Veva's ankle-length dress exposed the full length of her peacock tattoo, climbing her leg with its beak outstretched to an area I coveted. A hand on her hip emphasized her slender waist and curvy hips. My eyes travelled the rest of her as I approached, like a hunter narrowing in on the hunted. Two strips of fabric started at the waist, and veered outward and upward, cutting deep and exposing skin between her lush breasts. I hardened as I walked, imagining all the things I'd love to do to that skin from waist to neck. My eyes squinted, attempting to find underwear lines under the transparent fabric. They shot to hers in question as I drew closer.

"Heph." I nodded at another unfavored offspring, looking highly uncomfortable in a button down shirt with dark jeans, his dressiest attire.

"Persephone, lovely as ever." I reached for her hand and bowed to kiss her fingers. Dressed in a white, ankle length, halter dress, she looked virginal and innocent, but I knew the truth from Hades. Releasing her hand, I turned to Veva. With a clenched jaw and twisted lips, Veva watched me approach her.

"You shine brighter than the sun, Peacock." I didn't bother with her hand. I stepped into her space, wrapped a hand around the nape of her neck and leaned into her cheek. My lips brushed her warm skin, and I inhaled her after-rain scent. The muscles of her face relaxed and curved, despite her attempt to suppress a smile. Stepping back, I quickly swallowed the remaining champagne in my glass as my hand slid down her back, discovering the exposed warmth from neck to waist along her spine. At the base, my hand came to rest.

Heph nursed an amber liquor, and I decided it was time to switch alcohols. My heart raced with my hand on Veva's skin. My mouth dried at the thought of what I wanted to do to her. Reaching for Heph's glass, I rose it in the direction of the wait-staff and signaled for four glasses. Shots arrived shortly.

"Here's to another year," I said bitterly, clinking my glass against each one of my friends. I drank heartily, letting the sharp bite of whiskey enflame my insides. So many years lost before I knew who I was or what I was. Veva still held her crystal and stared at me.

"Get ready for the big announcement," Heph muttered, his eyes avoiding me.

"Heph, if you could join me." Zeke waved for Heph to come to him, as if calling a dog forward. Something didn't sit right with Zeke's tone or Heph's muttering.

"What's going on?" I questioned both girls. Persephone shook her head and Veva shrugged a shoulder, distracting me, and forcing me to wet my lips for the kiss I planned to steal from her skin.

"Family, if you could please raise your glass and join me in the announcement of my son's engagement…"

My head shot upward and I held my breath. *He wouldn't.*

"Hephaestus has agreed to marry the beautiful daughter of Aphrodite, Lovie."

My brow pinched as my brother struggled to force a smile. The wording of this arrangement was not spoken in congratulations of a mutual joining, but an agreement of some type. Zeke was not above arranging marriages and for the briefest second relief that he hadn't done that to me washed through me. Then my insides turned to stone at the reality of what he'd done to Heph.

"Heph's engaged," Veva interjected, as if clarifying the news. "I didn't even know he was in love."

Liquid sprayed from my mouth and I turned the best I could to prevent showering Veva.

"He's not." I choked.

"But he's engaged to Lovie." Persephone's sweet voice carried to my ears, but all I could focus on was the intense glare from my brother. How could our father do this to him?

"That doesn't mean he loves her, or furthermore, that she loves him." I took note of the awkward embrace of Heph's large hand around Lovie's slim shoulders. She was a stunning girl, flirtatious and fun. Her disposition was completely opposite that of Heph, not to mention her beauty compared to his mug shot. The cruelty of my thoughts pinched me. The alcohol throwing its own party.

"What, you don't believe she could love him?" Veva asked, defensive and protective in her tone. Their new bond included instantaneous friendship, and I didn't like it. I didn't understand it.

I turned in the direction of Heph's gaze, taking note of the dark-haired beauty with a slender form, who stood staring over at War. The intensity of clenched jaws and stony faces spoke volumes to the impossibility of Lovie being attracted to Heph. The match between Heph and Lovie was a terrible arrangement.

"I didn't say that," I backpedaled. "I'm certain anyone could love Heph, but the point is, she doesn't, and I don't think he loves her."

"Heph mentioned falling in love with the one, that he was waiting for her," Veva commented as she raised her glass to her peachy lips and then sipped her shot.

"That's destiny, this is something else," I snorted, but instantly knew I'd gone too far. Heph's shoulders slumped as I watched him. He would never be happy with Lovie.

"How do you know?" she snapped next to me. I hadn't even realized the flat of my hand had slipped inside the side of her dress. My palm cupped around her waist and I pulled her closer to me, as if I feared my father would marry her off next. I turned to face her, realizing suddenly how close we stood, as her face was only inches from mine. Our breaths mingled as Veva's agitation grew.

"Because I believe in destiny. I believe in finding the one. The one who will complete me. The other half of me. The one opposite and whole for me."

Veva's breath hitched at my words, and my mouth leaned for hers, ready to prove to her with my lips that she might be that destiny. The only way to know for certain involved joining together again, letting the rediscovery happen, if it will, as I hoped. I'd battled all week with the thought. I recognized Veva in that first kiss because she was the other half of me. She made me whole.

elda lore

"Lovie isn't that person for Heph," I whispered, but a sharp cough told me we were not alone, and I turned to face a weary-faced Heph.

"I'm sorry, man," I muttered, attempting to mend the spirit I broke in my tender brother. "If you love her, then congratulations." His response came in the form of swallowing the full shot and raising the glass for another.

That's what I thought, I mumbled in my head. Veva stepped forward to comfort him, but a raised hand told her to step back. The instant hurt in her eyes made me want to punch my brother. Our little foursome had fallen somber, despite the call for celebration. Veva stared at me, her eyes unnerving me. The intensity proving I'd said too much about my position on love. It's like she wanted me and wanted to throttle me, at the same time. I needed to do something to break the tension.

"We should swim," I blurted. "Liven this party up a bit." I pulled the hem of my shirt from my pants.

"You can't be serious. We don't have on suits." Persephone delicately sipped the hard alcohol in her glass.

"Oh, come on. We don't need suits." I pulled my dress shirt over my head and kicked off my flip flops. In the heat, I drew the line at dress shoes. My head cocked for Veva to follow my lead.

"Follow me," I urged. Veva's adamant shaking head fueled my desire to swim.

"You wouldn't," Veva gasped, as I reached for her. It was all the temptation I needed. I bent and swooped her up at the waist, hoisting her over my shoulder.

"Solis!" she screamed, beating my back. The loose, sheer material felt less than paper thin and swished over Veva's skin at the back of her knees.

"Gotta live a little, Veva. That's what your name means."

"Put me down!" Her hand smacked my ass, and I sprang to life with the delicate sting.

"Do you have on underwear?" I groaned, slowing my pace as I neared the pool's edge.

"I don't see how that's any of your business," she yelled with another swat at my lower back. "Put me down."

"What kind of bra do you wear with a dress like this?" I asked, ignoring her plea. As I neared the edge of the pool, I slid her down my body, but not far enough for her feet to reach the ground. Her toes kicked at my shins, but I refused to release her. Her body trapped against mine only reinforced my growing excitement. She squirmed and screamed, but I wanted an answer to my questions. From the feel of those firm globes pressed against my chest, I'd say no bra constricted those precious breasts. My hands slipped under her thighs and she willingly wrapped her legs around my hips in an effort to prevent me from releasing her into the pool.

"I'm waiting for an answer," I teased, hitching her body higher against mine. The thin material was so silky under my hands, if I inched them upward, I'd discover the answer for myself.

"I'm warning you. Put. Me. Down."

"Or what?" I threatened playfully. I twisted at the waist, swinging her away from the pool before twisting quickly, motioning as if I'd toss her into the tempting bath water.

"Okay," she screamed. I inched closer to the edge, feeling for the tile with my toes. I balanced on the precipice, knowing Veva did as well. I shifted her away from the water, still holding her under her thighs while her legs clamped around my waist.

"So?"

"You'll never find out if I wear underwear or not." Her threat only encouraged me. I spun, swinging her over the pool's edge. Only something happened—her weight shifted, and the momentum of the false toss tugged her outward from me. Instinct to protect her kicked in, and I grabbed onto her. We moved in slow motion, her eyes opening wide, as did mine. She fell backward as she held fast to my neck, and I was going down with her. I turned my body, angling to hit the water first, but it didn't matter. Within seconds, we submerged in the tepid pool. I held onto her and watched as her dress billowed outward in the warm liquid. It rose as we sank and I caught a peek of what I questioned.

It was only Veva and I underwater for that moment. Nothing else existed. Nothing else mattered with my arms wrapped around her waist, drawing her close to me. We pushed upward collectively and sprang from the water. I whipped back my hair, noticing Veva's fell in limp strands over her face. Her make-up trickled down her cheeks. That strange sense of only the two of us in the world surrounded me. There was no sound but our breaths gasping for air. Reaching out to wipe away the unnecessary paint on her face, she swatted at my hand. The moment abruptly burst.

"Don't touch me."

"I'm so sorry, Veva. That wasn't meant to happen."

"Of course not. Dangling me over a pool, threatening to throw me in because you want to know if I wear underwear, would never lead to me going in the water." Her sarcasm flowed deeper than the liquid around us. Ignoring her battling hands, I brushed back her hair, wiping down her face to remove the streaks of make-up. I stepped closer to her.

"You ruined my dress." Her hands futilely attempted to pull out the formerly billowing material. In doing so, one strap fell off her shoulder and dropped precariously low, threatening to expose her. I stepped even closer, but Veva stepped back. My eyes drew to her chest. Round, ripe globes outlined in sheer wet fabric highlighted the peachy center.

"Veva, I…"

"Forget it," she huffed, smacking the water as she released her dress. "I'm freezing." She stepped toward the edge of the pool, but I blocked her way. Freezing or not, the wet material enhanced her assets and I didn't need the whole party to see what I desired.

"Just stay put a second." I muttered, my eyes diverting from her chest, but the force too strong, they roamed back.

"Oh, now as if dumping me in here isn't enough, you want to keep me in the pool. What's next? Drowning?"

"Veva, no, it's not like that…it's…Heph?" I called out. His attention hadn't left the spectacle I'd made, and I motioned for my dress shirt. Not taking my meaning, Persephone brought the shirt to the edge of the pool. Before she reached me, Zeke appeared.

"Veva, honey, are you all right?" The concern for our guest weighted heavy in his tone, and on my heart. He'd mysteriously reneged his threat to send me to nowhere Nebraska, but this stunt might spark a new deal.

"I'm fine; I just want to get out of here." She stepped again for the edge of the pool, but I blocked her, turning my back to her to face my father.

"If you wouldn't mind?" I reached upward for my shirt from Persephone, and Zeke stepped back. I turned to face Veva, but Zeke still had the final word.

"Meet me in my study. You have some explaining to do, son." The endearment demeaned more than comforted. I placed a hand on Veva's upper arm to guide her toward the grand staircase. She shrugged her shoulder, yanking her arm out of my grasp.

"I'm so sorry, Veva. But you're more than cold at the moment, and I need you to put on my shirt." This direction stopped her, and she looked down at herself before glaring up at me. I held out my button down.

"Why? Why cover it all up?" She waved a hand up and down her soaked dress. "First, it's ruined, and second, isn't this what you wanted? To embarrass me? Show the party what I had under the dress, which you clearly know now is very little?" She huffed, and my heart sank. Exposing her to the party had not been my intention. I wanted her all to me.

"I'll replace the dress," I offered, but the words were wrong. She swiped the shirt from my hands and threw it in the water, releasing it to float away from us.

"Forget the dress. I just want to get out of here." She twisted away from me, dragging the water laden fabric of her dress behind her as she walked through the pool. When she reached the edge of the first stair, she stepped upward, took a deep breath and continued forward. Her uptight shoulders and straight back told me—she'd had enough of me. The dress clung to her as she exited the water. There wasn't a curve to be discovered or a crevice to be hidden. She continued forward, holding ramrod stiff as she regally left the pool. Persephone met her at the water's edge, arguing she should have taken my shirt, but Veva held up a hand at her friend. Shaking her head, she dismissed Persephone and walked toward the house, letting everyone get a glimpse of what I'd never experience.

+ + +

"If throwing her in the pool wasn't your intention, what exactly was your intention as you made a spectacle of yourself and her?" Zeke's tone admonished me like a five-year-old, although that had been several lifetimes ago.

"She shifted, and the weight forced the momentum toward the pool."

Zeke narrowed his eyes at me. "You seem to have a particular interest in Veva."

"No, sir." My eyebrows rose at the thought. "I was only joking around with her."

He nodded once. "What we all witnessed proved otherwise."

Something in his tone registered awkwardly with me. A strange sense of protectiveness crawled over my skin. My father had a player mentality, and age did not discourage him. Had he checked out Veva in her wet attire? All his professions of love and special care for Persephone and Veva I took at face value, meaning they were off limits because of his relationship and connection to their mothers. It hadn't crossed my mind that Zeke might desire one of them as his own. I shouldn't put it past him that he would.

"Are you saying…"

His hand rose to stop me from speaking.

"I'll stop you before you say something you'll regret. If you didn't want to show her off to everyone, you have an uncanny way of proving that. I don't think anyone missed her." His lip twitched as if he fought a smile, a smile of pleasure at what he saw, and my fists balled at my sides. I stepped forward.

"You wouldn't…"

"I don't think I care for your implication." Zeke's face turned stern and his booming tenor grew, but the twinkle in his eye told me wayward thoughts had crossed his mind, if only briefly. He couldn't have her. He was too old. For that fact, so was I. "I must commend you in one regard. You could have used your powers to stop things from escalating. As I'm not clear what Veva does or does not know, I appreciate that you did not expose yourself to her."

My power. I didn't fully understand it myself. I went to trainings daily, but I hadn't learned to control the inevitable.

"I apologize, again. It was not my intention to throw her in the pool."

"Don't apologize to me. Apologize to Veva. I see you always watching her. Your punishment should include spending time with her. In fact, that will be your punishment. I'm ordering you not to leave her side. You will be her entertainment and her escort for the remainder of the week."

"What?" However, the conviction of my dismay wasn't strong enough. "She hates me."

"And that's what you deserve. The rest of the week."

"She'll eat my heart out and serve it to crows for breakfast."

"Don't be dramatic, and besides, that's already happened to someone else."

Zeke's sense of humor was untimely, but his tone proved he was serious. He didn't care if she did carve me up in little pieces and feed me to the birds; I was to make up for what I had done.

"I'm adding another stipulation. She's off limits to you."

"Wasn't she off limits before?" I bit.

"She was, but now I'm making it clear. You are not allowed to have any relations with her."

"Considering how she feels about me, I'm sure that won't be a problem."

"Considering you're my son, it just might be." He winked at me and I hated the implication that we were similar. I was nothing like him. I'd never do the things he'd done, although in this moment, thoughts of killing him crossed my mind.

VEVA

The next morning, I woke with images of the night before in my head. A beautiful, star-filled evening. Candles glimmered around that elongated pool, increasing the aura of a magical night. Dressed in a manner making me feel sensual and seductive. Zeke had sent Persephone and I on a shopping spree, complete with a maid servant as an escort. She took us to several dress shops about an hour from the estate. Having a maid made me uncomfortable, but Persephone seemed strangely comfortable with the service. The girl's name was Maya, but at one point Persephone called her Mina. Tears filled her eyes as she reached for the girl, and stroked her arm, apologizing while she corrected her name. I didn't understand the interchange, but Persephone briefly closed her eyes, took a deep breath, and then opened them to admire her reflection. She wore a beautiful white dress. My dress, on the other hand, was completely ruined. *Solis*, I screamed in my head as a fist beat down on the bed. My gorgeous dress, something I'd never owned before, was a heap of blue disaster in the hallway outside our room. Like a spoiled child, I de-robed, and tossed the stunning material into the hall. I couldn't even think of it piled in our trash bin.

The door to our room opened, and Persephone walked in with a vase filled to exploding with whimsical, yellow flowers. She muttered some Latin name for them as she took a deep inhale of the fragrant flower before setting the vase on the stand between our beds.

"Those are lovely." The airy display was bright and cheerful, and looked handpicked from a meadow.

"They're for you."

My heart stopped. Literally, I choked on a breath. "What?" Persephone held out a card for me that had been tucked inside the arrangement.

*You still shone brighter than the sun last night. My deepest
apologies.*

That signature lightning bolt completed the apology, and I exhaled
a breath. I shook my head and closed my eyes. I did not understand Solis.

A knock interrupted my thoughts, and Persephone turned for the
door. I crawled to the end of the bed, peeking over the edge enough to
see the would-be visitor. Discovering it was Solis, I scrambled back up
the mattress, hoping he hadn't seen me. I had wild hair and tear-stained
eyes from crying myself to sleep. I didn't wish to see him, and I definitely
didn't want him to see me.

"Is Veva awake yet?" His voice was low, the jovial booming tenor
missing. My brows pinched at the change.

"She is. Would you like to come in?" I cursed Persephone in my
head. *No, we do not want him in our room.* I did not want him near me.

"Could she come to the door instead?" I shook my head in response,
although neither could see me. *No, I would not go to the door.* I did not
want to see him.

"Of course," Persephone answered sweetly, and I knew it would
only take five steps to cross the small hallway to our beds. My head
already shook adamantly as Persephone rounded the corner. She signaled
back to the door with a raised finger: *one moment, please*, and then she
rounded my bed.

"He looks so sad." Her whisper rang louder than expected, and my
head continued to shake without additional response. *No, I did not care
if he was sorry*. I did not want to hear his words. I had determined that
Solis was the devil, pure evil, but Persephone wasn't taking my refusal.
Reaching for my arm, she yanked me out of bed. I fumbled and tripped
into her. Smoothing my hair, I walked to the door, holding my head as
high as I could, to find a repentant Solis with his head dipped. I didn't
speak, just stood inside our door.

"I'd like very much for you to attend this afternoon's festivities."
He presented me with a gold envelope. I paused before accepting it, and
in that instance, his eyes were the only part of him that moved. Slowly,

he traveled over my feet and swirled up my ankles. He eyed the feathers inked on my leg, climbing higher as if he stroked them with each blink. He crossed over my short-shorts and scanned my thin cami, lingering on the hint of cleavage at the low neck-line. His hesitation reminded me of last night, the way his eyes drank in my body in my beautiful dress. He licked his lips as he had the night before. The reminder snapped me out of my haze. I snatched the envelope from his fingers. My other hand came to the door, preparing to slam it in his face. His foot came forward in anticipation of my intention, and one hand reached to the side of the doorframe, outside my line of vision. Drawing back, he presented me with a long garment bag. I froze. For the first time, his eyes met mine and he pierced me to the floor with the apology in them. Heavy lids and honey eyes implored me to forgive him, and all my resolve to not be near him, to not see him, not hear him, crashed to my bare feet. My body wanted to launch at him. Without a word, he held out the bag, bowed his head when I took it, and stepped away.

+ + +

The invitation included a full itinerary. Festivities involved daily activities to celebrate Zeke's guests. Persephone and I were honored to be included, and we crossed the large expanse of lawn adjacent the pool area, covered with billowing white tents and colorful flags. The arrangement was similar to a medieval festival. The atmosphere was celebratory, and the infectious prospect of a good time took hold of me. Lightened by Solis' flowers and apology, he had also given me a restored dress and a new one for the grand ball at the end of the week. I'd never had such lush clothing, as a simple farm girl, and the prospect of another disaster was quickly forgotten when I held the silky blue fabric that matched my tattoo. The color shimmered like water in the deep ocean, and the material flowed over my fingers, tickling them with promises.

Persephone and I found a trolley shuttle taking guests to the first destination. The invitation read to dress accordingly, but I didn't heed the warning. We travelled to an elevated height where the temperature dropped. In contrast to the heat in the valley below, the cool temperature brought goosebumps to my bare arms. In jeans and a T-shirt, I hadn't taken the warning seriously.

Our destination involved a flat cliff overlooking the great, brown valley below. Brightly colored, triangular canvases, larger than an awning, lined up, and pointed toward the opposite mountain range. The oversized kites looked like hang gliders, rippling and whining in the wind atop this cliff. The sound reminded me of horses primed for a race, their manes fluttering in the wind, their nostrils flaring with anticipation of the start. The colors billowed and contracted; the canvases poised and aimed for flight.

We found Heph under his, a rich brown color with a ring of fire on the back. He was locked into a five-point harness and held the triangle kite over his head by a metal support.

"Hi Persephone," he said shyly. "Hey Vee," he offered with more affection. Since the day in the library, a strange friendship developed with Heph. Being near him brought me comfort. He calmed my temper that day and a silent bond had formed between us. He found me before I entered the house last night and offered me his shirt as protection. By then the tears leaked, and his large arm encompassed me as he escorted me back to my room. His body language today held him rigid and preventative. It only took a moment to realize who he tried to block from my view.

Next to Heph stood Solis, under a gray canvas with a bright yellow lightning bolt splashed across the angry sky.

"You made it," Solis beamed in my direction. His face lit up then fell slowly as I stared at him. Dressed in a flannel plaid shirt, with shorts and construction boots, the outfit contrasted his bubbling appearance. He looked rugged, earthy, and too good. He reached out a hand in my direction and tipped his head for me to come to him. Like a moth to a flame, I ignored the warning of being scorched and walked to him.

His hand covered mine and he tugged me closer to him.

"I'm so happy you made it," he said to me, and then called over his shoulder. "Christoff, help harness her."

90

"What?" There was definitely an echo as I said the word at the same time as Heph.

"You can't be serious," Heph growled from feet away.

"I am," Solis stated. Instantly, a middle-aged gentleman tapped my foot to rise and I stepped unthinkingly into a contraption of several connected seat belts and clamps.

"What...what is this?" I questioned, blindly letting myself be clicked and snapped into the awkward binding. I shivered when a breeze caught under the canvas. Solis quickly unbuckled his chest clips and shimmied out of his flannel shirt. Holding it out to me, I blinked at him.

"I want you to ride with me." He paused, still dangling the shirt at me. "Please."

Not fully understanding the concept of riding anything, I took the soft material and stretched it over me. The arms hung too long and I rolled them several times to accommodate mine. The length gave me the appearance of wearing a dress. The warm material smelled like sunshine.

"I knew I'd get you in my shirt somehow." He winked at me, then tugged me forward by the chest buckle on my harness. I stumbled in front of him.

"What...what is this?" I repeated, grabbing the metal rod before me. Solis was at my back and an additional clack behind me let me know, he and I were snapped together.

"Solis? Oh, my God, what are you doing?" My voice rose with each syllable.

"It's a race. We fly to the other side of the valley." His breath tickled below my ear, exposed under the helmet Christoff placed on my head.

"I'm not flying with you, anywhere," I snorted, but based on my harness and current position, I was about to go where Solis went.

"Hold onto the rod, that's all I ask." His voice dipped deeper and a shiver rippled over my skin despite the warmth of his flannel shirt. Sucking in a breath, a whiff of sunshine caught my nose and the scent added to my tremors. I was surrounded by Solis. His arms wrapped around mine, bracing his hand on either side of mine along the metal support.

"Don't worry. Thunder knows how to fly." Solis reached up and stroked a hand down the underside of the gray canvas. The material rippled and the triangular point at the front of the glider tipped upward, as if caught in the wind. The strange sound of a horse whinnying followed by a hoof scraping dirt whispered around me. I had the eerie sense things were not as they appeared to me.

"Ready to lose this year?" Heph taunted from his ready position to our left. I turned right as well, to notice a line of people, braced with hands on the metal supports and canvases pointed forward. Turning back to the left, I noticed Persephone had disappeared from Heph and every other rider was singular. Solis was the only one with an additional rider.

"Solis," I warned, slowly, clenching the bar before me.

"Not going to lose, brother. You know I always win this race."

"What race?" I asked through clenched teeth noticing the sharp drop off of the cliff before me and the great distance to the opposing mountain. *He could not be serious.*

"You have an extra passenger this year," Heph teased, and I twisted my head to look at him.

"Not going to be an issue. She's as light as a peacock feather." The words brushed my neck like a light breeze.

"Oh my God," I blurted, realizing what we were about to do. I released the bar and with trembling fingers, attempted to unclick the harness at my chest.

"Besides, I think she's going to bring me good luck." Solis commented, ignoring me.

"You'll need it," Heph laughed. "But, of course, I always let you win."

"Let me win?" Solis scoffed behind me, paying no attention to my struggles in his jovial teasing with his brother. "Thunder rules the sky."

"On your mark." The booming sound fired over the kites and the sails dipped and rose in anticipation.

"Solis." My tone squeaked with panic. My fingers shook so rapidly they couldn't get a grasp on the buckle.

"I'm not going to let anything happen to you. I promise."

"Get set." Those two words rippled through my body and I struggled to decide if it was *I promise* or *Get set* that upset me further.

"Don't promise me anything, just get me out of this." My voice quivered. The frustration built inside me. Like a slow boil, panic and irritation collided within me.

"Oh my God, Solis. I hate you. Get me out of this." Full-on hysteria was about to hit me. It crawled under my skin, creeping to the surface. The anger was coming.

"Go." A shot went off and bright triangle shapes jostled for the edge of the cliff.

"No, Solis. Please. *Please*."

"I need you to run with me." He ignored my plea with his gentle command. Most gliders were passing us.

"Veva." He barked. "Run."

Not willing to follow his demands, I remained with my feet flat on the ground until one arm wrapped around my waist and he hoisted me upward. Jogging with me, jostling with the support one handed, the glider dipped to the left and right as he struggled.

"Whoa, Thunder," he called out. *He'd named his glider*, I mocked in my head to suppress the full-on scream preparing to escape me.

"Grab the pole." He yelled as we staggered to the cliff edge.

"No. As if throwing me in the pool wasn't enough, now you want to throw me off a cliff?" I yelled over the growing sound of clomping hooves and whistling wind.

"I'm not throwing us over a cliff, but if we don't steady this thing by you holding onto the rod, we're going to drop like a stone. Hold still." His command harsher than previous, I stopped kicking out my legs and reached for the steel pole.

"I'm going to swing you in front of me. I need you to wrap your legs backward on either side of my hips." His demand rose over the heightening sound of wind whipping the sails. We were closing in on the others, nearing the edge of the cliff.

"I'm not wrapping any part of me over you," I snipped, but his immediate bark of "Just do it" coincided with us reaching the ledge. My legs sprang outward like a toe-touch jump, and then flipped back so the full length of Solis pressed against me. My thighs straddled his hips in a position that felt strangely compromising and erotic at the same time. His center matched up with mine and I dangled precariously with only my legs over his and my hands on the steel.

"Jump," he commanded and the glider soared outward. No longer in control, the scream escaping my lips could have peeled skin off a horse. At the same time, we flew and Solis released my waist to steady the support. My hands sweat as I gripped the metal. It remained a lifeline between the sky and the valley, thousands of miles below me.

"Oh my God!" I let rip from my throat as Solis flattened out behind me. Afraid to move, I clasped the bar harder, but my hands slipped with the sweaty moisture.

"I'm slipping," I yelled over the rushing wind as we dipped and soared amid the other gliders.

"I've got you," he replied. "We're clipped together. You aren't going anywhere without me."

"My hands." Panic took full residence in me, and a tear fell from my eyes. I trembled, but was unable to determine if it was my fear or the shaky flutter of our kite and the thin metal that supported us.

"Let go, Veva. I've got us."

"I'm not letting go," I yelled. My eyes travelled down and the valley below loomed too far away. My stomach dropped and bile rose. "Oh God, I'm going to throw up."

"Point downward then, so it doesn't slap you back in the face." He chuckled behind me at my fear and the thought of vomit covering me dissipated the bile. I swallowed hard. My body stiffened.

"Why would you do this to me?" Yelling was the only tone of voice to use among the whipping wind.

"I want to experience things with you." The comment dropped my stomach in a different way. He couldn't mean it.

"Why?"

"You're feisty and stubborn and closed off. I want you to open up. Enjoy things. Trust me."

94

"I'm not having sex with you," I blurted, although that wasn't what he asked. It wasn't even what he implied. Maybe it was only something I desired, and I quickly erased the thought.

"Not asking you to. Yet. Just wanted to take you flying today."

My shoulders couldn't relax, but my legs tired. I was as ramrod as the steel support before us.

"Let your legs fall. The wind will hold them up and my legs will support yours. Unless you like this position. I mean, I do." He thrust forward at the hips and I took his meaning. It would be the most risqué thing I'd ever done. I wasn't opposed, I just wasn't there yet either. My legs slipped slowly from his and a squeak of fear escaped me.

"I've got you, Vee." The soothing sound reminded me of falling into his arms the night he had me paint the canvas. My legs flipped back to rest under his and the new position allowed him to lay flat over me.

"What is this, anyway?"

"A chariot race across the sky." His laughter boomed like it had at other times, and the familiar sound let me know he enjoyed himself. He truly thought flying across the sky, so unencumbered and unprotected, was pleasurable.

"You said you always win, but you're losing."

"I'm not losing today, Veva. I got you under me. That's a win, right there." He chuckled again. Without seeing his face, I sensed the wide smile and shook my head at his comment.

"Where do we go?"

"Across the valley. Straight ahead."

The distant mountain range looked close, and yet so far away. I didn't understand how we could make it across before we would lose steam and plummet to the valley below. There was no engine. No power source. Just us and the wind.

"Giddy up," Solis called out and jiggled the support bar. The front of the triangle sail dipped and we increased our speed. We passed two gliders after first flight. We passed two more with this change. Ahead of us, I saw the canvas for Heph and another one covered in vibrant yellow with a burning orange sun radiating to the very edges.

"Who is that?" I tried to incline my head toward the sunny sail but the attempt seemed futile.

"The only one we want to beat." The bitterness in his tone told me a rivalry definitely existed. The stormy kite above us had full intention to eclipse the sunny one ahead.

"What's his name?"

"Leos. Another son of Zeke's. In case you haven't noticed, he has several to spare."

"Is that what you think you are? A spare son."

"One of many." He snorted behind my ear.

"I don't think Zeke sees you like that. In fact, he seems quite in favor of you. When I suggested he didn't send you away, he agreed you were a leader, just didn't want to give you power yet."

"You asked Zeke not to send me to your mother's farm?"

Oopsy. I'd said too much.

"Why didn't you want me to go, Veva? Would you miss me if I was gone?"

I couldn't answer him. I didn't know. While one moment, I prayed for him to disappear, he consumed my thoughts too much lately, and I wasn't certain what I would do without the constant, annoying distraction of him.

"I'll miss you when you go," he stated.

"Oh, where am I going?" I smiled slowly.

"Back to school, right? When summer ends."

When summer ends. Ah, yes, back to reality when summer ends.

"Right."

"Vee?"

"What?"

"Why don't you trust me?"

"I don't trust most men who play around with lots of girls. Plus, men always walk out, like my father did, after they get what they want."

His silence behind me let me know I'd said too much again. Too deep a thought for hanging precariously in the air under a flimsy kite, holding onto a metal bar, and praying for your life.

"Never mind," I yelled over the wind. "You wouldn't understand."

"I totally understand."

My brows pinched with question. It was strange to have this conversation as we dangled over the valley, not to mention, I couldn't turn to see his face.

"What do you mean? You have Zeke. Spare son or not, he takes care of his children. Look at the elaborate home."

"I didn't always live there. He isn't exactly the father you might think."

I had more questions but we were picking up speed again, and Solis' body over mine stiffened into racer mode. We dipped lower than the others, no longer caught in their tail wind. The shift sped us forward, and I risked a peek at the ground straight below.

"What is that?" I called out. In a vast river, visible from our height, a line of fluorescent green streaked through the middle of the blue water below.

"Looks like Idon decided to attend after all. Means my cousin Triton is coming. It's gonna be a par-tee." He laughed wholeheartedly again, and I had to smile at the giddiness.

Solis angled us upward and the sail caught. We flew forward, cutting ahead of most of our opponents. One contender floated ahead of us. The other side of the valley loomed closer and Solis kicked out his feet, triggered the pole at his hands, and called out with a *yah*. We sped up as if the sail understood Solis' command.

"Come on, Thunder. You can do it." The sound implied Solis' teeth clenched as he spurred on the inanimate kite. We were suddenly side by side with Leos, represented by his sunny glider.

"No," Leos called out.

"Yes," Solis responded.

We flew point to point, so close the triangular edge almost poked one another.

"Yah, yah, *yah*," Solis called out, reminiscent of a master goading his horse, and as if the gallop increased, we pulled ahead of Leos. A large purple strip, what I assumed was a finish line, loomed below us, draped across a vacant field. As we drew closer, dots of observers became visible. The royal-colored finish line appeared brighter. Our speed ensured we could win if we only continued at this pace. Our front point was more than two feet in front of Leos.

The finish line came up quickly, the ground rising to meet us, a green strip of grass the path to follow. I feared our landing. *How would we stop?* I didn't have time to ask my question before we crossed the line and leapt upward, ignoring the expanse of green flooring before us. Distant cheers erupted behind us, and I could only assume they were for Solis as the victor, but he continued upward, climbing a new break in the mountain.

"What happened? We won, right?" Excitement filled my voice. The speed of racing dulled my anger, as it did at home. There was nothing as exhilarating as crossing that final line and claiming victory.

"We won, Veva. We won." He spoke close to my ear, pride filling his voice.

"But where are we going? Don't you have to stop after you cross the line?"

"I only have to cross the line to win. Now, I want to cross another line for true victory."

I didn't take his meaning, and we climbed only a moment more before another cliff came into focus.

"It would be easiest to land if you wrapped your legs around my hips again. It reduces the risk of getting our feet tangled and crashing."

Instantly, my legs wrapped around his hips as instructed, and we coasted feet above solid ground before his feet touched down. He galloped to a slow jog before calling out "Whoa," and pulling back on the support. We stopped, and Solis controlled the metal frame, dipping the sail forward to rest on the ground. We stood under the canopy for a moment, still locked together, and my heart raced with the combination of fear and exhilaration.

"What did you think, Veva?" His mouth rested temptingly close to my neck, and his hand cupped under my chin. The position compromised me again. I had nowhere to go, being strapped to him.

"I found it…invigorating."

He moaned behind me, and his free hand came to rest on my hip. We stood, back pressed to chest, hand cupping chin, bodies poised for immediate taking. I swallowed hard in anticipation of his lips on my throat, but his fingers dipped lower. Slowly cascading down my chest and dipping into his flannel, he unclipped the first harness. *The harness, right*, I cursed myself. My breasts heaved and sagged at the lack of attention. Another unsnap clicked, as he dropped between my legs and my thighs thumped. My center pulsed. He had to be teasing me, taking his time to torture me, before letting the sound unhinge me, literally.

His hand slipped around my hip, dragging over my ass, and sliding up the center to unclick another harness at my lower back.

"You're free, now." His sultry tone covered my skin, cascading and sliding down me like his fingers tempting tease. The voice heated my already-dampened skin, moist with sweaty fear and exhaustive flight. I hadn't moved. Neither had Solis.

"I…" His tone dropped another octave. A struggle in just one vowel sound. "I'm glad you came with me."

"I didn't willing come."

He moaned behind me.

"I hope, one day, you do." The fingers at the base of my spine slipped into the waistband of my jeans and tugged me backward. My ass brushed over the hard length of him, solid and strong like the metal before us. My eyes closed at the vision of him taking me over this bar. The image passed when he released me. I spun in time to see him wipe a hand down his face. He removed his helmet and his blond hair hung limp at the edges. His honey eyes remained closed for a second, but when he opened them, warm caramel met mine, and the desire to launch myself at him came to me again. But something in his stance held me back. I didn't trust myself, and I certainly didn't trust him. *He'd just flung us off a mountain*, I reminded myself, stepping to the side, ducking to exit the alcove created by the sail.

"Where are we?" My back remained to him as I took in the breathtaking view of the valley in its rich brown and deep dips of sandy earth. In contrast, we stood among cedars and pines with boulders encased between the greenery.

"Cliff Mortum. I just need to give Thunder a rest and then we can travel down to the trolley."

I spun back to him, crossing my arms, ready to accuse him of insanity in naming his glider and implying it needed a rest, but I stopped. Before me, the sharp, front point of the sail rested in a dish of water, and the sound of guzzling water forced me to tip my head.

"Morph," Solis spoke softly, his eyes not leaving mine, and the glider shuddered. First a head appeared. A horse's head. Then the sail folded inward. The metal rods fell apart and four legs solidified. With a jostle, and an unfolding, the appearance of a massive, solid creature stood before me: a gray horse, draped in a silver blanket with a yellow lightning bolt down the center.

My hand slipped forward and I waved in the direction of the thirsty animal.

"What...how...did you..." I couldn't get the words to form, all the while Solis' eyes never left mine.

"You asked me if it was true, and the answer is yes."

"I..." I couldn't remember the question. I couldn't remember my name. A full-size horse, formed from a flimsy glider, stood before me. I glanced to the right, taking in the great distance we traveled, over a valley, through the air, to reach this mountain cliff. I turned back, pointing again at the horse. My mouth hung open without words.

"I am a god." I blinked at the statement. If he was teasing me, this was an incredible joke. "An average glider would not have made it that distance. It would have propelled downward, not across." He stepped toward me, one foot in front of the other, as if pacing out the space. He took his time to approach me, cautiously, careful not to frighten me, because I must have looked like I would run. I wouldn't know where to go, but my instinct forced a reaction like a frightened filly. However, I stood thousands of miles up in the air, hundreds of feet from Zeke's home, and a million acres away from fully understanding what transpired before me.

"Veva?" He spoke calmly, like one would speak to a skittish animal. "Do you understand?"

"I've lost my mind, right? It's the lack of oxygen. Elevated heights. Thinner air. I'm hallucinating."

"Take my hand. It's real." Solis reached out to me as he stood before me. Inches apart, he didn't try to touch me, but offered his hand for my comfort. *Was he even real? Was I imagining everything around me? Was I still in bed, restless from the night before?*

His hand slowly came to my chin proving he was real. He was solid, but that horse. I didn't understand what it was.

"I'm so warm." The world began to spin a little. The ground tilted. Solis' hand slipped to my neck. His other hand brushed over the buttons on his flannel. He unbuttoned one button at a time, before sliding the too warm fabric off my shoulders. His eyes stilled on my throat.

"You're still wearing my rock?" Those honey eyes lit up and his lips curled. He closed his eyes momentarily and then slowly lifted his lids. The honey turned to molten caramel and my mouth watered like I could taste that flavor on my tongue.

"What's happening? The horse. The glider." I didn't even know what I was asking, distracted only momentarily by his comment on my necklace.

"The horse has powers to shift and change. He can only go from horse to glider. Different family members own different items that morph."

"Which family members?" His hands rubbed soothingly up and down my shoulders, but I wasn't allowing the physical comfort to distract me.

"I can't tell you."

"Of course not," I huffed. *Secrets.*

"Veva, don't shut down on me. Just listen. I can't tell you each of their tales, I can only tell you mine."

I nodded, although I had no idea to what I had agreed. Solis gently pressed my shoulders and I collapsed to the grassy cliff. Sitting cross-legged on the earth, he spread his legs to straddle beside mine. His presence surrounded me, attempting to ground me. I sensed the story he was about to tell would be unbelievable.

"I'm Zeke's son, and heir to rule the sky. I'm new to discovering my powers. I'm learning control and temperance. I don't want to ever hurt anyone or lose control of my strength. Do you understand?" I nodded, although I didn't. His hands slid up to my neck and his thumbs rubbed tenderly up and down the side, while his fingers massaged my nape.

"I'd never hurt you, Veva. You don't need to be afraid of me or my family."

"How many are there? Zeke plus what?" My mind jumbled through all the people I'd met in the last twenty-four hours. Were they all the same? Did they all share a secret, and Persephone and I were on the outside, looking in? My thoughts jumped to Persephone and her attempts to tell me that Harris Black was named Hades, and he was a god.

"Does Persephone know?" I answered my own question before I added the punctuation. Of course, she knew. She tried to tell me, and I ignored her. I thought she suffered post-traumatic stress. But if that was her case, what was mine? My heart rate accelerated. Adrenaline coursed through my body. I felt alive in the moment, but convinced I lived in a dream.

"Maybe you should talk to Persephone more about this? Tell her what you saw? Tell her what I said?" Something in his curved lips and the sound of Persephone's name on them jolted me to reality.

"This is a joke, right? You and Persephone concocted this story to make a fool of me. But why? Why do you dislike me so much? Is it her? Oh my gosh, it's Persephone. You're in love with her, and…" I stood instantly. He followed me upward, his face aghast, eyes open wide.

"You're kidding, right? I told you before I don't have a thing for Persephone. There's only one girl who consumes me." He took a deep breath and looked up at the glorious blue sky. "This isn't a joke. This is my life, and I am trying to share it with you. I'm trying to give you bits and pieces, so I don't scare you away, so you won't think I'm a monster when you learn it all. You said…" He waved a hand dismissively at the open air between the mountains. "You said…about your father…and I thought…you know what, forget it. Forget it all, Veva." He stepped away from me, turning his back and I watched him stalk away. He reached the horse and swiped a hand down the elegant neck. With the horse rested and revived, Solis stood beside Thunder with his back to me. His head fell forward and the troubled position pulled me to him. I stilled behind him, questioning if I should touch him or not. Afraid that if I did, I might never let him go.

VEVA

As if a race across the sky wasn't enough, the closing of day one involved a sunset dinner. We returned to the original cliff, and after a stomach-filling feast, guests wandered the grounds for places to watch the sun descend the valley. Boulders scattered here and there provided the perfect seating, and I followed Heph's lead to a large rock providing space for four. Originally, Heph sat between Persephone and I, but then Solis found us and slipped between Heph and me.

I wasn't certain where the overprotective, big-brother behavior suddenly came from, but Heph had been particularly doting after our return from the landing cliff. It was almost as if he wasn't letting me leave his side, glaring at Solis each chance he got. Clearly upset that Solis made me glide against my will, Heph was equally irritated that Solis took me up to Cliff Mortum, although I repeatedly assured him nothing happened between Solis and me.

I was still confused about what I witnessed earlier and decided to just watch the sunset, letting the beauty of nature perform for me. With my legs crisscrossed, I leaned back on my palms. Sitting next to me, Solis sat in a similar manner, only his legs stretched forward, crossing at his ankles. I sat forward, allowing my hands to rest on either side of my thighs. While the sun began its descent, Solis' hand inched closer and closer to mine, finally linking his pinky over mine. He gently stroked against my smallest finger as the sun turned to a vibrant ball of orange. Time seemed to stand still as the fiery core slowly slipped lower.

"What a beautiful day," Persephone voiced. My stare at that flaming orange didn't wane. The color matched the ink on Solis' arm, the rays a mixture of yellows and golds. Solis' finger continued to stroke between mine and my thoughts flicked to images of his fingers lingering lightly between my legs, taking their time to tease my thighs, hinting at having the heat of me.

The fire ball slipped further between mountains that looked like raised knees, and the muscles at my core clenched. Crisscrossed, my center felt exposed, mysteriously warming with the descending sun, flaming in its own way from the evening heat. The rippling orange circle hung in the sky, wobbling and wavering, like the emotions inside me: suspended fiery need and flickering flames of craving. The warmth filled me. Each infinitesimal crawl downward, I drew into me as if that heat entered me in the most primeval of ways. Solis continued to rub between my fingers, and I imagined it mimicked the prickle of passion possessed in that fiery ball as it slid lower, deeper, disappearing partially behind the raised-knee-mountains.

My breathing shallowed, and my chest rose, and Solis caressed his stroking. The sun dipped further and sexual energy seeped slowly into me. My core throbbed, swallowing the warmth as it pleasurably pierced me. The experience was like no other. Sweat gathered over my lip and my thighs trembled, but I forced myself to remain still, drawing in the pleasure building within me. An overwhelming desire for relief from *something* overcame me.

The surreal sense of conversation between the others sounded to the side of me, but I was too enraptured by the setting sun and the pulsing rhythm. When the sun finally set, absent from the sky but still sending out rays of fuchsia, lavender and gold, my channel was full to bursting, sensitive folds moist with desire, and an electricity prickled inside me. My eyes closed briefly, imagining heat to the hilt. My fist opposite Solis clenched and my center squeezed. Satisfaction was on the brink, but I needed more, so much more.

My eyes opened when Solis linked his finger to mine, bringing my imagination to a screeching halt, but the bass beat onward between my thighs.

"Veva, you okay?" Solis teased, his voice low and sultry, seducing, but smug. A shaky hand came to my forehead, and I swiped the thin film of perspiration from my brow.

"Vee, you look flushed." Persephone's concern forced me to face her, my head moving slowly, as if I were drunk. Solis' lids lowered. His smirk grew. He knew what happened to me, even though I couldn't describe it. Furthermore, I didn't feel satiated but saturated. The heat melted within me like wax dripping from a candle, but I wanted to spark. What I had was a flicker, when I wanted the flame.

"That was better than sex," I blurted. Heph choked on his beer as he spun to face me. Persephone stared, her brown eyes wide, but Solis, he glared. The honey color dark as molted lava. A volcano roared beneath the surface and his clenched jaw along with the removal of his pinky confirmed his irritation. He swiped his hand on his shorts and drew up a knee.

"The sky is almost dark. We should go. Night is coming."

"Night is coming," Persephone whispered beside him, and I stared at my friend in question. Her eyes remained focused on the absent sun. The sky had turned a deep navy blue.

"Pea?" Her eyes drew to mine and she smiled sadly.

"Night is never returning," she mouthed to me, but I didn't understand. She stood first and Heph followed.

"Veva, you coming?" Heph waited, but I needed a moment. I didn't trust myself to move. My legs quivered and my core ached. Tears burned in my eyes as well.

"We'll be just a minute," Solis answered for me, and Heph huffed as he followed Persephone. Solis didn't look at me, but continued to stare off across the valley.

"Know what happens when you play with the sun?" The tone of his question bit. My first thought was to respond with what I'd just experienced: The sun would fill me with a warmth I'd never known. Tame the fire inside me with its own flame. Rule over me with pleasures I'd not experienced. But instead, I said: "I get burned."

"That's right. Leos would roast your heart."

"Leos?" I wracked my brain for which brother, cousin, relative he was. *Oh, right, the one with the sunshine sail.* "I'm confused."

"Leos rules the sun."

"Ahhh." I shook my head. We were back to the super powers things again. "And you rule?"

"The whole damn sky, someday." He huffed and stood quickly.

"With a name like Solis, I thought you were the sun. You know, center of the universe and all," I mocked. He lowered a hand to help me rise. My legs trembled as I stood.

"The only sun I want to be is the center of your universe." He dropped my hand instantly and turned away from me. I followed, with nothing more than an achy need and a sudden loss for words.

SOLIS

I knew what was happening to her. The shortened breath. The intake of air. The tensing of her body. And it pissed me off that the setting sun had that effect on her. Women loved Leos. Sun worship continued even in modern times. The sky seemed inconsequential compared to the brightness of my brother, but the sky was more powerful. The heavens ruled earth. I would rule one day, and it overwhelmed me. My thoughts wandered back to earlier in the day, after I exposed my secret to Veva.

"We should leave." I sensed her behind me. Ridiculously, I longed for her to wrap her arms around my waist, lean into my back, and tell me she understood. But it didn't work that way, and I'd already told her too much. Zeke seemed to approve of Veva knowing the truth, while he refused the knowledge to be shared with any of the other girls I'd been with in the past. He reinforced that the right woman would accept me for who I was. I don't know why I told Veva. I don't know why I let it go this far and showed her Thunder. This was the reason Zeke didn't allow non-family to attend the week-long celebration. Certain events were exclusive to their privy, but not the race. When all the gliders morphed, carriers would transport them down the mountain and the distance back to the estate.

I'd already pushed Thunder too hard. Rode him the additional distance to be alone with Veva and show her who I was, thinking foolishly she'd understand. Turning to face her, I didn't make eye contact.

"I'll help you up," I offered, cupping my hands as a hoist for Veva. She placed her foot in my hands, but then her hand came to my head. Her fingers combed through the messy strands and her nails scratched tenderly to my nape. I kept my head lowered, willing her to continue the delicate touch. She removed her foot from my clasp and cupped my chin. I looked up at her and staring down at me were brilliant blue eyes,

swirling with questions and fears. In that moment, I sensed I'd worship this woman if she ever gave into me.

"It's a lot to take in," she sighed, "but thank you for sharing it with me." I dropped to my knees and wrapped my arms around her waist. My head rested on her lower abdomen as she continued to stroke through my hair. My palm lay flat at the base of her back. I just wanted to freeze time, and hold her. My heart rate lowered, despite the grassy dirt biting into my knees. I pulled back and kissed her covered belly. The strangest thought came to me. What if she carried my seed in there one day? I kissed her for a second time, knowing it could never be.

That strange desire for Veva's comfort and understanding haunted me the remainder of the day, and clearly into the night. While our pinkies wrapped together, I wanted to surround Veva in more than one digit and I certainly didn't want to sit by while she drank her fill of the sun. A storm brewed inside me and the clouds came quickly. By the time we returned to the estate, I needed to paint away my anger, but the sight of my cousin Triton dissipated my irritation.

"Solis, dude!" Triton clapped my back heartily and dragged me into a tight hug. I imagined this was part of his power, pulling people to his lair under the sea.

"Triton, I didn't think you'd be here." His father was Zeke's brother, Idon. As brothers, they interacted only slightly more often than with Hades, Sr., their third brother. Triton and Hades Jr. were stuck like me: eternally the prince, but never the king. Only the concept of ruling didn't particularly sit well with me. It did not excite Hades, either.

"My father wanted to visit this year. Heard there had been some trouble with Hades and wanted to discuss things with Zeke." I looked left, hoping Persephone hadn't heard Triton mention Hades.

"Is that her?"

"Who?"

"Your latest conquest?"

"Don't say that, man," I laughed nervously.

"Because they aren't conquests when they come willingly?" He punched my shoulder, and I flinched at the contact. Triton was strong, although strange looking. His skin glowed a luminescent green, his hair hung in exaggerated curls, like clumped seaweed in a darker shade of green. His lips were swollen and his eyebrow pierced. He joked he could easily be hooked by that ring, but nothing was going to catch my cousin.

"That's Persephone."

Triton stopped his teasing and straightened to stare. "She's beautiful."

"She is, but she's off limits."

"I know." Triton's voice softened.

"How?"

"I saw Hades in the early spring. A river near his home swelled and I traveled to visit. I heard what happened from the maid. I'd give up land and sea for a girl as beautiful as her."

"Yeah, well, he didn't have a choice." I turned to look in Persephone's direction and noticed Veva watching us. Near enough, she could have heard our conversation, I worried that she did. She already misinterpreted every move I made near Persephone. I didn't want her to overhear me calling Persephone beautiful, when I thought Veva stunning.

"Who is *that*?" Triton spoke loudly, and Veva's response proved she stood close enough to hear us.

"*That* is named Veva, and you are?" She stepped forward with a too-large smile. Her eyes roamed Triton. He leaned forward to kiss her knuckles, lingering to kiss all four individually, before standing and *not* releasing her hand. She didn't even flinch at his less-than-ordinary color.

"Triton, at your service, madam."

"You're green."

"It's my color. It looks good on me." He paused while his eyes swam up and over the waves of Veva's body. "It would look good on you, too, Veva." He rolled her name over his tongue, and I hated the sound of it crossing his lips.

"Hey," I snapped. Triton stepped closer to her, heedless of personal space. His arm wrapped around her waist.

"I like that name. Veva." He growled her name a second time, and Veva chuckled in response. The coquettish sound thumped at my chest. "Besides, you said she wasn't yours, dude."

"She's…"

"He doesn't own me. No one does." She glared at me and the implication she was a possession. She spun to face Triton, softening the light in her eyes and winking at him. Veva knew how to work a flirt, I had no doubt, but this was the first I'd seen her in action. She purred, and her hand came to his chest. The slightest pressure proved she wanted him to step back, but he didn't read the signal. Triton looked over at me and back at her.

"Well, then, Veva, you look flushed. How about a swim?"

Oh no, he doesn't, I thought. That slippery devil would lure her to the water and take her in the deep end. Literally.

"She doesn't care for the pool," I replied for her.

"Stop speaking about me or *for* me. I'm right here and, yes, I do like to swim," she teased. "I just don't like being thrown in. I like to control where I jump." Her eyes narrowed at me before she batted them at Triton and he fell under her spell. The blue swirls with turquoise rims told Triton she'd have her way with him, not the other way around.

"You can take the lead, girl. Howe*ver* you'd like it, I'm yours."

Gag. I was going to throat punch him if he didn't release Veva. She let her hand slid down his chest before she gripped his wrist and gently tugged him forward. Triton released his hold on her and she stepped back, dragging him toward the pool's edge by his wrist.

"Let's swim," she cooed, and Triton nodded.

"That's my language." He tugged off his shirt, exposing his radiant green skin and a hard-core swimmers body. Next, he slipped off his shorts, revealing swimwear that left nothing to the imagination. Veva stared. Her throat rolled and I cursed her interest in my cousin. To continue the flirtation, Veva pulled off her shirt providing those around the pool a second viewing of her lush breasts. A demi-cup bra hardly contained her. Next, she shimmied out of her skirt to reveal a matching set in light blue. *Well, fuck me to Sunday*. My zipper strained, but Veva had no interest in what lay beneath my shorts.

"Veva," Persephone warned.

"It's like swimming at home," Veva replied, cutting off her friend's concern. "Lead the way." She swept out a dramatic hand to Triton.

"I'm not taking the bait." In one swoop, he encircled Veva's waist and dove gracefully with her wrapped around him. She let out a playful cry before breaking the surface.

"What bait?" she laughed once she sprang above the water like a water nymph.

"I could see it in your eyes. You wanted to fool me." She splashed water playfully at him, while only a night before she cursed me for dunking her in the pool. Granted, she had on that beautiful dress that revealed everything about her, but the moment she stepped out of the pool tonight there would be nothing to the imagination again.

"You're right," she teased. "You needed to cool off." She giggled as he captured her wrist and tugged her against him. Her name crossed my lips but no sound escaped. I couldn't watch this display. I walked the length of the pool in great need of my cottage.

"Hey, where are you going?" Triton called after me. "Jump in, cousin."

As if Fate couldn't leave well enough alone, Mel cornered me at the pool's end. I don't know how she got on the grounds, as tonight was still a private affair.

"I need to speak with you."

"Perfect timing," I replied gruffly, gripping her arm and tugging her behind me. Two could play this game, I thought, as I peered over my shoulder to see Veva watching me, and noticed my cousin had disappeared underwater. The glowing green spot in the pool still gave away his position, but his identity did not need to be seen by this human. Mel was a nuisance.

"Look, Letty needs help, Solis. *You* have to help her." I continued to drag Mel away from the viewing of the pool, but not far enough she'd see my cottage.

"Why is this my problem, Mel?"

"She needs you. I need you." Mel's clawing voice matched the sharp nails tipping up my shirt. "You seem tense tonight. I could relieve that pressure." Her hand covered my shoulder and she shook me back and forth. The motion annoyed me, rather than soothed me, and I thought of Veva's fingers rubbing in my hair.

"How did you get in here?"

"I have my ways." Her attempt at a seductive voice ended with a tiny snort. How I ever found this girl attractive, I couldn't remember.

"You aren't allowed to be here."

"I can if I'm your guest."

"We aren't allowed extra guests until later this week, Mel."

"So, you'll invite me back?" *Shit.* She'd trapped me.

"I'd need to ask my father."

"Since when do you follow your father's orders?" Mel's voice turned serious. She didn't know me on a deeper level, so it shocked me that she knew enough to realize I didn't like to follow his word.

"Since his father gave him a direct order to be escort to another." The towering sound of Zeke's voice startled Mel. She flinched before me and I closed my eyes, taking a brief second to control my racing heart, before I turned to face Zeke.

"Melody, I'd love to walk you to the entrance." His outstretched hand was not an open invitation but a strict command to take his offer. Her hand slipped purposefully over mine before she reached for his.

"Solis, return to your post." He wrapped an arm around Mel, who peered back over her shoulder. Fear didn't fill her eyes, but hatred did. My father moved her hand to rest in the crook of his elbow, leading her to the front entrance like she was a normal guest instead of a pesky intruder. To prove I didn't follow orders, I marched on to my cottage instead of turning back to face my playful post.

+ + +

Sweat dripped at my hair line as I stroked aggressively. *Almost there*, I cursed, giving a final flick of my wrist and staring at the wetness seeping downward. My canvas mimicked the night sky. Anger, frustration, and a bout of fear resulted in a sudden rainstorm over the valley. The clap of thunder and a strike of lightning would clear the pool, and I calmed as I accepted that Veva no longer swam with Triton. New concerns took over as I pummeled and painted. My brush became the extension of my emotion. I envisioned Veva wrapped within my cousin's strange-colored arms, and I didn't like it. Exhaustion took hold, though, and my sweaty brow matched the spitting rain outside the cottage window. I stepped back to admire my work, and realized I didn't care for it. Spent from the exertion, I decided I needed a shower and my bed.

I crossed the low, plant-covered terrain under rainfall still spilling heavy enough to accumulate in puddles here and there. After passing through the trees that hid my cottage, I stopped. Amid the clearing stood Persephone, her clothing drenched and hanging off her shoulder. Her hair was soaked and plastered to her cheeks. Water riveted down her face, but I'd dare say it was more than rain.

"Persephone?" I approached slowly, not wanting to frighten her. Her body shivered, but she didn't turn to me. Her eyes cast off toward the shadows in the trees.

"Persephone, honey, you're soaked. Let's go inside." My hand brushed her shoulder. She didn't flinch, but she didn't respond to the touch either.

"We met in the rain," her voice croaked. "He saved me." Shaky fingers brushed against her cheek, making no difference in the moisture upon her face.

"He promised me he wouldn't leave me." She paused and turned her saddened eyes to me. "Why do men leave?" I feared her question dug deeper than just Hades. Persephone had no father, like Veva. A queendom of women ruled their farmstead back in Nebraska.

"Why can't he love me?"

"Oh, Persephone, I don't..." A snap behind us made me turn, my arm coming to rest on her shoulder in protection. My eyes met another sodden female. Veva's eyes turned the color of ice and glowered in the dark night.

"Veva?" I questioned, and Persephone turned to face her friend. The shift brought her closer to me, under my arm, and the position looked all kinds of wrong.

"I knew it," Veva hissed, her voice too low.

"Vee?" Persephone's sad tone did nothing to soften the anger in her friend's face.

"I knew you two were together. And after leaving with Mel, too." Her crossed arms slipped to her side, hands slapping her thighs in aggravation, and then retreating back to a folded stance.

"Vee!" Persephone's cry admonished her friend's implication, and I agreed. I grew tired of the accusation that I was attracted to Persephone. She was beautiful, but she did not call to me like the fire within Veva. I burned for Vee.

Spinning quickly, Veva headed in the opposite direction. I dropped my arm and raced after her, catching her within a few large steps. My arm encircled her waist and I pulled her back against my chest. To my surprise, she twisted without much strength, the fight flickering out of her.

"Let me go." She spoke calmly and the steady tone frightened me more than the yelling storm she could produce. Cold, wet fingers pressed on my wrist at her waist.

"Veva, listen to me. It's not what you think."

"Men always say that."

"Then good thing I'm not a man." She straightened with that comment. "I was walking back to the main house when I saw her standing in the pouring rain. I was only trying to bring her inside. She's soaked, Vee, and she's lonely." My voice softened. Veva's body relaxed and her head fell back against my shoulder. I dipped my face to rest near her cheek. "She misses him, and I can't help her again."

With that Veva turned in my arm, her wet clothing hugging her body in a sinful way, and she pressed against me.

"I'm so confused. I don't know what to believe."

"I'll tell you what I can, but let's get her out of the rain first."
Thankfully, Veva agreed with a simple nod. Keeping my arm over her
shoulder, I guided her back a few paces to where Persephone still stood,
letting the rain shower her. I released Veva and stepped toward
Persephone. My eyes focused on Vee while I wrapped an arm around
Persephone's back and stooped to scoop up her knees. Lifting her limp
body, I jostled her, still focusing on Veva, willing her to understand that
I simply wanted to help Persephone. I spun for the house and stopped.
Veva bumped into my back with the abrupt halt. Persephone kicked out
her leg and I let her feet drop to the ground. She stood still, but her body
trembled. Her voice cracked as she stared at the figure dressed entirely
in black among the edge of the trees.

"Hades?"

VEVA

I couldn't believe my eyes. Harris Black, or Hades, or whatever his name is, stood before us. Equally drenched in rain, the four of us stared, but only two sets of eyes connected. Persephone could not move. Hades remained focused on her.

"Hades?" Her voice, hardly a whisper, seemed to swirl out and circle the trees like a whirlwind before turning back and resting before him. The subtlest dip of his chin signaled it was him, and she raced for him. The distance short, she leapt upward, and he caught her under her thighs as she wrapped legs and arms around him. To my surprise, they didn't kiss as I expected, only embraced in the tightest hug I've ever witnessed. Hades' face buried in Persephone's neck proved he held her as tight as she held him.

Solis' hand came to my back, and he gently prodded me toward the path for the main house. He patted his cousin's back as we passed. "Take the cottage," he offered. Guiding me the rest of the distance, he surprised me by continuing toward my room. My thoughts scattered while we walked. Persephone told me how Hades was special, and that made Solis unique as well. I didn't share with her what happened on the cliff, fearing she'd think I was crazy, until she went into detail about her stay with Hades and her own fears of sanity. It didn't settle my mind, but fed my confusion. The estate seemed so normal. *How could things appear one way and yet not be as they seemed?* A flying, morphing horse. A green cousin. A man risen from the dead. It was all too much.

Shaky, cold fingers fumbled with the keycard when we reached my room and Solis took it from me, swiping it over the security pad. He didn't stop there, but followed me into the room.

"You shower first," he commanded and stepped back to lean against the wall. "But make it quick, or else there will be a flood in this small entry." With his back pressed along the wall opposite the bathroom, a raised foot let me know this would be a permanent position. He would

elda lore

stand guard while I showered. I was brief and wrapped myself in the thick robe hanging on the back of the door. His eyes scanned my covered body, lingering at the slight opening near my neck. He entered the cramped space, carrying a small bag I hadn't seen before, and I shifted around him. He closed the door after my exit, clearly making himself at home.

I quickly changed into the shorty pajamas from the other day, but tugged a loose sweatshirt over me to hold the warmth. He was equally brief in warming up and exited the bathroom dressed like a sports star. Hair slicked back, wet from a shower; dribbles of moisture rippling down his bare chest. Low-hung sweats dipped to expose hips, and bare feet crossed toward the end of my bed. He sat with a thump on Persephone's bed, letting water trickle down his firm chest, dripping ever so slightly off his nipples. He swiped a hand through his wet locks, rubbing back and forth, releasing more droplets. The mussed appearance made him even more enticing. *Lightning strike me*, sin sat across from me.

But my body was exhausted from the emotions of the day: the flight, the discovery, the sunset, the pool and the rain. A day of firsts plus too much information and my system needed to shut down. I stifled a yawn. My mind leapt from one thought to another as we sat in silence, looking at each other. I wanted to ask for more details about his strange scar, but when another yawn presented itself so rudely, Solis spoke: "I suppose we should go to bed."

"To bed?" I croaked.

"To sleep," he clarified with a teasing grin.

"You can't sleep here." I suddenly took his meaning when he sat back and slumped down on Persephone's pillows.

"Well, where else should I go? The cottage is taken, and I don't want to deal with Triton yet." His head swung to face me as I still sat on the edge of my bed.

"Why? What's wrong with him?" I giggled, knowing that I needed to learn more about that crazy skin tone, but his playful demeanor made me ignore the color.

"Obviously, nothing." Sarcasm dripped from his voice.

118

"What do you mean *obviously nothing*?" I snipped. Solis' head rolled back, and he stared at the ceiling.

"Meaning you seemed very into him tonight." My mouth fell open. He had to be kidding.

"Into him? What about you and Mel? She looked particularly appealing tonight. I didn't think outside guests were allowed. You didn't waste any time leaving with her," I growled.

"They aren't," he sighed. "And I have no idea how she got in here tonight." His focus remained on the ceiling, and I looked upward to see what held his interest. When I turned back, I found his eyes on me. The honey gaze reflected intensely back at me, and my breath hitched.

"Veva, can we just form a truce for tonight?" He sighed. "I can't fight you anymore today." The lowered tone seeped into me like a soothing warm bath after a long day. The silence lingered between us. The slightest movement of my head gave ascent, but his eyes lingered on me.

"I guess we should just go to sleep," I hurried to offer, saying anything to break the intensity of those eyes. Alone with Solis, I suddenly felt self-conscious in the close quarters of the room. Larger than my old dorm room and definitely more luscious, the walls pressed in claustrophobically with only him and me in the space.

I twisted to the nightstand and snapped off the lamp light. Swallowed in black, the darkness felt oppressive, but I curled under heavy covers anyway. Persephone liked to keep the air conditioning low, and some nights I froze in our shared room. Continued silence filled the room, weighing down the night. No longer sleepy, my mind raced and my body stiffened, tense yet restless.

"Vee?"

"Yeah?" My voice choked out so low I wasn't certain he heard me.

"What happened on the mountain tonight? At sunset?"

My face flushed and gratitude for the suffocating dark room filled me with relief he couldn't see my face. I heard the bed creak opposite me and the covering rustled with his movement. He still lay on top of the blankets, but I sensed him watching me. I rolled to my side to find his body prone and positioned to face my direction. The heavy shadows hindered me from seeing him completely.

"We are an ancient people," he began. "With a history longer than history." I sensed a smile in his tone. "I didn't even know all I was until I was older." Instantly, that cheerful sound disappeared. He rolled back to face the ceiling, but I continued to watch him. An arm rose to rest over his forehead.

"My mother was Zeke's one true wife. Meta was her name, and she was beautiful. They loved one another, I believed, until he learned of the prophecy. Then, I think, Zeke loved himself more." He snorted and paused. Uncertain if he would continue, he startled me when he spoke, "This is kind of boring, are you sure you want to hear it?"

I nodded before realizing he couldn't see me, and a squeaky 'yes' escaped.

"The prophecy told that what Zeke had done to his father would be done to him by a son. So when he had a son, he gave orders to terminate me."

"What?" I sat up in bed, balancing on my hand to peer over at him.

"He obviously changed his mind," he snarked, but I found no humor in what he said. "My mother decided to leave him, and so we ran. Everywhere. I can't even describe how many places we lived. How many awful places we stayed. I just wanted a place to call home. One bed. One roof." His voice lowered and my brows pinched at his pained tone. My heart ached, and the desire to reach out for him, connect with him, took hold. Like earlier in the day, I longed to touch him, giving him comfort similar to when we stood on the cliff.

"What did Zeke do to his father?" He turned his head to face me.

"He killed his father. Surely you know this story."

I didn't know. I'd heard the rumors, but my mother said not to listen to what others said. He continued without addressing his father's crime further.

"So the prophecy is that you would kill Zeke. That's crazy."

"Yeah, crazy," he sighed. Silence built between us only briefly before he began again.

"Anyway, my mother, eventually, she left me, too. I remained with a man I called a stepfather, but he never legally held that title. Father was the furthest thing he was to me." His tone dropped bitterly.

"What happened?" I couldn't imagine the story getting any sadder.

"Zeke found my mother. Gossipers say he kidnapped her. He swears she willingly returned to him. She produced a second heir for him. A daughter."

"Athena," I whispered.

"Athena," he bit out. His voice dipped lower, and I sensed there was more to the story. Waiting for the rest, I held my breath. When he didn't speak, I softly spoke.

"What happened to your mother?"

"She's dead."

"I'm so sorry." I didn't know what else to offer, other than my arms, which ached to reach out for him and draw him close to me. I despised him most hours, and yet this sadness made me see him in a new light.

"Yeah. Me too." His voice lowered to a whisper. He coughed once and began again, but he took a new direction.

"When I came to live here, I trained my body and mind. I had much to learn. The olive oil industry is an interesting business and I submerged myself in it for human interaction. The mechanics of my body, on the other hand, were my true heritage."

He was losing me again. I didn't understand.

"Are you saying you aren't human?"

"I've already told you; I'm a god." With those words, and a teasing tone, I fell back on the bed, thinking he was kidding me again. Our positions shifted as I lay staring at the ceiling and he propped up on his elbow. As I lay perfectly still, his legs swung off the bed and he crossed the short distance to mine. An agile body climbed over me.

"What do you think you are doing?" I rolled my head to glare at him as his solid form crossed mine, but my narrowed eyes had no effect in the darkened room.

"You were too far away." His voice lowered as a he positioned himself beside me, returning to his perched elbow.

"Thunder is…special. As you saw, he can convert. I can't do that. I look human. I feel human. I act human, but I'm not."

"How can you exist?"

"I just do. I don't understand it all, but I just do. *Exist*. That's a good word for it." He lowered his head to rest on his crooked arm. Fingers stretched and reached for a lock of my hair, twisting the still-wet tendrils around them. His eyes focused on the strands wrapping and unwrapping around his finger.

"How old are you?"

"Let's just say I've been around for a while." My mouth bit back a retort. I bet he'd been around… around the block a few times.

"So you're *old* old." I paused. "Eww…" I giggled, shivering exaggeratedly and swatting his chest. He flattened my hand to his pecs, and then slid it down the hard form of his abs.

"Do I feel old to you, Veva?"

My voice caught in my throat and I swallowed the lump of desire forming. My fingertips burned with the need to continue the path further down his body.

"Consider me wise." He paused. "I know what I want."

"Maybe I should consider you ancient," I retorted, my voice dropping lower. *What do you want?* The inside of my cheek grew sore as I gnawed at it, holding back this question.

"Your hair is so beautiful," he whispered, ignoring my tease. I attempted to thank him but my voice cracked at the compliment. I was used to boys telling me things meant to make me feel good about myself, but those were typically said in passion. Solis' voice sounded sincere.

"What happened during the sunset tonight?" There was no chance I'd tell him, and I rolled my head away, but his free hand quickly gripped my chin in a tender hold. He forced me to face him, and then cupped his hand over my cheek. His fingers brushed my hair behind my ear.

"Trust me."

"I…I'm not really sure. Something I'd never felt before, so I can't explain it."

"Never felt before?" His questioning eyes lit up, as mine adjusted to the darkness, his glowed in a feral way back at me. "*Try* to explain it. Paint me a picture with words." His voice roughened and the tone dropped from his typical boom to a low tenor. When a finger traced down my jaw, under my chin and up to my lips, I fell under the heat of his spell, blazing like the lowering sun. Words began to tumble out of me.

"It's like the sun came alive, despite its descent. It was a living, breathing thing. Its warmth crawled up my thighs and entered me." Solis' breath hitched at the mention. "It sounds silly, doesn't it?"

"I'd kill Leos if he touched you." His voice hardened. "Sit up," he demanded softer, and I did as I was told, embarrassed at my explanation. He sat up as well, and tugged my sweatshirt over my head.

"What are you doing?" My voice shook, but he ignored the question by pressing my shoulder, guiding me to lay back again.

"You're still wearing my rock." He hadn't been able to see it under the sweatshirt, and he held it reverently in his palm. His knuckles brushed over the top of my chest, and I shivered.

"It brings me peace." Using his word, from the night he gave me the canvas, truth filtered through my response. I liked wearing it. The weight calmed me. The backs of his fingers stroked over to my shoulder and flittered down my arm. Goosebumps rose.

"Tell me more about the sunset." His voice dropped so low, it rumbled up my legs starting at my toes. Relaxing into the sound, my center pulsed with a vengeance, demanding an encore of the earlier sensation from the sun.

"I…I…" *How could I tell him?* "A warmth," I offered, swallowing hard on the word. It was all I could explain. An image of the lowering sun increased the tingling of my thighs, and I shuffled my legs for friction. Solis did not miss the motion. His fingers skipped to my side, his knuckles brushed around the swell of my breast and curved down my waist. Fingertips finally reached the band of my shorts and drew a line back and forth at the entrance.

"Let me feel how warm you are?" The question rolled over me like clouds tumbling in an overcast sky. The words collided and thrilled me.

elda lore

A storm brewed between my thighs. A gray anticipation enhanced the desire. Solis wasn't black or white, yes or no. I didn't know where I stood with him or where this would lead, but *gods forgive me*, I wanted his hands on me. I hadn't answered him before his large fingers dipped to slide my shorts and underwear to my hips and then slinked forward to my most intimate area. Cupping me at first, I flinched at the contact. The warmth of his palm heated me like the melting sun. A nervous giggle escaped. The tenderness of his touch and the intensity of his gaze tinted the moment as raw and real and frightening.

"So hot, Veva," he whispered. "I burn for you." His lips didn't reach for mine, and a combination of relief and disappointment warred within me. He hadn't touched my mouth with his after our hasty kiss in the racing field, but my lips longed for another taste of sunshine. On the other hand, kissing increased any emotional connection, threatening to overwhelm me, and I didn't need emotion to take over my heart.

His curled hand relaxed to one slender finger slipping through sensitive folds. My breath caught again at the sensation. Heat sliced through me. Solis' eyes watched where his hand worked, carving out the craving in my body and a notch in my heart. The length of his finger circled and curled until it found the right spot, the spot only I had discovered. My eyes flicked wide, and then lazily the lids lowered as I melted under the heat of his touch. The warmth of the setting sun spread, blanketing me in a blaze of desire that increased with the pressure of Solis' fingers. As my breath hitched and my hips rocked, sparks kindled, creeping up my legs and catching at my core, begging to ignite. Solis took his time to tenderly tease me with tortuous twists and turns. A long, thick digit lingered at my entrance before lighting me up as it entered.

"Solis?" I whispered, as confusion collided with the most exhilarating sensation. Warmth burst forth. My legs trembled. My hips slowed to dance over his palm. When his thumb found that special spot, I clenched around his finger. I wanted to hold him in. I wanted him to drag it out. I didn't want any of it to end. My eyes rolled back. My fists clasped the sheets as my back arched. Animalistic and raw, I groaned as something powerful, wonderful and indescribable rippled through me.

124

Like clouds in a heated battle for control of the sky, I crashed and rained down on Solis.

"That's it, Veva." His voice tempted me, and his mouth found my shoulder as I rode the summer rainstorm. I soared through the lingering mist, floating a million miles from the bed. As I came down from my high, my eyes opened slowly to find a smirking Solis staring down at me. Torn between smacking him or kissing him, I cursed myself for letting him get under my skin. I swallowed, waiting for what would come next. My euphoric high threatened to crash into a full-on thunderstorm of tears at the sudden insecurity of that smirk. He'd gotten what he wanted. It would only be a second before he'd slink away. Liquid filled my eyes, and I fought off the tears with rapid blinks.

Instead, he pulled up my underwear and kissed my shoulder again. He shifted, and removed his sweat pants to reveal dark gray boxer briefs. My heart raced anew.

"I..." His finger came to my lips and held them closed.

"I want to paint a picture of you in this moment." He didn't say it in his typical snarky way, but instead like he wanted to remember this second as a snapshot. He waited, eyes begging. My response involved my tongue slipping out to lick the pad of his finger. His eyes opened wider and a slow curve spread his lips. I kissed the tip of his finger, and then opened my mouth to draw in the digit.

"Veva." He exaggerated the Vs, moaning them, and I liked the sound too much. I sucked harder, releasing his finger after a slow drag to the back of my throat. His haunting smile grew and he pulled back his finger. He sat back, separating my ankles, and resting a hand on the tattooed one.

"I've wanted to pet this bird for too long," he muttered and I giggled.

"You want to touch the peacock?" I teased.

"No, that's what I want you to do." His tone was serious, despite the joking implication. Nervously, I reached for him, but he stopped me. He slid forward between my thighs that willing opened for him and I cursed my body again. *What's wrong with you? Why are you moving in*

elda lore

unison with every command he makes of you? Bucking at the contact with the length of him, I had my answer. Only his briefs stood between the tip of him and the still-clothed core of me.

"I just want to press against you, Veva, to feel the strength of you against the strength of me." His hands braced on either side of my shoulders as he tenderly thrust forward, mimicking a motion I understood. Despite telling me he was a god, he wanted me to feel how real he was as a man.

"This is as far as we'll go, Vee. I just…I just…" A vein in his neck rose and his eyes closed as he drew forward. His head tipped back as he rocked against me. "I just need to feel you feeling me." Strangely, I understood what he meant.

"I want you to feel that I'm more man than god." His eyes begged me to understand, but I didn't. I was too wrapped up in painting my own image, one I knew would be permanently etched in my head. A snarky, cocky, powerful man, rocking over me, his face full of pleasure, his eyes filled with desire. This wasn't my typical romp. This was something more, and it frightened me that it felt so strong. It scared me that it would burn, and yet, I wanted the flame. Solis did not disappoint. He danced over me and my body followed his lead. I gave in a second time with a subtler cry. This time, it was Solis who released the god in him.

VEVA

I fell into a restless sleep of fighting clouds and lightning skies. There was an argument of some type in my dream, and I was sent away from the estate. I cried out for Solis to find he was the one banishing me. I woke with a jolt, alone, and not surprisingly. Solis had already surprised me enough with his tender touch. Wrapping me into him, holding me tight against his chest, and stroking my hair until I slept, my awe was complete. Being alone did not shock me. What did, was the ache in my chest that he left.

Why do men leave? I'd heard Persephone ask him in the rain. The same question haunted me. I'd been in enough compromising positions to know men didn't stay if they didn't get what they wanted, and once they got what they wanted, they always left. Either way, I lost. Solis was no different to me, and yet recalling his touch, I wanted him to be. The delicacy with which he traced over my skin, like he worshipped it, I wanted to believe he was different; that *I was different* to him, and that's when it hit me. This is how he made them feel – all those girls – they felt like me. Worshipped. Replete. And totally taken by him. Sitting up, I ran a hand through my messy hair, still smelling sunshine on the sheets. When I turned to the night stand, a small cairn of rocks stood at the corner. A marker. *He had been here.* My lips warred with a smile at the sweet gesture while tears threatened to flood my eyes.

I wandered to the breakfast room, wondering if I would find Persephone there. Instead I found Zeke again with Mel.

"Good morning," Zeke offered cheerfully, but Mel glared. "Did you sleep well despite the storm?"

I turned toward the three large windows lining the dining space. "There was a storm last night?"

"Yes. At one point the windows rattled. I thought the house would cave in." Mel's clawing sound ripped over my skin. Something seemed off about her presence at such an early hour.

127

"I hadn't noticed," I replied, shaking my head at the thought. I hadn't heard a thing outside of the breaths and groans of myself and Solis. *How could I have missed such a powerful storm?* "Well, it looks particularly bright and sunny today."

"It certainly does." The booming tenor filled the room and I turned in the direction of Solis propped against the entrance to the room.

"Solis," Mel squeaked before I could respond. The momentary smile on his sunlit face faded instantly at the address from his previous lover.

"Mel?" Solis' eyes shifted from Mel to his father and back. "I see," he muttered. The grinding sound of his voice made me shudder suddenly. My hands rubbed up and down my chilled arms. His eyes leapt to me.

"We should talk," Mel addressed him as she stood. She stepped toward Solis. My brows pinched in question. His body straightened and he raised a hand in her direction. I noticed Zeke lowered his head to his breakfast.

"Actually, I have plans." With those words, he spun on his heels and exited the room. Mel turned to glare at me again, but I returned the smirk. I had my own demons with Solis, for leaving me alone this morning. Facing off with Mel, only added to my displeasure. I reached for a chair, although I was no longer hungry. As my fingers curled around the back of the seat, movement caught the corner of my eye. From where I stood, I had a clear shot out the entrance of the breakfast room. Solis stood within the shadows motioning for me to come to him. My eyes pinched in his direction for a moment, but his waving insistence continued in earnest.

"If you'll excuse me," I coughed. "I'm not really hungry after all." I pushed at the chair before me and walked slowly to the exit of the room. Solis had already stepped farther away from the dining area. Once I crossed the threshold, he continued to walk backward motioning me to hurry. He turned slightly, holding back his hand, but continuing to pace forward, picking up his speed. By the time I reached for his hand, heels clicked on the tile behind me. Wrapping my fingers in his, Solis practically dragged me along behind him.

"Solis." The screech echoed off the hallway walls chasing behind us as we ran. We broke through the front door and Solis shifted behind me. With ease, he gripped my hips and hoisted me into his Jeep. He used the roll bar to hoist himself upward on my side and swung over me to get to his seat. Falling in the driver seat with a heavy thump, he twisted the key as the front door opened. With another shriek of his name, he hit the gas and the open vehicle lurched forward. I had no idea where we were headed, but I smiled at the fact that Solis picked me.

SOLIS

I shook with anger. My father slept with Mel. There was no other explanation for her presence so early in the morning. It might even explain her appearance last evening. She must have wandered off from him in hopes to tell me this morning. She continued in vain to tempt me with jealousy. The only person worthy of such an emotion sat next to me and the laughter escaping her lips as we cleared the dirt drive relaxed my tension. Bubbles floated upward and popping in surprise, and my smile grew that she produced that sound for me.

"That was crazy." Her hands clapped and she turned back in her seat, but we were too far from the front entrance for Mel to see anything. The estate gates parted for us and we hit the open road.

"Where are we going?" She yelled over the whipping wind. I'd hit eighty-miles-per-hour almost instantly and her hair blew wildly in the open air of the Jeep. Attempting to brush it back herself, I reached over and held a clump at the nape of her neck. Tugging at it forced her to look at me.

"I love to look at your neck," I blurted. "And I'm sorry you woke alone. I had training this morning and I didn't want to wake you." I smiled to reassure her as I'd seen the doubt in her blue eyes. Hurt filled that turquoise center as she looked at me across the breakfast room. A slow smile curled her luscious lips. I couldn't forgive myself for not kissing her first before I touched her last night. I hoped today would make up for it. Finally getting to massage the inked bird on her calf gave me the idea after I left this morning.

"What training?"

"The Olympiad games in two days. It's the highlight of the week, next to the ball." My grueling training sessions included more than basic calisthenics and boxing.

"I still have so much to learn about my powers," I offered. I drew closer to mastering my strength. I'd let the power control me. Once. The result was deadly, and I didn't wish to repeat it. The weight of that sin bore heavily on me. I had to be ready.

"What power?"

"I'll show you some day. When I'm ready." I wanted to be able to control it before I flaunted it.

"What are the games?"

"The games were the highlight of the week for my father's celebration. Traditional sports battled on an open field." They seemed like pin-the-tail-on-the-donkey compared to my personal training, but there was still a need to prove myself amongst the other competitors, most of whom were siblings or cousins.

"It's all cousins and siblings competing in good fun, but also to impress Zeke. Everyone wants his favor."

"Except you." I snuck a glance at her, as her eyes weighed on me.

"I want to impress him, too. I want him to know I mean him no harm, despite the things he does to me. He's still the one who found me and brought me here. He could have turned me away as he's done to others. I have that one bed, that one roof, that I mentioned last night."

"It seems like it's still not enough, though." How observant my little peacock was, as she sat, correct in her assessment. There remained a missing piece to my safety and stability. A final link to feeling whole sat under my grip at the nape of her neck. I just wasn't ready to tell her that yet.

"I'm working on it," I offered, sensing she waited for an answer.

"Speaking of the ball, I never thanked you for the dress," she said shyly. Her lids dipped and a small smile curled her lips.

"I can't wait to see you in it." Not only did I replace the dress I'd ruined by dropping us in the pool, I purchased a second one. Thinking of her in it, and then her out of it, strained my lower regions and memories of last night filtered through my brain. Veva under me painted a vivid image, but I needed more to complete the masterpiece.

I didn't release the hair I held at her neck, and we drove on in idle chatter after that. An hour later, we reached my undisclosed destination. Pulling into a parking space near a public park, Veva instantly noticed my surprise. Grabbing the roll bar at the top of the front windshield, she pulled herself to stand and stared forward. Her eyes gleamed and her mouth curved wide.

"Peacocks?" She questioned with a giggle.

"Peacocks." Dozens of the royal blue-necked birds filled the open space, wandering freely among the fences, bushes and grass. In an effort to migrate the peacocks away from the surrounding homes, the community built a bird park. The space worked. While the gorgeous creatures still wandered amid the clapboard houses of the community, the nuisance of their roaming dissipated with the new area. Veva continued to stare in wonder.

"I'd never seen one before." I stood to match her position, crossing my arms to rest over the roll bar.

"Really?"

"Yep. A first." A smile filled her voice as she continued to watch the creatures strut slowly amongst each other.

"Another one," I mumbled, proud of myself. I had no doubt the result of touching Veva had been a first for her. In many ways, it had been a first for me as well. I wasn't used to taking time. I rushed in, I claimed, I retreated. I didn't linger and I never stayed like I had last night. But the look in Veva's eyes as she watched me rock over her, the longing to trust me and the conflict to not, stabbed at my heart.

"Can we get out and pet one?" She asked, ignoring my comment. Her mouth twisted with the innocent question.

"I'm not sure. This is their natural habitat. I think they can be mean when frightened." Veva shook her head in understanding.

"They are so beautiful. Graceful and exotic." She sighed watching as a few pranced together toward a larger bird.

"Yes," I exhaled, watching her watch them. The peacock symbolized her. She matched the bird in grace and poise. Her beautiful eyes matched the brilliant colors of their plumes, making her exotic as well. She turned them on me, and the excitement at my gift intensified in their reflection. I was mesmerized. She cast a spell on me. The noisy cackling of the birds broke our connection and Veva twisted to observe them again. One rose its tail feathers, literally, and the elongated design spread to a full fan. Thousands of eyes stared back at us.

"They're looking at me," she said nervously. "The feathers are staring at me."

"They recognize a queen." The comment jolted her attention to me, but I turned away this time. All those eyes watching her. Watching me. That's how I felt on the estate. They were all watching, waiting for what I would do. *Would I fulfill the prophecy? Would I dispel it instead?* The question haunted my father. Keep your family close, your enemies closer, unless they were one and the same.

"What did you say?"

"I said they see their queen."

"No," she said. "After that. About enemies."

I hadn't realized I'd muttered the saying aloud.

"Keep your family close, your enemies closer, unless they are one and the same."

"Isn't it *keep your friends close, but your enemies closer*?" She chuckled lightly.

"Not in my case," I exhaled, letting my hands gently tap the glass beneath them.

"What does that mean?"

"My father says it." I paused, hesitant to tell her more. She loved my father. She trusted him, and I didn't want to ruin her relationship with him, but I didn't trust him around her.

"Let's get out and walk. We'll see how close we can get." Knowing she waited in anticipation to be closer to the birds, I decided I would deny her nothing. Hopping out my side, I hollered back for her to wait for me, but she'd already jumped down from her side of the Jeep. I came around to her and reached out a hand to guide her closer. She hesitated. More distrust.

"Take my hand," I commanded with a whisper. Her fingers shook as she reached for mine. Entwining our fingers, I led her a step toward the birds. Despite her intrigue at the peacocks, something weighed on her mind. Thinking my brave Veva was suddenly frightened of the unusual creatures, she stared down at our linked fingers.

"What is it?" I squeezed.

"She slept with your father. Doesn't that anger you?" Her question completely shocked me, referencing Mel who I did not wish to bring into our day.

"Not as much as the possibility he wants to sleep with you." I tugged her forward another two steps. The closest birds parted at our approach.

"That's gross. Zeke is like a father to me." Her brows pinched in consternation.

"That won't stop him."

"It will stop me." The conviction in her statement pleased me. I bent to pick up a long, lone quill admiring the varying colors in the feathery shape, in particular the one at the center that matched her eyes. I twirled the feather between my fingers, not letting go of hers with my other hand. Pointing the plume in her direction, I tickled it down her neck. She giggled in response to the touch.

"He's very persuasive."

"Then I see where you get it from, because so are you."

"Oh, yeah?" A smile graced my lips. I stopped our slow pace and stepped closer.

"Did you like me persuading you last night?" I drew down her neck, dragging the feather between her breasts, watching her chest rise as she sucked in a breath. She bit her lip and my mouth watered.

"Could I persuade you to do another thing?" I tugged her to my chest and her hand landed over my heart. She hadn't answered before my lips were millimeters from hers. "Kiss me."

The words exhaled over her mouth. She answered with a tender brush of peachy lips over mine, too soft and too brief. As she pulled back, I captured her mouth instantly, refusing to let her go. I wanted more, so much more and my lips demanded it of her. Tugging the deep bow of her bottom lip between mine, I held her still until our mouths matched in contact. The hand holding hers released and wound upward into her hair, tugging her closer by the nape of her neck. My other hand wrapped over her hip, pinching the feather with my fingers at her side. I had plans for that feather and the rest of her skin, but for now her mouth was my desire. Warm, wet, and willing, she dove into this kiss, responding to each nip with one of her own.

When my mouth took her lower lip, her tongue teased my upper one with a lick. The temptation triggered a full onslaught of lips on lips and tongues twirling with tongues. She pressed into me, and my mouth claimed hers, sucking on her tongue before beginning a delicate dance. Our mouths melded together as if her lips were made for mine. That strange familiarity overcame me, as if I knew her mouth, as if mine had been waiting to return to hers. This kiss answered my quandary. Her lips belonged to me, but even stronger was a sense she owned mine in return.

I'm not sure how long we stood among the peacocks and kissed, but when a feather brushed my ankle, I pulled back at the strange sensation. Looking down and around us, the birds surrounded us, as if we were part of their flock. Statuary and still, we stood amid a sea of royal blue and feathered eyes draped like a bridal gown train behind each owner. A vision of Veva dressed in white, with a tail of feathers following her, flashed before me. When a slow smile lit her face, warmth filled me and my heart ached at the thought of her marrying a real man one day. As if to drive the vision home, I turned toward the Jeep to find a rare, solid white peacock perched on the hood. Its beady black eyes focused on Veva, sharing a secret with her royal highness before taking a giant leap for the extended length of a wooden fence.

"Wow," Veva sighed, following the movement of the unusual bird.

Wow, I thought when Veva turned back to me, her eyes alight, matching the color of the creatures so connected to her. She leaned forward to kiss me again, with lips persuading me she might pick me as that future man.

SOLIS

Two days later, the games began. The yard bustled with activity. White tents circled the large expanse of lawn outlined for a variety of classical Olympic competitions. While the friendly banter among brothers and cousins included taunting teases and insinuating insults, an underlying tone of battle ensued. Each competitor wished to win and earn the good graces of Zeke, a true patriarch to his family.

In many ways, I was no different. I wanted Zeke's approval. I needed to prove I was not the prophecy. I was not his enemy; I was his son. I looked for Veva in all the excitement. I needed her strength and I envisioned her under me, looking up at me with those haunting eyes. She needed trust from me and I wanted to give her everything. But these were thoughts I had to suppress in order to perform. *Keep your head in the games*, my trainer admonished.

Political, athletic, and artistic, the modern event on Zeke's estate was no different than those original games in appreciation of the body. Descendants battled for Zeke's attention. Competitors fought for victory. Artists admired the athletes in song or modern artistry—photography. I found myself in the center of such a display, as a set of special-invitation media hounds took photographs, recorded interviews, and asked for autographs. *Let the games begin*, I muttered in my head.

"Solis, any comments on a special woman in your life?"

"No comment."

"So does that mean there is one?"

"No comment means no comment."

In that moment, my eyes found Veva's on the edge of the crowd. That pained look I'd seen before returned, but I didn't wish to expose her to all the attention. I wanted her attention on me. The opposite occurred—she turned away, with Callie, Di, and Ionia at her side. My insides roiled with the thought of ex-lovers comparing and sharing stories with Veva, but the first call to games went out, and the crowd dispersed as a whole.

Traditional sports recalled our heritage. The first events included racing, and the clear winner would always be Hermes. Known for his speed and agility, Hermes was a wily guy. A trickster at heart, speed was his sport, and car racing was a more modern interest. Our father disapproved. Leos presented a second disfavored son in car racing. His thieving ways added to our father's disapproval.

In wrestling and boxing, there was no match for War. A descendant of a close relative to my father, the military hero in him knew how to fight. He also fought unfairly in love. His interest lay with Heph's fiancé, Lovie, and their uncensored attention proved embarrassing. While Heph had no place in most of the day's events, the fight in him could be unparalleled if called to action. He saved his competitive spirit for long jump, an event he surprisingly dominated despite the bum leg. Triton would take all swimming events, which were added over time to appease Idon and his offspring. Dionysius remained uninvolved in all sports other than the skill to lift a glass to his lips and drink heartily. The final competition would be in discus and javelin throwing.

I still hadn't found Veva again, but I assumed her present. Everyone was. As I lined up against my competitors, I saw Veva standing near Leos. Smiling brightly at her, he pushed back a stray hair and held his hands behind her neck as he spoke. The position was a familiar stance of my own and it irritated me that he copied my move. Anger roared through me. Everywhere I turned, men were taken with Veva. More annoying was her interest in them. I wanted her attention on me. The clear sunny sky was slowly invaded with rolling dark clouds. A crackle of thunder off in the distance drew some attention. Zeke signaled to speed up the games with the opposing weather front. His eyes met mine across the field.

Discus was first. A circular object similar in size to a dinner plate, the object weighed over five pounds, in solid metal forged by my very own brother, Heph. I spun in the necessary circles and released the disc, watching it spiral to the projected target area. Several competitors followed me, but only one concerned me. Leos had strength to master this event, and his practiced arm threw the disc just far enough that it landed on mine, dangling off to the edge. The symbolic image wasn't lost on me. The sun overpowered the clouds most days, but my destiny included the complete sky.

The next event was javelin and my power would show who held the strength between Leos and I. His glorious, ray of sunshine javelin burst forth and flew quite a distance. The crowd cheered and applauded his tremendous ability. Leos exited the arena and walked straight for Veva. My father's eyes met mine again before shifting to Leos. He smiled appreciatively at his son's effort. Then his eyes narrowed. Reading my face, he knew my intentions. His head shook once in warning, but the caution came too late. I reached behind my back, closed my eyes, calmed my breath and removed the scar. The air crackled and sparks lit from my back as the jagged rod fulfilled its destiny and became a lightning bolt with my touch. Held high in my hands, I aimed for Leos' ray of sunshine. Poised for the throw, I released the bolt with a mighty thrust and watched as it far surpassed Leos' reach. The bolt hit a tree, splitting it in two before igniting it in flames. The earth rumbled with aftershocks and the dirt shuddered at my feet. A mighty roar of wonder exploded among the observers. My father stood, unimpressed.

"Holy crap," Triton laughed, clapping a hand on my shoulder. "How did that feel?" He understood my struggle. I had the strength to kill within me, and I'd worked hard to suppress the ability. Seeing Leos flirt with Veva after Triton's attempt only a few nights before drove me from valley to mountain top in range of anger.

"Amazing," I sighed, stretching back my shoulders at the release of the weight. The bolt lay dormant until I needed it. I'd only used it once, in extreme anger. The results had been deadly.

Adrenaline rattled through my body and prickles of electric shock worked their way to my fingers and toes. The energy would release slowly and rebuild within me. There was another way to remove the electric energy faster. I turned to find Veva staring at me. Her hand covered those peachy lips that belonged to me. I strutted for her, never losing connection with her eyes. The instant I reached her, I didn't stop, but reached out for her wrist and tugged her behind me. Sweating and shaking from the heat, I pulled her toward the backside of the pool house. A row of semi-private showers lined the back wall.

"Solis?" she cried behind me, but I continued onward, ignoring her. "Solis, where are you taking me? What are you doing? Are you all right?" Her last question lowered an octave, full of concern after the initial shock began to wear down.

"Solis, you're…you're…" She wouldn't have an answer. I wasn't exactly bleeding in the true sense of the word. My back would appear wounded and open, but the natural course of my skin would heal and repair quickly. A smell of burned skin lingered like a person too long in the sunshine. I needed a shower. And Veva was coming with me.

I yanked open the wooden door and gently dragged Veva inside. Slamming it shut behind me, we stood close in the tight confines. I spun the faucet and instantly we were drenched in warm water.

"What do you think you are doing?" she yelled, but her throat caught on unquenchable laughter and her hands cupped water before pushing back her soaked hair. I reached for her neck and tugged her to me, my mouth claiming hers as water pelted us. Her shirt plastered to her luscious shape and her jean shorts, cut too high, slowly retained the water hitting her side. My hand found her backside and cupped one succulent globe, forcing her to crush against me. Our mouths fought, hers mixed with irritation and concern, mine searching for comfort and relief. We carried on for several minutes, kissing and sucking and licking at lips before we heard an undeniable sound.

"Oh Heph. Yes, Heph." A corresponding grunt or two or five accompanied the cries. The wooden wall of the shower stall at Veva's back began to rattle and shake. Veva giggled, and I covered her mouth with my hand. My forehead came to rest on hers. The noise continued at her back. Heavy breathing added to the disturbing symphony, and Veva's eyes opened wide at a tender moan. A final huff of weighty breath and the rumble of the stall stopped. Veva's eyes hadn't left mine. When the door to the used stall opened, and then creaked closed, I removed my hand and Veva bubbled into laughter.

"Oh my God."

"Yes, well, even a god wants to be treated like a man." I chuckled and Veva gaped at me a moment before launching herself at me. I fell against the support behind me and her legs wrapped around my hips. Holding both delicious backside cheeks, one in each hand, our mouths crashed together again before I winced.

"Did I hurt you?" She pulled back from my lips and I longed for her immediate return, but my tender back bumping the wooden wall pinched. Her hands wrapped over my shoulders and she paused.

"Does it hurt?" Her eyes searched my face, longing for understanding of the un-understandable.

"It stings. It will take a little while before it feels normal again, whatever normal might mean." Still perched in my hands, pressed against my waist, she watched my mouth as I spoke.

"You just pulled that off your back." It was a question and a concern rolled into one, and it gave me pleasure that she cared.

"I did. It's what I've been training for."

Her legs slipped but I hiked her upward, not wanting to let her go.

"I'm too heavy for you."

"Never."

"Let me go."

"Never ever."

She smiled slowly. "How about, put me down?"

"You know all I want to do is light you up."

She laughed heartily, jiggling in my arms and jostling herself against me. Her arms wrapped around my neck and she pulled herself to nuzzle into the crook at my shoulder.

"I can't believe you can joke after what just happened. It must hurt." Hesitant fingers skimmed my shoulder blade and reached for the wound that had already almost closed. She forced herself free of my hold. Placing her hands on my shoulders, she nudged me to turn. All the while, we ignored the streams of water pouring over us, but the direct contact made me flinch as my back, facing her, centered under the spray. She reached to turn it off but made no other move. Without seeing her, I felt the weight of her eyes taking in my back. My spine crisscrossed in a jagged line, raw and red from the release of my energy source. When her hand came to rest at the base of my spine, I flinched again.

"Did I hurt you?" Her tender tone relaxed me, and my shoulders fell.

"No. Just surprised me." I took a calming breath and looked over my shoulder at her. Her hand returned to my back and delicate fingers traced up the line of the removed bolt. Taking her time to outline the length and then cross the width, her fingers soothed the lingering burn. My hands came forward to rest on the wall of the stall and I hung my head, allowing her fingers to explore. Eventually, they deepened into a massage. Pleasuring pressure worked from the base of my spine upward, until a hand delved up the nape of my neck and into my hair. Tugging it gently, my head pulled back, and Veva stepped closer.

The brush of her wet T-shirt against my skin sent shivers rippling through me despite the heat. Her mouth came to my shoulder blade and small pecks increased to full sucks of skin up and down and over my back. She worked her way along the scarred skin until she reached my shoulders. Standing shorter than me, her mouth could reach no further, and I spun with the intention to capture her lips again.

"I know he's around here somewhere." The clawing screech of a familiar voice stopped us both just millimeters from meeting mouths.

"I don't know why you keep chasing after him." Another, deeper, female voice responded. Veva winced in my arms.

"I'm not chasing him. I'm saving him. His father's making him do it."

"I don't know, Mel. He seemed pretty intense when he looked at her."

"He didn't look intense. He looked pissed off. I know that look. He doesn't want her."

There was a pause as the voices drew closer.

"Besides his father's making him babysit her."

The separation from Veva was instantaneous. Her shoulders fell and her feet lowered. As we stood in our perpetual pose of anticipation, Veva had been on her toes. She stood flat-footed and pressed on my chest to release her.

"Vee," I whispered shaking my head adamantly.

"Babysit her?" Di asked.

"Yeah, Zeke told him he has to watch over her during the week to make-up for throwing her in the pool. He's almost free of her. Tonight, after the ball, he's released from his duty. He's only doing it so he isn't kicked off the estate."

With those words, Veva stepped away from me in the small confines, her back pressed against the wall behind her. Not letting her retreat more than a few inches, I followed her, filling her space.

"Veva, don't listen to that. It's not true..." But she pushed against me hard enough I fumbled backward. The slam of my back against the opposite wall forced a sharp cry. In my weakened moment, Veva reached for the door and pushed outward. She exited the stall, the door slamming in her retreat. I instantly followed, to find a startled Di and a smirking Mel a few feet from the shower. Pleased with herself, Mel turned in the opposite direction of Veva, who stalked back toward the competition field. Di stood still and stared at me. Silently standing beside her stood Letty, with a tear slipping down her face.

VEVA

"Where have you been?" Persephone entered our room the next day.

"Where have you been?" I teased in return. I hadn't seen my roommate in nearly four days. Her face instantly blushed and her swollen lips spoke a truth her mouth would not mention. Reunited with Hades, I imagined their solitary confinement created a world for only the two of them.

"You have some explaining to do." I used my best accent to further tease my best friend.

"I don't even know where to start." She giggled as her fingers covered her lips, but her eyes told a different story. Troubled and sad, I sensed their rendezvous was short-lived.

"He can't stay long. And he's only here because he's been summoned, as was his father, for the party tonight. He heard I was present on the estate. I never knew this was one place he could visit freely."

I stared at my friend, too overwhelmed and confused by all the details I'd been learning.

"Harris Black wasn't real." The statement sounded like a question, but I had my answer. A dead man cannot revive, and the man who captured my friend in his arms the other night stood very much alive.

"Hades has powers…" I raised a hand to stop her. I nodded, as if I understood.

"Did you see what Solis did the other day?" Pea lowered onto her own bed, sitting opposite me. My heart sank as I remembered what I'd heard. *Babysit me?* He was only with me because his father told him to watch me? How dare Zeke, but furthermore, how dare Solis? He'd played me well with his romantic gesture to steal me away and show me the peacocks. I couldn't even allow myself to think of all the kissing we shared. *How dare you*, I cursed myself. I'd done just what I told myself not to do. I fell for Solis. But despite my aching heart, the uncertainty of his being and the presence of his back haunted me.

"I heard. Are you okay?" Her brown eyes questioned mine. She didn't seem concerned by what she'd heard as much as worried about my response.

"It's a lot to take in." I sighed.

"It certainly is," she smiled slowly. Her cheeks fell softly. "But I love him," she whispered, "and I see you falling for Solis, too."

My head shot up and my back straightened. "I am doing no such thing."

"Vee, I see…"

"You see nothing." At the curtness of my words, my friend straightened in response.

"I see more than you think. I see my best friend, whom I love and adore, throwing herself at men all the time in attempts to prove her mother wrong."

My mouth fell open in disbelief, but Persephone rose her hand to stop an interruption.

"And repeatedly getting her heart broken, despite the bold front. And I see you fighting Solis, whatever the attraction is between you, you're fighting it. Afraid of it, when maybe you should embrace it. Let him in."

"He used me. Or rather, he's only with me because his father told him to watch me."

"I don't believe that."

"Yeah, well, there's a lot I wouldn't have believed either, but after spending time here, I think anything is possible."

"Why do you think this?" Persephone shook her head, still not trusting my words.

"Mel and Di were talking outside the showers behind the pool house. I overheard…"

"You overheard two jealous girls making up a story to discredit Solis and his affection."

"Affection?" I snorted. "Solis and I…" My voice faltered. *Had he been affectionate?* My lips tingled where he'd nipped them. My tongue brushed at the back of my teeth, knowing he'd invaded my mouth with his. My thighs clenched, recalling tender fingers between them. Despite all those attentions, it had been the look in his eyes as he hovered over me. Tender. Questioning. Trusting. In me.

"Veva, what did you do?" My friend's voice sounded nearly pained as she asked. Something in my face must have given away my thoughts. My eyes drifted to my lap and a tear splashed down to my bare thigh.

"It wasn't like *that*; it was just sweet, actually. He was sweet, and I guess I misunderstood." I swiped briskly at the moisture on my cheeks and faced my friend. I shrugged a shoulder like it didn't matter, but my heart began to squeeze, and I couldn't take in air. Persephone shifted to my bed and wrapped an arm around me.

"I don't believe he didn't care. I don't believe he isn't falling for you."

"I don't know what to believe," I whimpered into her shoulder and let the tears slip slowly.

"I believe my cousin is a fool." Persephone and I both spun to face the cold glare of a blue-faced man. A white scar crossed his lips, and another curled down the side of his face. His lips pursed, his deep eyes softened as he looked at me.

"Hello, Veva. I didn't mean to intrude." Persephone and I both stood. I wiped at my cheeks again.

"How did you get in here?" Persephone admonished, but the smile in her tone wasn't forceful. She stepped to him, and he opened his arms to her.

"I came to see if you were getting ready. And if you had found Veva. I heard she ran off." His eyes shifted from glowing adoration as he spoke to Persephone to stern pebbles of blue as he looked at me.

"Did he tell you what happened?" I closed my eyes after asking, cursing myself for caring.

"He told me about a bunch of silly girls who set a trap to hurt you. He's been looking for you."

"Well, he didn't look very hard," I snorted. "Besides, I've been right here."

Persephone eyed me. "Actually, it's been nearly two days. Where have you been?"

I didn't respond. I didn't want them to know that I'd taken the liberty to wander the grounds, and I stumbled upon some of the homes of the migrant workers. I applauded Zeke's effort to give them comfort, but I still disapproved of their missing amenities. I helped several children with infected cuts and scabs, and talked with a few women who were pregnant. I held an infant, showing a young mother how to hold the baby to relieve pressure from gas. The presence of these people, and their appreciation of my time spent with them, calmed me. It was another reminder of home, and how much work I'd done among the children and women who spent time on our fields. I missed my mother in moments like these, although she'd never understand my predicament. She'd admonish me for giving into a man with a track record for broken hearts. Then she'd scold me for using my body as a tool instead of a temple. *Let them worship you, and revel in what they will never have.* Her words haunted me. *What about what I would never have in return, then,* I wanted to ask.

"Is it almost time for dinner?" I changed the subject, focusing on the other part of Hades' questions.

"It is. I don't think either of you look dressed." His eyes roamed up and down Persephone, and without a thought, he kissed her neck. He spoke softly to her and she blushed, her eyes shifting to me to see if I'd heard what he said, then lowering as her skin flushed darker.

"Well, I think you need to leave so we can get dressed." The words teased him and his head shot up. My smile reassured him I wasn't kicking him out, just asking for a few minutes. "Unless you are going like that." I waved at his dark appearance: black jeans, black hoodie, black T-shirt. He nodded at me and turned to kiss Persephone on the lips.

"I leave you two to dress."

+ + +

An hour later, we walked down the hall, Persephone and I each linked with an arm through Hades'. I felt like a third wheel, but Hades insisted and Persephone agreed. She looked lovely in another dress of white, cut over one shoulder and dipping precariously low over one breast. Wrapped around her, the material belted at the waist, then fell straight to the floor. She looked Grecian and regal, and together, in Hades' opposing black, they stood as the epitome of black and white, night and day, king and queen.

I, on the other hand, wore a dress of royal blue silk. Bright and daring, the slit up the side revealed the ink covering the length of my leg, highlighting that feature of my body. The neckline dipped low, and two thick straps covered my shoulders. The back draped to my waist, leaving my skin exposed. It was sinful and sexy, and when I walked, the silk seduced my legs while it slid between my thighs. The exposure of my back made me feel seductive, not like I revealed something to anyone who noticed, but instead offering temptation. They would never have the full view of me, and in response to any question Solis might ask, I wasn't wearing underwear or a bra. Demi-cup tape strips held me in place. Nothing covered my lower region. It felt risqué and freeing, but the electric current of achy need poked and pecked at me with every luxurious step.

We met Solis immediately, as he stood to the left of his father. His sister, Athena, stood on the right. She was an anomaly to me. Solis spoke of her, but I hadn't spoken much *with* her. In the receiving line of greeters, she posed proudly next to her father, who kissed each cheek and shook each hand. When I reached Solis, his hold lingered on me.

"You look stunning." He leaned in to kiss my cheek as the custom directed, but stopped. His clean-shaved face, slightly out of place for him, rested against mine. Warm breath tickled under my ear.

"You're the blue sky to my gray." When I pulled back, I noticed his charcoal gray attire. He gave suit porn the label: Dress pants and an open coat, with a white shirt underneath, made my mouth water. A rainstorm did not compare to the deluge of desire that overtook me. I cursed my body, hyperaware of his nearness, charged by the attraction. "Save me every dance. All of them belong to me." I didn't think he was referencing the dance floor of the ball room, but the slow rhythm of a few nights ago, private and intimate in my room.

A cough beside me signaled I'd lingered too long on the host, and I turned to see Mel had squeezed her way between me and the next guest. Solis' arm wrapped around my waist, and he dragged me to his side. "Stay with me," he muttered. "This is torture." To our surprise, Mel slipped her arm through Zeke's, but turned to rake over the protective arm Solis held on me.

"I think I'll leave you to your godly wonders." I patted his chest, playfully, so as not to make a scene, and broke free of his arm. I hadn't taken two steps before a lingering weight of warmth rushed down my spine. The pressure so real, the presence so warm, I turned. To my surprise, Solis still stood by the entrance, but his eyes were on me. The corner of his mouth turned upward. My heart fell to my toes with his heated stare. Desire filled those eyes, but I wanted an explanation before he could have any part of me. I turned my back on him to tell him as much.

SOLIS

The party was torture. Dinner, a feast of gluttonous proportions, only delayed my getting near Veva. She avoided me at every turn. The whole night was turning into a dance. One step forward to the bar where she pressed on her side waiting for a drink. Two steps back when I finally reached it to find her gone. One step left when I saw her talking to Triton in a corner. Two spins to the right when she disappeared before I made my way to their corner. The room was aglow with enough candles to start an inferno. The circular tables smattered here and there kept people close but allowed each table their privacy. Finally called to dinner, from the main table, I had a clear shot of Veva seated at the nearest table along with my father's two brothers, Idon and Hades. Hades Sr. epitomized an older rock star with his long dark hair, streaked with gray. The open shirt and longer jacket over leather pants rocked his stature as ruler of the underworld. Idon, on the other hand, wore a linen shirt, dark dress pants and slides on his web-toed feet. Not used to wearing a shirt, I noticed my cousin, scratching occasionally at the material covering his greenish skin. Veva retreated often during the meal, only to return finally with two beautiful women, one on either side of her.

"Hera," my father exhaled as he stood. Instantly I recognized a woman who could only be Veva's mother. Regal in stature, feminine and pure, her face held an edge of distrust as she scanned the room. She was an older version of her daughter. Her eyes were a rich, bark brown matching Persephone's, but that acorn hair was signature to Veva and her mother. Mel flinched next to me as she'd taken a seat at my father's left, forcing me one seat from my customary position. "Demi." He added, stepping around our seats and retreating to the two women who had entered our gregarious feast. The second woman had hair the same color as the first. They could have been twins for the similarity in figures and stance, only the second woman had a livelier expression on her face and embraced her daughter, Persephone, the instant they connected. Veva

149

and her mother did not touch. A table was set at the back of the room, as all tables were full, and the women took their seats, as did my father. Veva joined them there.

After several minutes, I stood, too curious about the back table to concentrate on the second course. At the same time, Heph stood. He took his time to reach the back of the room. He addressed the table, being acknowledged by all, but the cold glare of Hera's face left me questioning. Veva's head spun from Heph to her mother and back. Something was said before I appeared at the table, and Heph retreated. A heated word crossed between Veva and her mother, and Veva followed Heph. I'd lost her again, but I felt obligated to meet the two women my father had never been able to tame, and the two women who claimed his heart.

"Good evening," I addressed the table, and Zeke stood.

"Ladies, it's been so long since you've been to the estate. Allow me to present, my son, Solis." Hera eyed me warily, knowing the prophecy, I assumed. Demi, on the other hand, stood and circled the table to embrace me. She smiled weakly as she pulled back, her hands lingering on my biceps.

"Take care of our girl," she spoke, and tipped her head subtly toward the exit where Heph and Veva passed. Instantly, I took her meaning and jealousy reared at the thought that Veva would comfort Heph or vice versa. As I walked down the hall, remembrance of her tender kisses down my back and soothing caresses on my skin prickled up my still-healing spine, and my feet picked up the pace. Her lips sucking at my skin and her fingers working in care tickled over my back and I suddenly raced down the corridor, spinning my head into every crevice of privacy. I was at a full run when I found them standing in the main foyer, caught between the residents' hall and the guest wing.

Veva's delicate fingers brushed down Heph's large face, crossing over his growing scruff, her eyes gazing upward at him as her second hand came to his chest and held over his heart. Heph lowered his head, the stance a form of submission from him. He stood too tall to match their heights, and my heart hit the floor envisioning his mouth drawing close to hers. As the click of my dress shoe hit the tile, I heard Veva's soft, questioning words, and I froze.

"You're my brother?"

VEVA

The question lingered between us as I stared into eyes that did not match mine. They were my mother's, only deeper in color. Heph's body stature was pure Zeke—broad, bold, and tall—but his eyes were all Hera's. My mother. His mother.

"How?"

"A long, long, time ago, Zeke and Hera were together."

"A long time ago, but you and I are roughly the same age." I was only twenty-three to Heph's twenty-seven-year old appearance, but how often had things not been as they seemed on this strange estate?

"That's not exactly true," Heph's voice, typically gruff, softened. His eyes lowered, and my forehead pinched. At the same time, I heard a tap on the tile floor to my left. Twisting at the neck, I saw Solis standing on the edge of the circular foyer. His eyes begged me to understand all the mysteries I learned.

"Did you know?" I barked. I released Heph and stepped toward Solis. My fists clenched at my sides, fighting for permission to strike out at him. "Did you know the truth and not tell me? More lies. More secrets." My voice rose and echoed through the round hall. Under our feet, a mosaic tile portrayed the sun in garish golds, yellows and orange. I stomped my foot in attempts to crush the brightness.

"I had an inkling. Zeke has so many offspring, it's hard to keep track."

"Well, I think this one would be particularly important to remember," I shouted, my voice echoing in the circular space. Solis lowered his head to agree.

"How?" I snapped again, turning my frustration to Heph, who I adored for his gentle giant ways and didn't wish to frighten with my anger. Lowering my voice, I stepped back to him. "Heph, please, I need someone on my side. I need to understand."

Heph nodded once. Looking over my head, he spoke.

"It was so long ago. They always fought. Zeke loved her, but he couldn't tame her. And he couldn't tame himself. They were too young. I was too big. Born deformed and ugly, Hera didn't know what to do with me. Zeke got angry at her lack of motherly care and she disowned me to spite him. He brought me here, and I didn't travel much after the accident. One day Zeke and I fought. I wanted to know her. I wanted to hear from her that she didn't want me. In my travels, my uncertainty about the world, I suffered…travesties…" He pointed to the scars on his face, covered by his scruff. He kicked his leg, forcing a snap of his prosthetic. A large hand wiped down his solid face.

"I didn't mean for you to find out this way."

"But you knew? When we first met this summer, before I even came here, you knew. That I was hers." He nodded once. "And in the library, when you…when you…"

"When he what?" Solis stepped forward primed for a fight. His body tense, his fingers circling my wrist to draw me near him.

"When you recognized my eyes were different, you knew then. Why didn't you tell me? When did you come to see her?"

"Before you were born."

"Zeke isn't my father." It was a fact I knew well, but in questioning everything, I suddenly questioned this again.

"Zeke is not your father. I'd never seen him so angry to discover Hera had a daughter from another man. But it wasn't you he was upset with." Heph's large hands covered my shoulders. "You can never think it was you."

"But I feel guilty toward *you*," I emphasized. "Why me and not you? You're…you're amazing. And I adore you, and there is no difference between us." My voice was adamant, and tears filled my eyes. I saw nothing different in Heph. Despite his slow speech and subtle ignorance of women, he had a kind heart, regardless of the large exterior that would frighten a lion. I meant what I said. I adored him.

As I watched his face, with my words, his eyes welled. He blinked rapidly, releasing his hold on my shoulders.

"Thank you. Thank you so much, Veva." He blinked again and shook his head, as if to rid the potential tears. "I think she did it all to spite Zeke."

"She did." Zeke stood at the edge of the foyer. "And I think we should discuss this all later. For now, I have a party I'm hosting, and I wish for my sons to be present. People are curious."

"What people?" Solis snipped. "Aren't you the center of enough attention? Three missing people won't make a difference."

"It makes a difference to me, and I'd like you to return to the dining room." He stood straight in his gorgeous tuxedo, a man of strength and power with one weakness. I'd like to think it was his heart, but I knew another part of him caused all his troubles.

"How could she do this?" I questioned Zeke, like I had so many times as a child, looking up to him as a father-figure.

"Later, my child." The soothing words hit me wrong.

"Not later. I'm not a child, and I want answers now." I stomped my foot, disproving my statement. Zeke's lips fought a smile.

"So petulant, like her." He scoffed. The comparison to my mother irritated me more. I was nothing like her. *Nothing.* I would never disown a child.

"Zeke, your guests are speculating." Mel's nails-on-a-chalkboard voice ripped at my skin. Anger boiled upward. I was ready to lunge for her, feeling the need to choke someone. Sensing my building rage, an arm locked around me, and my back hit the chest of Solis. Bare skin rubbed at his dress shirt, but heat still emitted through the cloth. A warmth overcame my body, and I relaxed against him.

"We'll be right in," Solis addressed Mel. "Can you give us a minute?" He spoke over my shoulder addressing his father. Zeke nodded, holding up one finger. He spun and gripped Mel's upper arm, spinning her to retreat with him. She didn't miss the chance to peer over her shoulder, though, and eye the three of us. Still holding onto me, Solis spun us as one to face Heph.

"Heph, go back." Solis' voice encouraged but Heph hung his head.

"I'm done tonight. I'm going to the stables." With that he turned one-eighty, and exited the front door, leaving Solis and I standing over the blinding sun design.

"If I'm her daughter, and you're his son, but Heph's our brother, that makes us…" I choked. My mind raced, logistics long ahead of reality.

"Whoa, Veva, slow down. Think of it like his, hers, and theirs. You and I aren't related. There is no blood connection." My breathing sharpened and my chest rose. My hand covered my beating heart. "Besides, all that happened between Zeke and Hera, resulting in Heph was ancient history."

"History? You mentioned destiny. Aren't all those crazy, ancient Greeks interrelated or something? And each one is destined for…" I stopped. Those crazy, ancient Greeks included him…and suddenly me. "Are we some kind of history due to repeat?" I gasped.

"I have no idea what you're talking about." But the pinch to his voice proved he understood.

"Are we destined to be together, although you're a cheating cad, and I'm a raving bitch, and we never get along?" I stopped, realization hitting hard. "We're like Zeke and…" The sharp intake of breath choked me. "Oh my God, it can't be true." Both hands covered my mouth while my eyes opened wide. "This is too much for me."

"Slow down, Vee." His hands rubbed up and down my arms. A satisfying warmth wrapped over me.

"Don't play games with me," I snapped, sensing he had done something to my body to trigger the calming response of his touch.

"I don't play games."

"Oh, yes, you do. And I free you of your obligation to spend time with me."

"It wasn't an obligation, and I'll never be free of you." He released me with those words, turning me to face him. His hands circled my upper arms, pinning me with his stare, braced for my flight.

"You and I are destined to be together." The way he spoke, the words circled me, confident and assured. That warmth of a setting sun spilled over my body, coating me in heat for a man I loved to loath.

"You and I are nothing," I spat.

"You and I are everything." His mouth crashed mine, and we battled for control. It wasn't pretty. I bit his lip. He gnashed back at mine. He forced his tongue in my mouth and my teeth covered it. He sucked back a breath, but I followed his lead. My tongue swiped his lips, and he captured it with his teeth. Our eyes remained open, too close and unfocused. One of us would have to give as we stood in this ridiculous position of his teeth holding me captive by my tongue.

His eyes shuttered closed. His lips molded around my tongue and drew backward. His teeth released me. Initially prepared to fly away from him, I remained to fight, giving into the sudden freedom. My mouth met his. He stilled. We stood, holding our lips together for a moment. Neither of us moved. I don't think I even breathed. Then his lips led as they formed over mine, and I gave into the capture.

The softening touch melted me like the rich caramel of his eyes and I relaxed into the kiss. Our lips danced slowly, sucking gently at each other in turn before coming together again to a spiral and twirl as one. My hips joined the dance and I pressed forward in need of connection. The peacock at my leg broke free of my dress and my knee rose against his gray pants. His hand instantly cupped under my knee, drawing my leg upward and opening me to him. The kiss deepened.

His other hand found its home at the nape of my neck. A powerful position, it controlled me and yet I reveled in the comfort of its placement there. Our mouths danced. Our hips swayed. Our thoughts one.

"Veva?" My mother's voice crashed me back to reality.

"Mom?" Solis released me so quickly, I stumbled backward. His hands still on me, he helped balance me.

"Solis, could you excuse us for a moment?"

His eyes met mine. I wanted him to stay. I was afraid I'd break under her. She'd ruin something. Something I'd never felt before. She would smother it, smother me, but my mother and I needed to talk. I

156

nodded for Solis to go and defeat came to his honey eyes. He released me and stepped around my mother, but her hand came out, and she motioned toward his lips.

"You might want to wash that off." Her stern voice implied disgust. Solis let his eyes burn at her before excusing himself.

"Mom, I still can't believe you are here."

"Demi and I needed to visit. It's been years since we've been here. I became concerned for you. You know I don't trust Zeke's philosophies."

"What *philosophies* are those?" I retorted.

"His morals on sexuality."

I laughed without humor.

"Judging by the position I just found you in, I see my concerns are justified."

"Mother, please," I sighed, dismissing the fact that another second and I would have let Solis take me against the wall of the entry way.

"I didn't raise a slut." The words slapped me, but it wasn't anything I hadn't heard before from her. Anger built anew in me, like a slow kettle boiling water. My fists clenched at my sides. I stood taller.

"No, you didn't. You raised a woman afraid to commit to a man. Afraid that a man would never commit to me, and provided me with every tool to distrust the opposite sex."

The sharp intake of breath in response was as if I slapped her back. Her brown eyes opened wider before narrowing to slits.

"Don't talk back to me. I see I've made a mistake allowing you to come here this summer."

"A mistake?" My voice rose. "Allowing me the freedom I deserve at twenty-three years old?" I scoffed again, humor being the farthest emotion from my thoughts. "On that note, I thought you'd be happy to get rid of me. You got rid of Heph." This time the words struck harder. Her hand covered her mouth.

"How dare you?"

"How dare you?" I snapped back. "I can't believe you never told me I have a brother. Why?" The whine in my voice proved I was on the verge of tears. The anger, the frustration and the betrayal all coming to crash, like boiling water frothing up and over the pot.

"Heph is a complicated story and none of your concern."

"None of my concern? I just learned I have a brother, and it's not my concern?" Taking a deep breath, I straightened my shoulders. "My *concern* is for a child you dismissed because of your hatred for a man, an innocent child that didn't choose to be part of your sick game with Zeke. A child who grew to be a man who's been nothing but kind and protective of me since I got here. I never knew about him, and he knew all about me." My palm slapped against my thigh, reminding me briefly of the sensual dress I wore, the party that played out down the hall, and the celebration we were supposed to be attending.

"I didn't mean for any of this to come out like it has." Her voice softened, but the sympathy I had for her vacated years ago. To harbor such bitterness, such hatred, all her life, had to be exhausting. It exhausted me.

"When did you mean for it come out? There is so much happening here, and I don't understand any of it. And I sense you know. You know all about this place and the people who live here. So many secrets, Mom." Like boiled water, I went over the pot and singed the stove flame. "Is there anything special about me?" My voice dropped, feeling inadequate compared to the rest of the people at Zeke's estate. Maybe they all have something unique about them, and I was the outlier. The ignorant outlier.

"Oh course you're special, honey." My mother stepped forward and reached for my hair, like she would when I was a child. She'd brush it behind my ear, but I didn't want her touching me, and I flinched back from her outstretched hand.

"I don't mean like that, Mom."

"How do you mean?" Her tone deepened as her hand lowered. Her eyes narrowed again.

"Like Solis, Leos, and Hades. Am I special like them?"

Defeat took control. My mother's shoulders fell, as did her head. Her hands clutched before her.

"I don't think tonight's the time to discuss all this. Let's just return to the party, and we can talk tomorrow."

"No, Mom."

"No?" She questioned.

"I'm not waiting anymore. Tonight. Now." I held firm. If she didn't want to talk, she'd have to be the one to walk away.

"Fine." She exhaled and looked up at me. A comforting brown did not meet me, but swirls of displeasure like a murky pond did.

"One day, your power will come to you. I have no way to predict what it will be or when that will happen, but a Day of Discovery will occur. Like a birthday, it will be the awakening of your gifts and talents."

I stared at my mother. *Who was this woman?* I suddenly wondered. My whole life felt like a lie, but then I recalled what Heph said. A long, long time ago. How old was my mother? She looked less than double my age. She'd been eighteen when she got pregnant with me, or so I thought. I realized, facing a woman who was an older version of me, I knew nothing about her. The front door opened, and Heph entered. His boots were caked in mud and dust covered his thighs. A piece of hay graced his dark hair. He stared at the two of us. Nodding once, signaling to excuse himself, he crossed the hall for the corridor.

"Heph?" My mother's voice was the meekest I'd ever heard. He stopped with his broad back toward us. "Could I speak with you?" A veined hand fluttered over her hair and her fingers trembled. Heph turned to face her, uncertain and hesitant to speak with the woman who rejected him.

"Tomorrow." His gruff voice surprised me. Full of hurt—I recognized that pain—set to bubble.

"Tomorrow." She smiled weakly, and he dipped his head again before turning back for the family's residence.

"Well," she offered to me, "I think we've made enough of a spectacle this evening. I hear music. We should rejoin the party."

I stared in disbelief. *That was it? A Day of Discovery? She'd talk with Heph?* Did she think this made up for everything? Two seconds of explanation and a promise to speak with Heph. The boil in me lost its steam. I assented to her request and followed her like a dutiful daughter down the hallway.

SOLIS

Thank the gods. Veva's prolonged absence put me on edge. Her mother's scowl told me Veva was in for a verbal lashing, and I didn't even know Hera. With her head hung, Veva separated from her mother, and headed straight for the bar along the back wall. The party had moved from the dining room to the ballroom dripping with a crystal chandelier and more candles. I crossed the room as if a magnet pulled to its pole. I wanted to comfort her in any way. Despite a tough exterior, Veva had been through too much over the last few days: Witnessing my powers; hearing Mel, and her vicious lies; and learning Heph was her brother were all too much information for one human girl to withstand.

I reached the bar at the same time Veva downed a shot of sweet whiskey. Her cheeks were sallow and her lips puckered, but she swallowed the harsh liquor, and her shoulders relaxed.

"How are you?" I asked, resting my elbows on the wood structure. Veva stared forward, shaking her head. *System overload*, I confirmed, from her lack of words.

"Let's dance." Her fingers gripped the edge of the bar, and my hand covered hers. I had to remove her fingers one at a time, the tension was so tight. Veva was wound; I recognized her temper.

"Hold onto me," I encouraged, and her delicate fingers curled into my palm as she nodded in agreement. Gripping my hand, I led her to the dance floor. The music pulsed. Afraid to release her, I was relieved to see the music melting into her, and her curvaceous body began rolling to the beat. Her arms lifted and her hips swayed, and my dick strained. Veva's moves seduced without trying. She spun in a half-circle, and I tugged her back to me. Her backside brushed against the strain at my zipper, and I nipped at her neck.

"That's my girl. Let go," I whispered. Our bodies moved as one in a rippling motion, like waves lapping at the shore. My palm flattened on her lower abdomen, and her arms rose again. We rode the rhythm until the song ended. My cousin's band had rocked the room.

"So, we're going to break for a bit and I hear there's a karaoke machine to entertain you for a few minutes. I'm volunteering my cousin, Solis, to get us started."

I laughed and shook my head. *No way.* While I could hold a tune, there was no way I would sing in front of these people. Before I knew it, Veva left me on the dance floor and walked to the machine. She scrolled the songs, asked a question, and picked up two microphones. Stalking back to the center of the floor, she handed me one. I laughed harder. She had no idea what she was in for, until she sang out the first line.

"You don't own me."

My heart dropped. A classic from 1963 by Lesley Gore, Veva broke into a song I knew well. She handed me the mic and I took over adding in the modern rendition responding to her call: she didn't know boys like me. For Veva, it wasn't about owning her. She owned me. The first moment I touched her, sitting on the lounge chair by the pool, the electric shock instantaneous—I knew Veva was like no other. Then when we first kissed, heated and heady, Veva was a drug to me, and I needed another hit of her. When I finally got to touch her, the familiarity of her body blew me away. The refreshing scent after a rain storm, Veva filled me with something I hadn't experienced before. Calm. Comfort. Care.

I cared about her, and despite her stormy exterior, I sensed she cared about me in return. Her tender kisses down my back returned to my mind as I watched her eyes alight with glee as she reprimanded me with song. No, I didn't own her. She owned every inch of me, including my heart, and it frightened me. More than my training or the prophecy, loving Veva scared me.

Together, we put on quite a show. Veva berated me while she sang, admonishing me and wagging her finger in my direction. I pretended to be wounded and rapped my confidence back at her. I even fell to my knees at one point and hung my head. Our little audience applauded at the end, and Veva's tension broke into that bubble-popping laughter I adored. I stood instantly and lifted her in the air. I wanted my girl to fly like bubbles. I wanted her to be light and carefree, and love me, but I couldn't guarantee I wouldn't hurt her.

The night carried on for a while, with more rounds of shots and more entertaining karaoke before Veva, breathing heavily, said she needed air. Taking her hand with mine again, I led her out of the ballroom and onto a low veranda. A single set of steps led down into the yard and I continued to guide her away from the chaotic celebration.

"That was invigorating," she laughed, holding her hand over her chest. "I haven't sung like that in a while."

"You were pretty good in there." I brushed back a wayward strand of hair falling loose from the pile on her head. I wasn't wrong when I called her stunning earlier. She looked surreal, with her sculpted neck exposed and her spine teasing me.

"You can sing, too. Is there anything you can't do?" she giggled again as she stopped and turned to look at me.

"I'm not sure I can tell you how I feel about you." The words tumbled out of my mouth too quickly to take them back, and the wide eyes of Veva proved her surprise. She looked down at my lips, as if expecting more or willing them to take the words back. I couldn't read her, suddenly.

"It's been a long day." Her voice softened, and the hand at her throat slowly cascaded to the deep V of her dress. I swallowed hard as I watched her blaze a trail over her own skin.

"I'd like to help you. What do you need?"

"I need to forget all of this for a little while. Maybe we could paint?" Her statement a question, asking me, could I help her? Trusting me to help her forget, warmed my insides and I fought the goofy smile threatening to fill my face.

"Follow me," I said, crooking my arm, and watching as her smaller hand slipped around my elbow. We walked to the cottage. Once there, I offered her an old dress shirt to use as a smock. I slipped it over her arms and slowly buttoned the front. Her chest rose and fell as each button trapped her gorgeous dress underneath. My mouth watered, filled with a thirst to kiss her, but I sensed Veva needed some time and space. She needed to paint.

I stepped into the small bathroom to remove my suit and returned to the room wearing only jeans splattered with paint. I didn't have a T-shirt to spare in the place, so with bare chest and bare feet I stood before her. Veva drank me in, her eyes slowly sipping over my abs and down the center of me to a low trail leading to my zipper. If her eyes lingered, she'd see the full length of my thirst for her in return. In appreciation of a beautiful thing, I admired her, as well. She'd removed her dress from under the smock. Hanging off her like a too-large shirt, her backside was covered, but those sexy legs ran from the hem to the floor, exposing that damn bird straining for the core of her, like me.

"Paint?" she asked, breaking my perusal of the ink travelling up her leg. I spun to retrieve brushes and hung a new canvas. At one point, as I stretched upward to hang the large material, my jeans slipped lower on my hips. Behind me came a sharp intake of breath. I spun as I tugged my pants upward but the dilation of her eyes could not be missed. The crazy center was almost solid blue, ringed in turquoise with a touch of green.

"What should we paint?" she questioned, staring at the blank canvas as I moved next to her.

"I don't know. Just start flinging paint again, if it helps."

She dipped the brush in the bright orange and flipped it at the spread. She stared at the color. She bent down for gold next and splattered it forward. The combination reminded me of a cloud ripple over a setting sun. Watching her face, I questioned if she noticed the same thing. We bent in unison this time and dipped more paint. Flinging it at the same time, splotches of colored liquid came alive within the existing patterns. We continued for several seconds in our own thoughts, forming our combined design in silence.

"Veva." Simply, saying her name, she spun to me, brush in hand and swiped across my chest. A large slash of bright orange crossed my pecs and painted my nipples.

"Oh my God." Her free hand rose and covered her mouth. "I'm so sorry." Bubbly laughter popped around her and her eyes glittered.

"Am I your new canvas?" Holding my arms open wide, dangling the paint brush from my fingers, the orange color dripped slowly down my front.

"I so did not mean to do that," she giggled.

"Well, then I feel it's only fair…" My voice faltered as I took my paint brush and stroked across her covered breasts. Her breath hitched.

"You didn't just do that." Her voice lowered. I returned the brush in the opposite direction confirming I'd done exactly what she had not expected.

"I think I did." I stepped closer to her. Her chest rose and fell, and my eyes dropped. "Although, it wasn't exactly fair play."

"Why not?" she exhaled slowly and her breasts rose higher, exaggeratedly slow before dipping downward.

"You got my bare skin. All I got was the smock." Our eyes held one another as my lip curled. Veva didn't break her hold on me as her fingers rose and unbuttoned one button on the covering. Then a second one.

"Veva," I groaned. It wasn't my intention for anything other than painting to relieve her mind, but watching her slowly undress, my self-control only went so far.

Another button and I could see the full exposure of skin between her lush breasts down to her waist. Then she slipped the smock off her shoulders, and before me stood a goddess, naked and exposed in her smooth skin glory.

"No bra or underwear tonight," I teased, but choked on the thought. "Have you been like this all night?" I questioned similar to the night I threw her in the pool.

"All night," she whispered and my eyes flicked up from the gorgeous globes and flat stomach.

"Veva?" I questioned, begging her to let me touch her.

"Persuade me," she whispered, and I fell to my knees before her like the goddess treatment she desired. I devoured one breast, suckling and lapping at perfect skin and a puckered nipple. My hand supported the effort, cupping under her and drawing her deeper into the warmth of my mouth. Her fingers slipped into my hair, combing and stroking as my attention intensified. Not wishing to ignore the other breast, I drew a trail with my tongue to the other and repeatedly filled my hunger for her. Her hands cupped the back of my head, holding me to her as her hips rocked forward. My name muttered across her lips, and I drew back to find her gazing down at me.

Still on my knees, my hands circled her ankles and slipped upward, covering her calves, then rounding her knees to climb up her thighs. The slightest pressure forced her to open wider for me. Her hands cupped the back of my neck for stability and I kissed over her waist as I stroked through an area damp and eager for affection. I painted a picture with my finger over tender folds and into her warm channel, where she clenched around me.

"I want to paint every detail of your body, Veva."

"Solis," she breathed out and her legs quivered. "I'm going to fall," she whimpered.

"Never, Veva. I got you. Always." I continued to stroke, brushing lightly and swirling intensely until the pressure built. Her thighs clamped together and she held me in.

"Solis," she moaned, her head lowering to rest on top of mine as her hips rocked over my fingers and she found the warmth of a setting sun. Kissing her waist again, I removed my fingers slowly when I felt her set completing. She lowered to her knees, placing her hands on my chest and tipping her head up to kiss me. My chest pressed against the heat of her breasts as our mouths took their time to discover one another. That sense of familiarity returned, and I took pleasure in each drop of remembrance, like a distant memory restored, refreshing me like a summer rainstorm.

She pulled back first, but I wasn't finished with her. Looking down at her breasts, splotches of orange dappled her skin.

"You got paint on me." The horrified words didn't match her playful tone. I dipped a finger in gold paint and drew a circle around her breast, trailing a blaze of golden sunlight as I went. Her chest heaved at the sensation of cool paint rounding her skin. Swooping between the globes, I circled up and around the other breast. Her eyes watched my illustration, enjoying the artistry, the pleasure of her body my new canvas. I tipped my finger in orange, prepared to add to my design. After pressing her back to lay on the canvas covered floor, I began an intricate portrait on her golden skin in accents of orange. Circling breasts, teasing close to the nipple, I brushed. Down the center of her body, I line-drew until I came to a rich mound near her legs. I poked tenderly at her waist, stringing dots to form breadcrumbs on a trail. I rolled her over, and took the brush to stroke up her back in a light coat of glittering gold. Her spine was the perfect element to follow and my mouth joined the mastery as it kissed in places paint missed.

She rolled to her back after I nipped at her shoulder. "My turn." Her voice hoarse, she sat up and pressed me down with one hand. Veva wouldn't do anything lightly. She flattened her hand in the paint and placed giant handprints over me. I laughed, breaking into the seductive moment of body sculpting.

"What are you doing?"

"I'm marking you."

My laughter faltered.

"I'm already permanently scarred." I circled her wrist and dragged the paint covered hand up to my heart. With my other hand, I flattened her palm to cover above my left pec. "Here." She held her hand over my racing heart for a moment. I lowered a free hand to my jeans, unbuttoning them to relieve the strain inside. Teasingly, I tugged her unpainted hand lower and forced it over the zipper region.

"And here." My attempt to lighten the mood after she didn't respond to my heart failed. Veva squeezed me and my breath caught. I choked as she maneuvered over me, tugging and pressing. My head fell back. I reached behind me, looking over my head for a rag. Enough of the finger paint play, I needed more of Veva. I covered her hand and wiped off the excess paint.

"My hands can't touch you like this," I offered as explanation.

"That's okay, I only want one part to touch me."

I finalized unbuttoning and removing my jeans, and Veva stared at the length of me. Her perusal approving, her clean hand wrapped around me, and I was a goner. Mark me, scar me, whatever Veva did was going to be permanent.

When the warmth of her mouth encased me, my eyes rolled back as she worked her magic taking me to the back of her throat. Sensing the build of a rising sun, I tugged her up and over me. I shifted again, fumbling for my jeans pocket. The uncanny ability of my father to impregnate multiple women was not something I wished to repeat. I sheathed myself while Veva watched.

"Take control, Vee. Own me." My hands slipped to her hips, willing her to be in charge of how things went with us. With trepidation in her blue eyes, she looked at me. My hands flapped to the sides, wanting her to possess me. Splat went the sound of my palm falling into something wet and I raised it to find it covered in paint.

"You wouldn't," she squeaked.

"Oh, I would," I teased, threatening to paint her if she didn't take me in. My hand gripped her hip. Skimming up her side, the cool paint slathered over her and I continued upward to cover her breasts. Tugging the heavy weight forward, I pinched her nipple, forcing it to ripen to a point. Dragging my hand downward, covering the front half of her belly, I returned to her thigh, one half of her body painted orange.

"You're the other half of me," I spoke, low and rumbling. I chuckled, and the jostle of my body renewed the desire of her straddling over me. "Vee," I warned, desperate to fill her.

"I..." Her eyes shifted down. Lifting up on her knees, she balanced over me. Pressing down, she winced, and my head tilted in wonder. My hands gripped her hips and pushed her against me.

"Vee?" I questioned. Something wasn't right. I spun us so she lay on her back and I settled between her thighs. Her face turned away from mine. I pressed forward again, but her eyes pinched. Cupping her chin, I gently forced her to face me.

"Veva, you're so tight." The statement was a question. I'd misunderstood. "Are you..."

"Forget it," she snapped, pressing her hands on my chest, attempting to force me off of her.

"Are you a *virgin*?" My tone softened on the word despite my shock. "I just thought...I mean you're always flirting..."

"Just forget it." She attempted to press me off her again, but a tear rolled from her eye.

"Vee." Her name choked out of me. She was about to give me everything, and I didn't want to lose this moment. Suddenly, she struggled beneath me.

"Get off," she groaned, but there was no fight in her, and another tear escaped. I gripped both hands in one and tugged them over her head. Perching on my elbow, I looked down at her.

"Slow down, Veva. It's okay. I've got you."

She huffed a few times, as if trying to calm the tears that fell in earnest.

"Don't cry, Peacock." I lowered to kiss each tear, sucking the salty liquid to clear them. Then I moved to her mouth. The kiss was a struggle as her lips quivered.

"It's okay," I soothed against them. "I've got you, Veva. I won't hurt you."

She nodded.

"If you don't want to do this, we don't have to. I just misunderstood. I thought...and I was wrong."

She looked away from me, but I chased her with my mouth. Gently kissing her, prodding her mouth to open and accept mine. I stiffened, the taste of her mouth hardening me further. I ached for her, but I'd follow her lead.

"Veva, tell me what you want to do?"

"I want this."

"Want this? Or want me?" I tilted my head to question her, suddenly feeling self-conscious.

"I want you, but I don't even know why." This gave me my answer. I pushed off her hands and rolled off of her, falling to my back. My arm came to cover my eyes. Veva could cut like a knife, that was unquestionable.

"I didn't mean it like that." Her voice spoke softly to my ear, but the words already pierced me. "I mean, I don't understand myself. There's something about you. An electricity. A familiarity. And I keep coming back for shock after shock. It pricks but it feels good and it frightens me."

My arm slipped from my face and I turned to Veva.

"Yeah?"

"Yeah." She smiled weakly. "I mean, I don't even like you sometimes, and you loathe me, and…"

"Vee," I huffed out. "I don't loathe you."

"You don't love me."

My eyes opened wide, and I stared at this infuriating girl. Why was I lying here naked while she insulted me? *Oh wait*, because I think I do love her. Or I thought I did.

"Not like that. I mean, you know, you don't need to love me, *love me*, just…oh God, I'm just messing this up." She flung to her back and stared up at the ceiling. I rolled right to remove the wasted condom and balled it into the paint-covered rag.

"Vee, why don't we just lay here for a bit, okay?" I'd pushed too fast, I realized, recalling all the things she'd gone through in the past days. This was one more thing she didn't need, and neither did I, because if Veva didn't want this from me, I couldn't force it. I threw my arm over her waist and pulled her into me. The paint had hardened on our bodies, and it would certainly itch if it stayed on us all night, but for now I just wanted to hold her against me. What Veva needed most was safety. I understood this need. I'd been abandoned before by both my father and my mother. One bed. One roof. One love.

"You're my destiny, Veva. I've waited a long time for you, a little longer won't hurt me." I inhaled the scent of her hair.

"Your destiny?" she laughed.

"You're my other half. Heaven and hell. Day and night. Love and war. They all go together. I'm gray skies and you're sunshine."

"How am I sunshine?"

"You light my world."

VEVA

This would go down in history as the most awkward first attempt at sex ever, and I blamed myself. I wanted Solis so badly I ached for him. A few minutes ago, I proved it by weeping, but when he discovered I was a virgin, something changed. I thought he'd just go for it, and hardly notice. He was a player after all, and the decision to sleep with him probably wasn't the best, considering I knew this fact, but I wanted him. Every time I turned he tried to take care of me, and I decided he'd be no different in this situation. When he fell to his knees and paid homage to me, I knew I was right. Then I opened my mouth and it all went wrong.

Despite the heat coming off of him, I shivered under his arm wrapped over me. He pulled me tighter. "I'll get a blanket." Then he stood and the loss of him felt like ripping off part of me. I missed him instantly and cursed myself further for ruining what could have been a sexy moment. He returned with a large comforter and tossed it over me. Climbing back in behind me, he curled around me again and kissed my bare neck.

"I'm sorry," I whispered.

"Don't be. There has been too much. My back. Mel. Your mother. Heph. This was just one more thing."

"But I want it."

"And I want you to want *me*, Vee." His voice saddened and a new tear escaped. I wanted him to want me too, but I couldn't say that. *Don't have expectations of men, Veva, they'll only disappoint you.* I wasn't expecting anything of Solis. He didn't have to love me to have sex with me, and I shouldn't have expected love to be part of the equation. But a nagging piece of me wished that it was. I wanted to be loved wholeheartedly. I sighed and kissed his arm over my chest. He didn't stir, and I realized he'd fallen asleep.

My mind raced backward in time. Tonight. My mother. The day. Mel. Heph. My beautifully awkward, unknown brother. How strange to

171

learn of his existence. When I thought of my mother's kindness to all the children on our farm, and then to learn she turned away her only son, I couldn't reconcile the thought. Then I thought of Solis. Disowned at first by his father, for fear Solis would kill him. Zeke should have loved his son, and then he would have no concerns.

I couldn't sleep. The more I tried, the more awake I became, each new thought messing with my mind. I gently tried to remove Solis' arms from around me.

"Where are you going?" he muttered into my shoulder.

"I think I should go."

"Why?" His groggy face popped up to look over my shoulder at me. With his hair rumpled, he looked sexy even in his sleepy state.

"I just…I feel so awkward. I ruined everything and I think I need to be alone."

"Don't run, Vee. Stay with me." He kissed my shoulder again.

"You don't really want me to stay."

"Vee, don't play these girl games with me. Don't run off and hide."

"I'm not hiding. I don't have anything to hide."

"You're scared, and it's okay."

"I'm not scared."

"Veva, stop fighting me. It's fine." He huffed behind me.

"It isn't fine." I spun in his arms and glared at him. I didn't understand why I was picking a fight with him, or what we were fighting about, but my heart raced, and I reached for his face, tugging his mouth to mine. Instantly, I took control, kissing him like my life depended on it. His hand fisted in my hair at the nape of my neck, and the connection brought me comfort. He tugged gently, but if he wanted to remove me, his lips still attached to mine proved otherwise. I rolled to straddle him, and our mouths fought for control. This is what I needed. I didn't think I could do the sweet, seductive style he'd been giving me. I needed hard and fast and reckless, but he pressed me back.

"Vee, slow down." He rolled me to my back, then slipped off of me, cradling me against his chest as his arms enveloped me.

"We aren't doing this. Not tonight." His tone teased, but his words were stern. He kissed my neck one more time, and although I felt his rejection, I also felt peace. Warmth spread over me and my body calmed. I slept.

+ + +

I stretched like a happy cat waking in the sunshine of a new day, and then realized I was alone. Warmth surrounded me, and a thin ray of sunshine slipped through the heavy shades. I sat up, covering myself with the comforter we slept under. I didn't know how I'd get back to my room without making another spectacle of myself, but I suddenly sensed I needed to leave. I didn't want him to return to find me waiting for him, like some lovesick girl or one of his other lovers. The thought of additional lovers sickened me and I reached for the paint smock, opting for it versus my dress as attire to return to my room. I stood on shaky legs with a heavy heart. Reaching the door, I jumped back when it opened. A slow smile greeted me at first, and without thought, I smiled in return.

"Good morning, Peacock." Solis' face beamed as he closed the door behind him. A large basket in his hand grabbed my attention. He walked toward me, and covered my hand in his. Guiding me to the makeshift bed, he lowered us to sit. Slowly, his expression fell. "What's going on here?"

"I was...I was just leaving." I looked away, embarrassed as thoughts of the night before raced through my head.

"Why?"

"Well, you were gone and I thought I should get back to my room." I moved to stand but he blocked me.

"I came back. I left you a note." He reached to a slip of paper I hadn't even seen. A line drawn sunshine covered the paper with a lightning bolt through the orb. The paper read: *You own me. Be back soon.* My shoulders fell in relief as I read.

"I went to get breakfast." He patted the basket. "And a change of clothes for you."

I nodded slowly. "I should change," I suggested, reaching out for the basket, but Solis pushed it aside.

"I want you to stay." He read my mind, knowing if I changed clothes, I would still attempt to leave. We stared at one another for a moment: myself shy, him confident.

"And yes, you should change." His voice dropped lower, and his eyes sparkled mischievously. "I wanted to give you breakfast in bed, and you're overdressed." Thick fingers with tiny specks of paint reached for the messy smock and unbuttoned it. His eyes remained trained on mine.

"Slip back under the blanket," he ordered, the command tender despite the rugged sound from his throat. Like being blinded from glancing at the sun, I followed each delicate demand. Naked once again, I pulled the cover to my chest. His mouth curled, pleased with himself, before he opened the basket and removed bread, so freshly baked it steamed, a jar of olive oil, and a bowl of mixed fruit. He unscrewed a thermos and poured me a cup of tea. The aroma undistinguishable, the taste divine, I let the warm liquid fill me like his presence. I sipped slowly, and silence danced lightly around us.

"I'm sorry again about last night," I began, but he gave me a look that stopped my apology.

"We don't need to talk about it, Vee. Today's a new day. Let's enjoy it." His smile grew larger as he drank me in. "But I do want to ask about the leaving thing. I'm not going anywhere, so why do you keep pushing me away?"

My head dipped in response as I collected my thoughts. The answer would be raw, but I already sat before him naked.

"My mother. She always spoke as if men only wanted one thing and then they'd leave. Once they got it, they were gone. It must have been how things happened for her and my father. He disappeared shortly after I was born. On the other hand, it could be lingering effects of a failed relationship with Zeke." My eyes flicked nervously up to his. It was still so new to digest the facts. He and I were not related, but we shared a common brother: Heph.

"I still can't get over that she abandoned Heph," I whispered. It was so contradictory—her attitude of being abandoned, yet she abandoned a child.

"I don't know the full story, but I'm certain she had her reasons. Spiting Zeke could have been number one. Heph would be a reminder of all she had lost. Rather than keep him, she rejected him."

It made sense, in a sick sort of way. I couldn't reconcile my mother being so cold-hearted, but then again, she'd never been warmly affectionate either. The irony was, I craved affection, and often took it under false pretenses. I trusted limitlessly until proven otherwise, much to my own downfall. I'd been burned too many times by the attention of men, and while I usually blew off the afterburn, the flames of betrayal and the sparks of hurt still stung.

Solis dipped a warm piece of bread into a small dish of olive oil and handed it to me. I reached for it, but he pulled it back.

"Open," he demanded. His beautiful, chiseled face lit up as he teased me, and I leaned forward to bite. Drawing in the savory warmth coated with oil, a drop slipped over my lips and dripped to my chin. Solis' fingers swiped up the oily liquid and coated my lips with it. My mouth covered the pad of his finger and lingered. He pulled back slowly, his eyes locked on mine.

"Your mouth is heaven, and I want to live there." He leaned forward and kissed me, only briefly, relieving my lips of their oily sheen. Pulling back, he caught me scratching at my arm, flicking chips of paint from the crease of my elbow.

"We should shower." He held out a hand for me, helping me stand. He removed his T-shirt, and I noticed the cracked paint on his skin. He swiped a hand over his chest and the flakes flittered to the floor. I followed him to the bathroom, which seemed small, but held a shower stall big enough for two and a bear skin rug before the sink. He shrugged his shoulder as I raised a brow at the fuzzy floor covering.

"I like soft things under my feet after I shower, not a cold tile floor."

I giggled in response as he turned on the shower. A thick stream of water fell like rain from a dinner plate-sized shower head. The spray would easily cover two people. He guided me toward the shower, giving me a moment alone as the water caressed my body in a loving spray of warmth. Solis' eyes were on me, but I was distracted by the decadence of such a shower experience. Only a minute passed before Solis removed his jeans to join me.

He tenderly washed me, cupping soap in his hands and massaging it over my body. The scent revived my skin while relaxing my body. I melted under his touch and the heated water. He soaped my neck and shoulders, moving in circles down my spine. At the base of my spine, his hands spread and worked toward my sides. Covering my hips, he pressed against me, the hard length of him brushing lightly over my ass. I purred. My hands covered his, and I leaned into him. My head rested on his shoulder as his mouth sucked at my shoulder and neck. He reached around me, lathering up more soap, and stroking over my stomach, washing away the crusty paint. Moving upward, he circled the golden designs around my breasts.

"You are luscious," he whispered as soapy fingers encased heavy, achy orbs. My eyes fluttered shut and I sighed. His fingers pinched my nipples at the same time, and the double shot of pleasure sent a bolt of electricity straight to my core. Always aware of my desire, he rinsed his hands before slipping downward to an area ripe for more than a cleansing. My hips jolted at his tender touch. The caress of the water and the steam of the heat heightened my sensitivity, my body pliant to his lead. He stroked me, fingertips tenderly teasing, before entering me. I gasped, and my head fell forward, my hands braced over his wrists.

"I've got you," he murmured to my neck. "I'd never let you fall."

Fall from grace, fall from the sky, fall in love. He'd protected me from all these things, and at the same time, made each one happen. He flew me across the heavens. He made me fall in love with him. The only thing left to take was my virginity.

He was hard behind me, but the distraction of his fingers vibrated through me, and I lit like the night sky before a thunderstorm.

"Vee." He bucked behind me. "Sweet gods, you're a goddess." His typically booming voice lowered, and his hips rocked against my backside. I didn't want to disappoint either one of us again, so I spun to face him and took his mouth with a force I didn't know I possessed. Empowered by the morning, I claimed his lips, and he let me devour them. I tugged at the bottom, releasing it only long enough to lick the seams of his lips, which opened, allowing me entrance. Sweeping the inside of his mouth, our tongues tangled as he twisted us so his back rested on the shower wall. He lowered us as we kissed until I straddled him, water gently pelting my back like a summer rainstorm, the length of him trapped under me like a lightning bolt. I brushed forward, letting my naked core slide along his solidness.

I released his mouth to bend forward and taste his neck. I nipped and soothed a trail of kisses down his chest, and then bit his nipple. He yelped quietly.

"Sorry," I muttered.

"Don't be." The words sparked me onward, and I scooted back to continue my trail. As I neared the length of him, he pulled me up to face him.

"If you go there, I'll lose it faster than a thunder clap. Stay up here with me." His mouth took mine as he returned me to straddle over him, our most intimate parts resting against one another. My hips rolled. His hands stilled. I rocked forward. His fingers pinched. Our mouths increased the pressure. A thundering collision of emotion crashed and coiled between my thighs. My pace increased, thirsting for friction.

"Vee," he mumbled, his lips still attached to mine.

"Just do it," I commanded with a whisper. "I trust you." My voice lowered and his mouth found mine, increasing the intensity of his kisses. An urgency arose between us and he twisted us sideways, fumbling for his jeans outside the shower.

"I need a condom." Then he sat us upward, with a puzzled look on his face. "Actually, I don't. You're the last girl I plan to be with, Veva." The words surprised me, their meaning too deep, too raw for us.

elda lore

"Well, you're going to be my first," I admitted shyly, letting my eyes fall from his. My fingers traced a random pattern over his wet chest.

"And I'm going to be your last, also." The intensity with which he said those words made me believe him. In that moment, there was nothing more I wanted. Nothing more I wished to trust, and I fell. *Fell from grace, fell from the sky, fell in love.* Right there on the shower stall floor. I leaned forward, positioning him between me, letting myself balance on a precipice.

"You're sure?" He whispered, his voice shaking, almost frightened in his own right, which was ridiculous, as he was no virgin. I nodded, gripping his shoulders for strength. Uncertain of the pain, a touch of fear slithered through me. *This is Solis,* I reminded myself, and whatever that meant, comforted me as he eventually plunged upward. I clawed his shoulders. He pinched my hips.

"Hold still." His words went right in my ear as his teeth nipped the lobe. "Get used to me."

I sat perfectly still, breathing slowly as I held him deep inside me, so deep, it was more than physical. He touched my soul. Our eyes locked and the connection was profound. I felt electrified, like a current conducted by water, as I sat under the warm spray, straddling the heat of him. My eyes hesitantly looked where we joined in the most intimate way.

"You're the other half of me." He kissed my cheek. "Now, I'm whole."

My throat caught and I blinked away the silly tears. I took several deep breaths and then I felt him flinch inside me. It sparked a pleasurable prickle, a different kind of current, and I wanted to feel the sharp crackle again. I leaned back and he moaned. Bracing on his chest, I dragged my hips upward, then lowered down. He filled me completely and I groaned at the fullness. He completed me. The strangest calm entered me.

"Solis?" I questioned the sensation.

"Move, love. Or let me move you. It will get better." His voice strained. He needed more. Raising my hips, I dragged to the tip of him then lowered to be filled again. I grunted at the feeling. Repeating it

178

leisurely at first, my pace quickened until I found a rhythm, a friction that ignited me. Solis' moans of encouragement spurred me onward.

"Slow down, Vee, or you're gonna lose me too quickly, and I don't want to lose you. Not yet." His arms tightened to wrap around my lower back. I continued, rolling like clouds in the sky, gathering speed as they collided, our bodies crashed together. I climbed, cresting, and all the while Solis rumbled under me. My heart raced and matched the galloping movement of my hips.

"That's my girl, Peacock."

The thought of being his pressed me harder. I rode faster, and an eruption struck. The lightning began, crawling from my toes up to my knees. I raced onward, and the thundering sensation built, gathering between my thighs and rumbling low in my belly.

"Solis," I screamed as the heat burst into bolts of light, striking and igniting me. I saw stars, sparkling and speckling, as I rained over him. He stilled beneath me, holding my hips hard, locking me to him, while groaning my name. He was my other half, and joined in this manner, we were one. My eyes stared at where he curled inside me, and I marveled at the wonder of feeling so complete. His own release reached its pinnacle and I shivered at the sensation of him showering within me. The control I'd had over this man empowered me. I felt alive and energized, but my shaky arms collapsed, and I fell on top of him. We weathered the storm of one another and the afterglow misted down my spine, as tender fingers and soothing water fell along my back.

"Veva, I…"

I love you, I wanted to interrupt. *I love you*, I wanted to hear.

"I…" His hesitation ripped my heart in two, but the rest of me was too replete to care. "I've never felt anything like this before. Is it strange that from the first moment I met you, there was a familiarity with you, as if I knew you? You complete me, and this isn't some cheesy movie line. You are my other half. My destiny. My sunshine on a cloudy day."

My eyes closed as I pressed a kiss to his chest, the racing of his heart kissing me back under his skin. He'd bared his soul to me, but I remained quiet in my fear. Absorbing the words, I let them caress me, and hoped beyond hope they were true.

SOLIS

"Today's the final day of festivities," I said as I rubbed over her body with a lush towel to dry her beautiful skin. Looking up at her face reflected in the mirror, I wanted to capture the glow of her cheeks forever. I couldn't imagine a color so pure, so satiated, so stunning.

"It's Sunday. Zeke's last call to worship him," I snorted. "He'll expect everyone to be present."

"Hades can't be, though, can he?"

My eyes found hers in the reflecting glass.

"He could. But he won't let me give him my powers again." She nodded like she understood, but I didn't know how much of the story Veva believed.

"And those powers are?" Her teasing tone brightened her face.

"The only power you need be concerned with is letting me please you." Her mouth opened forming a subtle O, and I imagined all the ways I'd like those lips to take me, but we had to be on the field soon.

+ + +

Baskets large enough to hold humans filled the grassy space, presently empty of all tents and Olympic games. The hefty puff of air and burst of fire filled the gigantic balloons with the necessary propane gas to lift a dozen gondolas, or baskets, into the sky. The colorful, nylon balloons represented any series of twelve: twelve zodiac signs, twelve months, twelve important people to Zeke. My place was number thirteen. I led Veva to one reserved just for us. Zeke pulled out all the stops to make sure we were alone, but I no longer felt his obligatory babysitting. I wanted to be with Veva night and day, in every way.

"This is frightening, but exciting." Her voice shook, as I helped her into the gondola. Her delicate hands gripped the basket edge and I recalled Veva's continued fear of heights. My girl was a brave goddess,

181

though, and she'd temper through this ride to prove to herself, and me, that she could handle the heights to which I'd take her. I looped my arms around her, after setting my camera bag on the floor. Not as proficient with the camera as I was with the paint brush, I still loved to capture images for inspiration. I wanted to capture Veva, but I'd never be able to recreate an image that would do her beauty justice.

I tugged her hair, twisting it into my fist and lifting it to the top of her head. Placing a kiss on her bare neck, my nose followed, rubbing over the sensitive skin.

"You have the most gorgeous neck." I kissed her again. "You might want to pin this up or it will blow all over the place." She twisted to smile back at me, grateful for the suggestion and produced a band to wrap around her hair. The basket jostled and a burst of air into the envelope lifted the gondola off the ground. Her hands tightened on the woven rim, but I pressed her against me with a palm over her stomach, forcing her back to my chest.

"I like you in my sweatshirt." I rubbed a hand up and down the too-long sleeves covering her arms. It would be colder where we traveled. She shivered, but I didn't think it was the air temperature.

"I'll never let you fall. I promise." I meant the words. I'd never let her go.

"What if I did fall, though?" Her voice shook as she tried to tease me. "What if something tripped me up, and I fell? What if I can't handle all of this?" She waved a hand at the elaborate estate below us, slipping further and further away. Her question wasn't literally. She still questioned me and all that she'd learned.

"I'd follow you. Wherever you went, I'd go too." Her neck twisted, and she looked at me over her shoulder. I leaned forward to kiss her lightly. It wasn't enough to reassure her, but we had an audience with our pilot, who I hoped was too busy conducting his business to care what I did to Veva.

"I want to make love to you in the sky, Veva," I groaned, allowing the truth of my thoughts to escape. She sighed, pressing her behind against the solid length straining my zipper. "Not fair, Peacock." I nipped at her neck, and she giggled.

We floated over the estate, a sprawling ranch shaped like a giant V. The pool reflected upward, centering the outdoor space. For miles, the olive groves stood in rows, stretching out to the ends of the earth. The small wooded area on the property hid my cottage.

"My grandmother lived there," I blurted, pointing to the area. "My father was very protective of his mother. He wanted the world for her, but he despised his father. They were continually at odds with one another. Something about his siblings and the greed of a parent to remain the center of attention."

Being up in the air gave me the freedom to tell Veva my story. Maybe it was the lightness of the thinning oxygen.

"I inherited the cottage when I came here. Zeke said I was special to his mother, even though I never met her. She wanted me to have the space, Zeke told me. She wanted me to know someone believed I would not repeat the sins of my father. I don't think my father was convinced. I think he just wanted me close where he could watch me."

"What happened to your grandfather?"

"I told you, Zeke killed him."

Veva spun in my arms. Her hands gripped my biceps, holding onto me to support her fear as well as balance the irritation in my voice.

"He grew tired of his father's jealousy and rage, much like me." My voice lowered. "For my stepfather."

"Solis?" The pain present in her tone encouraged me to continue.

"He hurt me." My eyes lowered. I couldn't look into the depths of those crazy blue colored eyes and see her pity for me. "One night, we were outside. He'd locked me outside. I thundered and roared at the door, hoping the house would protect me. I screamed and pounded at the wood. A crackle and a spark and lightning struck the yard. It hit the tree but the current carried. Something most people don't realize. Standing under a tree is dangerous in a lightning storm." I sighed. "Anyway, the electricity crawled up my legs and settled on my back. My body burned. My skin prickled. I screamed and he hit me. Rage I'd never felt before rippled through me, and I...I just instinctively knew what to do. I took the burning energy of my back and pulled it from me. I struck him." My voice caught and my heart raced. Veva's fingers dug into my skin, holding me steady as I finished my tale.

"I killed him." A breath swished out of me. "Zeke found me. He said he knew I didn't mean to do it, but I had to. I couldn't take the beatings anymore, Veva."

"Shh, I understand," she whispered, tugging me toward her, but I pressed her back. I had to finish.

"He explained who he was and what I was, and then I came here to train. I've been restless and reckless, on the verge, always waiting, wanting something more. I thought it was the prophecy. I thought it was the lingering doubt that I hadn't fulfilled it with the man I called father." I sucked in air. "But I realize now, after this morning, what I've waited for is you. The missing piece to me is you, Veva. You're *life* to me, and I don't have to fear that I'll kill again as long as you're with me." I pulled her to my chest, pressing her against me, holding her as tight as I could. Her arms circled my neck and she rose up on her toes to match my height. The need to make love to her, to show her how I felt consumed me, and I cursed the pilot's presence.

"I love you," she whispered, meek and hesitantly. I pushed her back to look at her face, but her eyes lowered.

"Veva?" I questioned, my heart soaring with hope. Slowly, her lids rose and the brightness of those peacock blues blinded me. Lightning struck in a different way, and my heart nearly burst from my chest. "Were you scared to tell me?"

"I was." Her lids lowered again, but I tipped her chin, forcing her to look at me.

"Even before we met, I loved you. I've been waiting for you, I just wasn't certain you would recognize me, but then we kissed. It was you. You and me. Destiny." My mouth took hers, wishing to invade her, wanting to crawl inside her and complete both of us again. Her lips responded in kind, matching my desire, understanding my struggle. I needed Veva, like the earth needs the sun; like the clouds rule the sky;

like a rain storm refreshes. I pulled back abruptly, her mouth still rounded to kiss me.

"I love you, too, Vee. I love you." My emotions poured out of me. I was a new man after Veva gave me everything, and confessing my sins to her, absolved me of them. My mouth returned to hers, breathing her in like the oxygen surrounding us.

A gentle cough behind me reminded me, we were not alone. Veva lowered her head and giggled into my chest. I leaned down to kiss her hair.

"I want to take some pictures. Hold onto me, if you're scared, but I need my hands."

"I'm not scared." She circled her arms around me as she stood at my back. Her head rested on my arm, peeking around my bicep to see the direction of my camera. I snapped photo after photo of the valley, the mountain ranges, and the olive groves. I spun to face Veva and clicked madly one image after another of her peachy cheeks and loose hair and swollen lips. She laughed and the film would never do justice to the sound floating out and popping in the thin air.

"Storms rolling in, Solis. We need to head down." I turned back to see the heavy darkness of clouds travelling toward us. My brow pinched, questioning where the angry gray had come from and what caused the argument of those puffs of deep black. The pilot released the pressure and the balloon began to descend. I held my hands over Veva's as she returned to standing before me. My mouth couldn't resist her skin and I peppered her neck with kisses. Her subtle moan told me she enjoyed the attention. A crack of lightning made her flinch.

"Did you see that?"

"It's beautiful." My voice faltered. The vivid yellow ripped the sky, reminding me of the first painting Veva designed in my cottage. "But not as beautiful as you."

She laughed heartily. "You're rather romantic."

"Me?" I chuckled in response. "Don't tell anyone. It will ruin my reputation."

She spun to face me and stumbled as we dropped again.

"And what reputation is that?" Her lips twisted, and distrust teased from her.

"The reputation of being a player. I'm not. Or at least not anymore."

Veva's brow pinched. Her eyes roamed my face.

"Why?"

"You, Vee. I only want to paint with you."

"I only want to paint with you, too." Her tone dropped and her hands slid down my chest.

"I want to love you. Let me be the one to love you." I tipped her chin so she'd see me. I wanted her to read it in my eyes. I meant what I said. I wanted her to trust me.

She smiled slowly and my mouth fell to her lips again. How little did I know the impending storm was a warning, a foreshadow for the hell we descended upon as we landed back on earth.

VEVA

We landed with a jolting bump and I laughed at the jostling, until another clap of thunder straightened my spine. The negative energy rippled through the hovering, dark sky. My skin prickled with things unknown, and that thing was Mel, waiting for us.

"Solis," she shrieked. "You must come quickly. It's Letty."

"I don't see how Letty is my concern. We've discussed this." Solis stated as he hitched a leg over the gondola and slipped out of the basket. He turned back, placing his hands on my hips, and lifted me as if my weight was nothing to him. He set me on the ground and my knees shook like sailors' legs. His hands did not release me. I stood positioned before him, as if a shield from Mel with her crossed arms, her tapping foot, and a stern look on her face.

"She's in a lot of pain, Solis." Mel's voice spoke of more than a heartache.

"What happened?" I stepped forward.

"Letty's pregnant."

The air swooshed out of me as Mel's words cut deep. I couldn't breathe. Great gulping gasps for oxygen choked me further. I was drowning in air.

"Veva, Vee?" Solis' panicked tone did nothing to soothe me. Suddenly, I didn't want him to touch me.

"I'm training to be a midwife. I might be able to help. Have you called a doctor?" Two pairs of eyes stared at me. I didn't understand their confounded glare and I no longer wanted to. My concern was the girl.

"Can you take me to her?" I directed to Mel, ignoring Solis' hand on my back, ignoring his presence next to me, ignoring the racing promises of love. I stepped forward as Mel's eyes softened, and she nodded once, trusting me. The heavens opened, and rain teemed down on us. I followed numbly. My shoulders straight, my head high, I would not let them see the ripping of my heart.

A small row of cottages stood near the migrant housing. Inside, Letty lay in the fetal position, knees pulled up to her chest. She shook violently, sweat pouring down her forehead.

"Letty?" My hand touched her arm, the heat of her skin burning, and she flinched. Wide eyes filled with fear stared at me over her shoulder. "Letty, honey, tell me where it hurts."

"My-y-y-y stomach." Her teeth chattered. "No-o-o-o. Lower." Shaky hands slipped down her body to her lower abdomen covered by a blanket.

"Okay, honey. I'm going to examine you. Can you trust me to do that?" I pulled Solis' sweatshirt over my head, suddenly shaking myself, itching to remove him from me. This was Solis' child. How could he ignore this poor girl? How could he play me like he did? I tossed the clothing to the floor and turned to Mel. Solis stood behind me, staring down at Letty.

"Mel, can you go to my room? Get Persephone. I have a small medical kit. It's not much, but she knows where it is. Have her bring it to me?"

"I'll go," Solis offered. He spun on his heels and stalked out the door. I turned back to Letty. A door to the left opened into a small bathroom and I rose to clean my hands.

"Don't leave me," the girl whimpered, gripping my wrist with weak strength. I sat again. The wait would nearly kill me. My thoughts raced too much.

"I'm sorry, Letty. Can you tell me what happened?"

"I'm-m-m-m pregnant. Or I was. I went to a priestess Solis-s-s-s recommended."

"She cursed Letty, hexing her like a spell." Mel interjected, and I shook my head. I couldn't really believe this happened. "She started bleeding instantly. It looked like a crime scene." Mel's face turned paper white. Her eyes closed, sealing off the vision.

"Okay, honey. I'll fix this." I rubbed her warm leg as the time ticked slowly before Solis returned with both Hades and Persephone.

"Veva." Persephone's concerned voice did not surprise me. She knelt instantly next to the bed. I opened my bag. Removing a syringe, I injected Letty with a pain reliever, hoping to subdue the aches and chills.

I heard Solis suck in a breath when I removed the blanket from Letty's waist. Blood stained her dress. Separating Letty's knees, I gently forced them to spread and found blood on her inner thighs.

"Okay, everyone out," I commanded.

"I want to stay and help." Solis' offer pushed me over the faltering edge I stood on.

"I think you've done enough." I stood taller, my tone low.

"Veva!" Persephone admonished as Solis' eyes opened wide in disbelief. The honey color I'd seen turn to molten caramel lightened to a fierce gold. Letty moaned, and our stare broke.

"Okay, Letty. Let's take a look." I separated her legs again, as I heard a door slam to my side. I allowed the flinch to rattle through me, then got to the business of helping a woman in need.

+ + +

Vomiting was the first thing I did upon leaving Letty. My nerves shot to hell, I trembled uncontrollably. I'd not experienced anything like what I'd done. Certainly, I birthed calves on the farm, and assisted my mother in delivering babies, if necessary, but Letty had miscarried. I didn't understand the purpose of a priestess. Why hadn't they sought out a doctor? The healing process would take a while, both physically and mentally. I cursed Solis over and over, setting a hex on him for his dismissal of this girl. A second wave of nausea released with that thought.

Solis. How could he have done such a thing? And how could he justify all those pretty words in the sky knowing this girl suffered at his expense? How could I have been such a fool to believe what he said to me? My body vibrated with the need to hit something or race a million miles. Anything to rid my mind of the damning thoughts and the hollow spot where my heart once beat.

After cleaning up, I asked Persephone to take my bag back to my room.

"Vee, you don't look so good. Maybe you should come back and rest?"

Rest was the last thing I'd be able to do.

"I just need to walk a bit. Let my mind clear." Concerned brown eyes focused on me. Her brow pinched, but she didn't argue. That was the great thing about my best friend. She knew when to let me be. Hades took my case from her and wrapped an arm around her, escorting her back to our room. Jealousy pinched my chest. Not at my friend and her love, but *because* of what she had, and I never would.

I wandered around the pool deck and out across the expansive field. Hours ago, it was covered with large air balloons and a dozen baskets. In the growing darkness of night, the space lay barren and open like my chest. A female wandered toward me and I recognized the shape of my mother. Regal and suave, her grace displayed poise and wisdom for a woman who worked a farm field. Next to her walked a large man with a subtle limp.

"Mother," I greeted her. "Heph."

"Veva, darling, I've been looking for you."

I nodded without answer. I had nothing to offer my mother. I couldn't explain where I'd been or what I'd seen, or even how I'd helped heal an ailing woman. I had no fight left in me, and I braced myself to take any admonishments my mother prepared to sling at me.

"We've spoken." She addressed Heph whose eyes remained lowered. I didn't ask for more information. I didn't need to know what she said. Nothing could change my disappointment in her for doing what she did to him, especially in my fragile state. After seeing the loss Letty suffered, my arms wrapped tighter around my abdomen. I'd never want to lose a child by any means. My body would become a machine. I would be the protector of children.

"He's trying to understand, but I don't think I have the right words to explain decisions made too long ago." She offered without my asking, still staring at my brother. His continued silence, and her reference to him in the third person, crawled over my skin.

"Is it ever too late?" I questioned without thought. "Can it be too late to fix things?"

"I'd like to think, no. I'd like to believe that time heals wounds, and actions speak louder than words." She spoke directly to me. I thought of pretty words spoken to me. My stomach roiled. "What actions will you provide?"

"I've invited Heph to come to the farm."

My eyebrows shot up at the invitation and I looked at Heph. If my mother had rejected him all those years ago, an invite to visit was a big step for her.

"He refused." My shoulders plummeted as I stared at him, waiting for some reaction. He tilted his head and looked off in the distance. His large lips twisted. Pain written at the corner of his eyes spoke volumes. He appreciated the invitation but didn't trust it. Saying he refused was harsh. Heph needed time to accept my mother's sudden interest.

"I'm headed north to Hestia's." He spoke off to the trees on the edge of the property. "I visit every fall." Hestia was my aunt. Hera and Demi's oldest sister lived a reclusive life in the northwest. Her home was cozy, I recalled, although it had been years since I'd been there. To think Heph had visited as well gave me hope of a shared history. I could only look toward to the future to build our sibling relationship.

"Hestia was always the perfect mother," my mother snipped bitterly. I didn't appreciate her tone, and Heph closed his eyes before responding.

"She's the only mother figure I've ever known." The words cut deep. My mother's eyes opened wide, abashed at the tone of his voice, but she bit her lip, holding back a sharp retort.

"I think I've had enough fresh air today." She nodded to him and looked at me. "Come back to the house with me." It wasn't an invitation but a command.

"I'm going to walk a bit longer. I've decided to return to school tomorrow." Heph's eyes sought mine, questioning me. My mother's tone bit. "I just got here, but I'll drive you."

"I'm going alone." To soften the rejection, I added. "I need to get some things in line for my fall clinicals." My mother didn't argue with my education. She agreed that an educated woman was a wise woman, one who could fend for herself in the world. *How long had my mother held this attitude? How long had she been lonely?* I wondered. While I wanted to obtain a skill, I didn't wish to pass my life feeling incomplete. Thoughts of Solis flitted through my mind, but I shut them off.

"You shouldn't be out here alone. It's almost dark." My mother's fears for the darkness were unfounded, I knew. Persephone was my best friend. She loved the darkness, literally. Nothing would harm me while Persephone had Hades.

"Heph can walk with me," I volunteered. Dark circles of deep chocolate set wounded in their sockets. My mother reached for me and embraced me. My arms did not leave my stomach. Her touch did not comfort me. She pulled back and kissed my forehead like I was a child. Abruptly, she stepped around me and left us without addressing Heph further.

"I'm so sor –"

"Don't." Heph's gruff tone didn't startle me. He had every right to be upset. He looked away again. My shaking hand reached out for his forearm, resting tenderly on the thickness.

"I don't want to be angry with you." He turned back to me. "I'm not angry. I just can't wrap my head around everything."

"I totally understand that feeling." Heph's eyes fell on me.

"What happened?"

"Solis got a girl pregnant." I sighed. I didn't think I could tell the story.

"He did not."

"He did." I snorted in response.

"Are you talking about Letty?"

"Yes." I dragged out the word, irritation filling in as more secrets were kept from me, suddenly angered that Heph knew such a secret and kept it from me.

"Hades didn't impregnate her."

"Are you sure?" I elongated the words again, frustration adding emphasis.

"I…" He stopped.

"That's what I thought."

Heph's stature grew before me. He straightened to his full height. His fists balled at his sides and his eyes narrowed. "I'll kill him for hurting you."

If I had a heart, it would snap in half at this brotherly outburst of protection.

"Awww, Heph. You don't need to do that. I'm a big girl." I dismissed the attention with a wave, but the tears swelling in my eyes betrayed me. His protectiveness and Solis' betrayal merged together. If Solis loved me, he should be the one protecting me. A traitorous tear fell.

"Don't cry, Vee." Using the casual term for my name broke me. A sob escaped and I bent forward, resting my forehead against his solid chest. Awkward hands patted my back before settling in to rub hesitantly up and down my spine. I cried for Heph, Solis, Letty, and me. The world was a clusterfuck, and I didn't want any part of it.

+ + +

An hour later, I sat on the edge of Cliff Morteum, my legs crisscrossed as I stared into the abyss of dark night and sunken valley. Off in the distance, somewhere in those lights on the opposite range, stood Zeke's estate. I took sobering breaths of the cool air and rested back on my hands. Reflective of all I had learned the past month, thoughtful of all that transpired the last forty-eight hours, I knew it had to end. I'd reached my human limit for trauma. Afraid of heights, the irony of sitting on a cliff, looking down into a foggy valley, wasn't lost on me. So many unknown lives under that cloud, just like the veil that covered my eyes from the truth of my being. I wasn't one of them, but my life was intrinsically interwoven, but I did not feel special. I did not feel extraordinary. I felt plain and inconsequential and unloved. My chest hollow, the ache deep and my hand covered it, squeezing at skin that covered nothing.

"Veva." The harsh breath exhaled behind me, and I stood rapidly. The heel of my foot rested on the edge of the cliff.

"Vee." A hand stretched out in the dark, visible by a flashlight pointed at me. Solis stood a few feet away with Persephone and Hades at his side. The nickname from his lips felt wrong and dirty. My arms wrapped around me, and I scrubbed at them.

"Vee, honey, have you been here all this time?" Persephone stepped forward, her concerned tone warming me, but I liked the chill. I needed the cold of this mountainous air to prevent me from feeling. I didn't want to cry anymore. I didn't want to waste the tears.

"Don't." I raised both hands before me and my foot slipped back. A brush with the edge of the cliff sent pebbles tumbling downward. The sound ricocheted through the silent night, skittering toward the valley like tiny boulders.

"Oh my God, Veva. Don't step back." Persephone's voice rose an octave as her hands covered her mouth in horror. Her head shook slowly side to side.

"Veva." The soothing tone of Hades called out my name. He nearly blended with the black night in his dark attire. He stepped toward me, hand outstretched, but Persephone reached for him.

"Don't frighten her." Tugging on his forearm sleeve did nothing to halt his approach.

"She's not going to do anything." Hades spoke to me, eyes fixed on mine. "It isn't her time." His head dipped, understanding me.

"Veva, come to me." Solis barked, and my connection with Hades ruptured. My head swung in his direction.

"You don't own me, Solis. I don't jump when you say fetch, like your other girls."

"There aren't any others, Veva. I've *told* you this." His voice took on boredom as he emphasized the words.

"You told me lots of things." I snorted. "Lies."

"What lies, Veva? When have I lied to you?" His voice rose and rumbled out into the emptiness at my back. *I love you* echoed with it. I flinched at the sound, and my foot pushed back. A clump of dirt broke under my heel and my ankle gave way. I slipped, but caught myself by my outstretched arms.

"Veva," Persephone screamed and Hades stepped closer, but so did Solis. My hands pulled forward again.

"Don't come near me." The fear in my voice radiated out and around us. If Solis touched me, I'd disintegrate. I'd dissolve like ashes after a fire, and blow off in the mountain wind. I didn't trust his touch, and my skin bubbled with thoughts of his hands on me. *Lies*, my head screamed.

Solis stopped short, but Hades continued forward, moving at a snail's pace. He drew closer, but my eyes remained fixed on Solis.

"Veva." His voice strained. He stood close enough that I could see the piercing pain in his honey eyes. "Veva, please." His eyes begged for something I could not give him: understanding.

"I don't understand how you could do that to Letty, and do this to me."

"What did I do…"

"I don't understand why men can't love me. I mean, what's wrong with me? Why am I not enough for one man? Just one." I shook, cutting him off without allowing him to explain. I didn't really want answers. I wanted understanding.

"Veva, you're more than enough. I love you. Step back from the edge."

Shaking my head, I answered vaguely: "Do you think I can fly?"

"Oh my God! No, Veva!" Persephone cried.

"Veva." Sternly, Hades repeated my name, shaking his head slowly.

"And what is this place where Zeke lives? Why didn't that girl get help? If we are all part of some sick tale and this is us, someone explain it to me. Am I'm destined only to have a cheating, lying man? Do I have special powers too? Can I fly as well?" My thought rambled as did my questioning and my foot slipped on the loose edge, forcing more pebbles to fall to the valley below, scattering and plinking as they hit larger rocks in their descent.

"Veva, step away from the ledge," Solis commanded. His voice made me flinch, and my foot slipped again. A large chunk of earth broke away under my feet. I pitched forward, but recovered my balance. Solis had taken several steps toward me, his hand outstretched for mine. Responding with a raised, flat palm, I signaled him to halt.

"Poor Letty." My lips quivered as I said her name.

"It is sad, Vee. But it's over."

"How could you be so callous?"

"Callous? I feel awful for her."

"How could you have such disregard for your child?"

Solis stopped. The flashlight in his hand dropped to the ground.

"My child?" His booming voice lowered to a rumble. A drop of rain splattered on my cheek.

"Yes. Letty and your baby."

"Letty's baby wasn't mine." His eyes opened wide before his brow pinched. "Is that what you think? That her baby was mine?"

"I don't know what to think." Suddenly, I questioned everything. My hands lowered to my sides. The wind picked up, and another drop of rain hit my forehead. I swiped at it before a light mist fell around us. The ground at my feet quickly softened, and the soil at my heels loosened. I rocked forward on my toes.

"Is it raining?" Hades interjected, turning to face Solis. "Stop it."

"I'm trying," Solis yelled back.

Several things happened at once.

Balancing on my toes, my ankles gave way. My feet fell flat, but my heels had nothing to bear my weight. The back of my feet slipped and my arms came up to catch me. My mouth opened in preparation for the descent. Persephone screamed and Solis lunged forward.

"Solis," I cried out before my mouth could stop me. My legs kicked as I dangled with nothing under me but a valley miles below.

"Stop kicking," Hades commanded. He'd caught my wrists.

"Don't drop her," Persephone's voice shrieked, but Hades was already dragging me upward. "I told you, it isn't your time."

When I was level with the ledge once again, arms encircled my waist and I fell forward, landing with a heavy thump on a warm body. Those arms didn't release me as we rolled to my back. Hands brushed feverously over my forehead.

"Are you okay? Tell me you're okay, Veva?" Solis' breath blew over my face as he peppered me with questions and tender pecks over my forehead. The weight of his body crushed me, but I had no fight left to force him off me.

"I'm…" I couldn't get the rest of the words out of me.

"Veva, why would you do this?"

I shook my head. I'd done nothing. "Slipped," I choked out.

"I told you to stop the rain." Hades' voice softened to water over river rocks as he stood over us.

"I…" Solis' eyes searched my face. "I…" His voice broke and he lowered his face to my neck. We rolled once more. Without releasing me, he sat up, tucking me against his chest as I sat cradled in his lap. My cheek pressed warmly against his chest. His mouth speaking to my hair.

"I love you, Veva. I love *you*. How could you do this? How could you doubt me?"

"I just came here to think." The words came out slowly, my heart still racing and my chest ached.

"If you had gone over that cliff…" He shivered. "I would have followed you. I told you, I'd follow you wherever you go. You are the other half of me, and I can't live without you."

"Letty?" I whispered.

"That baby wasn't mine. It was Zeke's. He slept with her after me. The baby was his."

I sat for a moment, drawing in deep breaths as the misty rain continued to wash my face and wet my hair. Solis' arms tightened around me.

"But you slept with her. How can you be sure?"

Solis drew back at the question.

"I won't lie. I did sleep with her, but I couldn't finish. My thoughts were filled with you."

I pushed back against his chest.

"Thoughts of me? While you were with another girl?"

"That didn't come out right."

"Oh man, shut up," Hades groaned beside us.

"Dude, go away," Solis barked.

"You're burying yourself here," Hades admonished.

"I can't think," Solis snapped. "I just want to hold her and make sure she's real. She's safe. Can't you understand that?" Solis' voice grew louder, and Hades lowered his head.

"Yeah," he mouthed with a nod. He turned to face Persephone, her face streaked with silent tears. She watched me.

"Vee, I love you," she stated. The fear in her eyes brought tears to mine. I hadn't planned to kill myself.

"I slipped," I repeated again. *Slipped from grace, slipped from the sky, slipped from love.* My head fell forward, pressing into Solis' chest. How many mistakes I'd made, and the only person who hurt repeatedly was me. The rain continued, and my hair grew heavy with water. I shivered. Shock set in, and my body trembled. My missing heart had nowhere to beat. I felt broken and alone, despite the arms around me.

"I'm so tired, Sunshine," I muttered.

"I've got you, Peacock. I'll always have you."

SOLIS

Relief should have filled me as Veva rested in my lap. I refused to let her go while Persephone drove my Jeep down the mountain. Instead, my thoughts raced backward over the past hours of hell searching for Veva.

God damn it all to Hades, I cursed in my head as I paced outside the door of Letty's room. I wanted to kill my father. He made everyone his plaything, and it backfired once again. Poor Letty. She was a sweet girl. Innocent. Guilt wracked through me at the reminder that I'd taken advantage of her, too. But not like this. I would not ignore such tragedy. I said Letty wasn't my concern because I hadn't gotten her pregnant, and I didn't want to step in where my father should. Obviously, he ignored his responsibilities once again.

Veva's accusation was unfounded and unfair, but arguing with her as Letty moaned and bled wasn't the time. After all I'd said to Veva, all I admitted, I'd hoped for a little more trust. My heart split in two, knowing Veva was the half separated from me. Her lack of faith in me cut deep.

I stormed off to find my father, rather than wait for Veva's unwarranted wrath. Finding him lounging in his office, the rain pelted his windows. He sat back in his desk chair, rocking forward and back, the end of a pen tracing over his lips.

"You've heard." His statement stopped me.

"This could have killed the girl." Rage unfurled in me. "I sent her to your priestess, and she didn't take care of her."

"It is not the place of Athena's women to save them all."

"It isn't the place of Athena to take care of your responsibilities, either. It's unacceptable."

Zeke had the grace to look chagrined briefly. His eyes lowered and he sat forward. A thick hand came to his forehead and fingers pinched at his tan skin.

"Why can't you leave the young ones alone?" I snapped. "Must you have every one of them after me?"

"Not every one of them." His head rose and his eyes narrowed, but the gleam in them taunted me.

I stepped forward. "I'd kill you if you touched her."

"Fulfilling the prophecy, I see." He sat back with a thud, and his chair rocked. A thick digit came to his lower lip. My breath hitched at the threat. He knew I wanted to believe I'd already fulfilled it. He wanted to believe it as well, hoping the term father *within the prophecy was stated loosely. "I worry you might enjoy that, son."*

The endearment did not endear me. It made my skin crawl. I'd never been his son, not really. Even after all these decades, after all the training, a division stood between us, a great divide of power and fear. Another set of opposites attracted. My father was another sort of destiny. He held power and wanted to instill fear. In me. It hadn't worked. I had the potential for the same power he held. Perhaps even stronger, my trainer had warned me. A strength rested within me, not separate from me, like his talisman lightning bolt. My back sizzled and warmed along my spine. Anger fueled the energy. Zeke would know this about me. He was the first to tell me of my gift.

"You need to make this right for Letty."

"I'm actually allowing it to be right for Veva."

"Veva?" My eyes opened wide. "What does Veva have to do with this?"

"Two things. Veva needs to learn her gift: the power within her to heal and cure. She also needs to see you for who you are."

My mouth fell open. "You talked Mel into this game, didn't you? You wanted her to make it seem like it was me. How?" But I had my answer. My father fucked Mel as well, and Mel's jealousy over Letty fueled her vengeance on both me and my father.

"How could you?" I sighed, frustrated with his attempts to tear me down, to strip away the one thing that had potential to be everything to me.

200

"Veva's a smart girl. She needs to get back to school to continue her training. She needs to get out of the clouds with you and back on her path. Her destiny."

"I'm her destiny." I stepped forward again, resting my hands on his desk.

"You will only hurt her, as I've hurt her mother."

I pushed off the desk and stood straighter. *"No, you wanted to hurt me, so I wouldn't have what you didn't have with her mother. You took from me, because you never had what I could have had. You've destroyed me."* I spun away from him and then turned back.

"I think the prophecy stated it incorrectly. The son would not kill the father. The father would sacrifice his son, forcing love out of the equation."

"What equation is that, smart boy," Zeke mocked.

"Veva plus me equals destiny. I won't let you play god here, Father," I spat. I could twist fate just as easily.

She didn't believe me, and my chest ached. Veva's human heart couldn't handle more drama. My feisty girl had lost her fight once again, and I wanted to battle every war for her instead. The rain deluged downward and Hades cursed me, but my emotions rained with fear and relief that Veva. While she hadn't cascaded down the mountain, though, I didn't believe she was safe with me. Even wrapped in my lap, she felt distant.

We returned to the main house, and I took Veva to my room versus the cottage. Wet and shaken, she needed to be submerged in warmth, and the tub in my room was the perfect spot. Lifeless, she sat at the edge of my large bed as I ran the bath, filling it with a fragrant oil. I returned to undress her, and like a ragdoll, Veva gave me control.

"Let me pamper you." Shaky hands unbuttoned her shirt as if they'd never undressed a woman before. Veva sat silent, complacent to my attention.

"Stay with me, Vee," I begged, meaning more than physically. I didn't want to lose her. I couldn't be without her. I didn't feel whole, knowing she was missing. I couldn't exist, if she left me permanently.

elda lore

Removing my own soaked shirt, I stood to slip out of my jeans. I helped Veva to stand and dragged her shorts down to her ankles, tapping them for her to step out. Her skin goose-bumped with cold.

"I'm going to take care of you, Vee."

Her hand on my shoulder stopped me. "Thank you." She mouthed the words, but no sound came from her whitened lips. Scooping her up in my arms, I carried her to the tub. I stepped in, still holding her, and sunk down, placing her between my legs. The space was large enough for two, and the jets steadily circulated the warm liquid around us. I scooped up handfuls of water and poured it over her head, warming her hair and washing out the rain. My fingers massaged her shoulders and up her neck.

"Vee, talk to me." Her silence disturbed me. Grown too comfortable with her fighting nature, a silent Veva concerned me. I worried a storm roared fiercely under her skin and any moment she'd thunder and leave me.

"Okay, I'll talk. I tried to sleep with Letty. It was before I knew you, but that sounds lame because the second I saw you, I knew you. The familiarity unsettled me, and I thought drowning in another girl would rid me of the prickling energy inside me. Stupid. I'm stupid."

"You are," she muttered, and I smiled to myself, leaning forward to kiss her shoulder. Those words brought me ridiculous joy. She could insult me all she wanted, as long as she spoke to me.

"I couldn't finish what I started with her. I couldn't get you out of my head. I didn't really want you out of my head, but I didn't know what to do. No one frustrated me as much as you." I swiped a hand through my hair and held it behind my neck. "Jeez, Vee, you were under my skin instantly." Her mouth twitched with those words, and I brushed my cheek against hers. My hands lowered into the bath and skimmed over her stomach.

"I know what you mean."

My hand cupped her jaw, and I turned her to meet my face. "Kiss me."

"Not yet." Her lips curled slowly and mine responded.

202

"There's my Peacock." My nose rubbed over hers. I filled the silence that followed by telling her what happened with my father.

"He's not going to get to me." She shivered under the water. "I don't plan to fall for anyone again."

The finality of her tone forced my forehead to pinch. With those words, Veva stood abruptly and turned to face me. Water cascaded down her large breasts like waterfalls and rivers teemed over her stomach to the mound at the apex of her legs. Tiny streams rippled off her hips. She rivaled the goddess of water. Holding out her hand to me, I stood as well.

"Fall, Veva, and I will follow you." I lowered my head to emphasize the words. She stepped from the tub, not releasing my hand, and led me to the bedroom without drying us. Standing at the base of the bed, she faced me.

"Can you make love to me?" The words softened as she spoke, but I sensed her hesitation. She left off the rest of the words. *One last time.* It had only been this morning that we shared a first. I didn't wish to argue with her. I only wanted to give her what she needed from me.

"Persuade me," I teased, using her words from only last night. When her hand landed on my chest, I fell under her spell. Less than a second it took. Slowly, her hand dragged upward, over my racing heart, to cover my shoulder, eclipsing the sunshine tattoo briefly before slipping to my wrist. Circling it, she lifted my hand and placed it over her breast. The invitation was clear. I took control, massaging the heavy weight of her and tweaking the nipple to a peak. I lowered my head to suck her in, and her hands found my hair, producing a comforting stroke that brought me to my knees.

Veva was the temple of life for me, and I planned to worship at her altar. My mouth trailed kisses to her core and took her with my tongue. Her hips danced over me, undulating to a rhythm in her head. I glanced up to find a mesmerizing scene, her lids dropped low and her body rippling softly like water down a stream. Fingers kneaded through my hair and held me to her, accepting my meager offering. My sacrifice accepted, she sang out her praise before her eyes opened and pierced me with their intensity. I sat back after a final kiss to her thighs and stood before her. She sat.

Resting only briefly on the edge of the bed, she slowly crawled backward up the sheets, luring me with her eyes to follow her lead. Like a sacrificial calf, I answered her call. My body would complete the feast. She opened her legs, drawing me to her center, and I speared forward. A breath caught in my throat, and I cried out sharply at the teasing pleasure of entering her slowly. This wasn't a race across the sky; this was a gentle rain caressing the earth. Slipping into the warmth of her, her legs wrapped around my lower back, my mouth covered hers, and my tongue took her again. Our movements were a dance of epically rhythmic proportions providing a symphony. My tongue a tingling clap of thunder; my dick the pulse of lightning, I drew heat from Veva as my earth. I took my time to enter and tease, drawing back before sliding home.

"You complete me," I muttered against her mouth, feeling safe and accepted in a way I'd never felt before. "I love you, Vee."

"I know." Her lids lowered as she drew in air with the glide of my entrance.

"Don't leave me." The plea lingered between us.

"Shh." Her mouth reached up for mine as her fingers found my hair again. She hadn't answered me, and even buried deep inside her, I felt her slipping away. I didn't know all her sounds yet, but I wanted to learn. When she stiffened and her legs slid off my hips, her mouth released me, and she whispered my name. I recognized what was happening and drove deeper, hoping to keep the connection as long as I could. The motion set me off. Drained of my seed, the remains of my sacrifice consisted of tired bones and an achy heart. I knew she'd leave me.

204

VEVA

In the morning, I found Persephone on the edge of the olive grove. She stared out at the newly risen sun.

"It's not the same as home, is it?" I stated, glancing out at the thickly trunked trees. In Nebraska, our fields looked flat compared to the haphazard, bushy display.

"Nope." Her short answer brought my attention to her.

"Where's Hades?" I hated to ask. The way her arms wrapped around her, like she held herself together, prefaced her answer.

"He's gone."

I didn't want to say I was sorry. She'd heard it enough before, the first time he left. She turned to face me and smiled weakly.

"If he keeps surprising me, there will be no place left for me to live without a memory of him haunting me."

"Pea, I don't know what to say."

"I know. You'll learn."

I continued to stare at my friend.

"You think you're leaving him, Vee, but you aren't. Not completely. I know that look on your face. Slinking off, you feel you've left him behind, but he'll always be in you. You won't be able to explain it, and you won't want to. Who can put words to such a feeling, except maybe Shakespeare?" She laughed at an internal joke, and I smiled weakly in response.

"I don't think he was ever mine." It was the truth, but oh, how I wanted to believe he was. I couldn't bring myself to accept that Solis belonged to me in any other way than being my first. While he spoke of familiarity, and I felt it too, but I didn't think that feeling would follow after we connected. He called it destiny, but I wasn't certain destiny favored me in a positive light. I believed in love, I just didn't see how love could follow me. How Solis would follow me.

"There's no denying him, Veva." We had started walking through the trees just like we strolled the fields back home. "He is yours, and you are his."

I let the statement linger, chewing at my lips as I considered her thoughts.

"I'm afraid, Pea. He makes me feel—whole. It's the only word I can think of to describe him. I don't feel that creepy, crawling anger inside me when we are good together, but I worry he'll keep ripping me apart, just to make me whole again. Letty was only the tip of the mountain. There are so many others."

"Does he want the others? No." Persephone exhaled. "Hera did such a job on you. She scared you into thinking it could never happen because it didn't happen to her. She's bitter, Vee, and it takes so much energy to be that negative."

Ignoring her admonishment, I changed the subject. I was too tired to argue about Solis or my mother.

"Did you hear about Heph?"

"I did."

We strolled onward, and I heard a branch snap behind us. Turning to look, I noticed the trees had brightened to a ripe green. I turned forward to find the leaves of the ones ahead of us still dusty. It struck me mostly because all the other trees had the same feathery color to them, but the strip we walked stood bright and erect, ready to drop olives. We walked a little farther, and something called at the back of my brain to turn again. The few trees we had passed had shifted to stand at attention and lightened their leaves to a glossy glow.

"Pea." I stopped her with a hand on her arm. I spun her to look back.

"What?" Her hand swung side to side. "What do you see?"

"Notice the trees." I whispered, afraid to disturb whatever was happening. "They've changed."

Persephone stared for a moment. "I don't see it."

"Here, walk ahead of me. Pay attention to that tree and then walk past it."

Persephone did as I asked, glancing back at me, questioning me until she saw the leaves visibly rise and salute her. The color radiated as she passed the tree.

"Oh my God." Her hand covered her mouth.

"What did you do?" I shrieked with half excitement, half fear.

"I don't know."

"It's the Discovery." We both spun to face Zeke a few feet behind us on the path. His white hair slicked back and his beard trim, a wide smile graced his face. "It's happened for you." He stepped forward slowly, reverently, reaching out to clasp both Persephone's hands in his. "I'm so excited for you."

Pea stared as did I.

"You have quite the green thumb, as you've learned in your botany courses, but there is something more to it." He waved a hand at the trees blossoming in respect to Persephone. "Your gift has bloomed."

"How can that be?" Persephone questioned, and I waited, holding a breath for his answer.

"It's simple, actually. Love makes your talent blossom." A tear trickled from Persephone's eye as she nodded in agreement with Zeke. For me, my boiling temper simmered at his answer. *If I had a gift, I'd never discover mine then*, I thought. But the lie rolled back to Solis, who I left alone in his luscious bed, sleeping in his godlike glory, replete from a night of endless lovemaking. I loved him, but I didn't believe in myself. I didn't trust my love for him, and I didn't trust that he loved me, exclusively. It was easier to walk away before he would leave me.

Zeke turned to face me, as if reading my thoughts.

"And you, my princess, have much to learn, as does my son. Let's pray your lessons don't waste more time. These storms wreak havoc on my crops." He raised his eyes to the sky before glancing over the grove. Here and there a split tree lay open, presumably struck by lightning. My lips twisted, confused whether to smile or frown at his comment.

"Happy Discovery Day, Persephone." Zeke leaned forward to brush her cheek with his lips. His lips lingered a moment too long, and an eerie emotion rolled up my body.

"It's time for us to leave, Pea," I interrupted and Persephone released Zeke's hands. His eyes sent glaring bolts of light in my direction, but I fired back. His secrets haunted me.

VEVA

We hardly pulled out of the main entrance when Persephone spun back to gaze one last look upon the estate.

"Veva, stop the car." Her hand came to rest on my forearm and I slowed, pulling to the side of the road.

"What did we forget?" I feared Persephone wanted to return, hopeful that Hades would remain. She'd already explained to me that with the ending of the festivities, so too was his stay. He'd returned to the underworld. It reaffirmed that I needed to get as far away from the Olympic Olive estate as possible.

"What the hell?" I'd swung my head back and realized the estate had disappeared. We hadn't gone more than a few feet from the entrance, but the entrance no longer existed. The gate was missing and all that remained were miles and miles of olive trees.

"But…" I stared, blinking in disbelief. Two tire trails veered off the road and dead-ended into nothing but the edge of an olive plantation. It was as if a driveway should be there, but wasn't. The ground dipped and the grass folded in two strips. No evidence of the paved drive. No entrance gate. No estate. It was all missing from the eye.

"Are you seeing what I'm seeing?" Persephone asked for confirmation.

"I don't see a thing, so if that's what you see, then we see the same thing." I wasn't even sure what I just said, let alone what I no longer saw.

"The estate disappeared." Persephone's voice faltered as it fell. "Not again." She sighed and spun in the passenger seat. Her head fell back and she slowly beat it against the headrest. "He's done it again."

"Done what?" My hand reached for her arm this time.

"He's made it impossible to return."

My eyes shifted back to the olive grove.

"I don't think Hades did that." My finger pointed behind us, circling for emphasis.

"Not alone, he didn't, but it's clear we can't return without an invitation."

I stared in disbelief.

"Are you saying you think we've been kicked out?"

"I'm saying they aren't ready to let us in."

"Who is 'us'?

"You and me." Her head rolled on the headrest to face me. "You and me, Vee. We're modern descendants, but we have to prove ourselves."

Modern descendants? There was no way I was a descendant of any of this crazy. Maybe Hades could rise from the dead, and Solis could fly across the sky, but there was nothing special about me. My thoughts jumped to this morning and the shifting of the trees as Persephone walked along the lane. Maybe she was a descendant of something powerful and strange, but certainly not me.

"Pea, please, just five minutes without this stuff." I shifted to face the windshield and put the car in drive. I wasn't jealous of her. I loved Persephone, and she clearly had a talent developing, as Zeke mentioned, but there was nothing for me on his estate, and I wanted to get back to the real world with no more talk of gods or gifts.

+ + +

The weather shifted drastically as we left the country roads leading to the invisible estate. Hitting Highway 99 through central California, the wind changed, and rain released from the heavens like a shower head. I refused to think of what I'd left behind. Persephone sat beside me in silence, her thoughts a million miles away and apparently under the earth. I was slow to understand all that Pea told me about Hades; what I didn't understand the most was *why* he couldn't stay. Whatever his reasons, my best friend sat grieving once again. She twisted a ring on her third finger while I swung the rock at my neck back and forth on its leather strap.

The windshield wipers swished as fast as they could but still weren't clearing the glass, and we slowed to a crawl. I couldn't see two feet in front of me. A crack of thunder shook the car and lightning struck to the left. I screamed and swerved. Persephone screamed as well. Suddenly something hit the hood of the car with a heavy thud, and I slammed on the brakes, foolishly squeezing my eyes shut for a moment. As we came to a sudden halt and I hit the emergency hazard lights, a large object rolled off the front of the vehicle. In slow motion, I turned to look at Pea. We hadn't hit something, or the impact would have forced the airbags. Something hit us. Without thought, I opened the door, instantly soaked to the core, and raced to the front of the car. My headlights lit the narrow visibility.

"Solis," I screamed, as I recognized the body slumped on the pavement. Falling to my knees, my hands gripped his open jacket.

"Solis," I shouted again over the deluge of water pelting me. I shook his limp body, realizing as an afterthought that I shouldn't be jiggling him. My hand brushed back his waterlogged hair and rubbed over his cheeks.

"Veva." His voice strained as he rolled to his back. His hand wiped over his stomach, rising hesitantly over his chest. He winced once but continued until his hand covered mine.

"Veva," he croaked again.

"Are you insane? What are you doing out here?" I yelled over the roaring rain ripping at the road around us.

"I told you, I'd follow you anywhere." His voice strained further as he formed a complete sentence. I blinked as the water blinded me.

"Where did you come from?" I shouted as he slowly sat up, gripping his ribs, and facing me. I couldn't believe he could move, let alone sit up before me. "Did you...did you just fall out of the sky or something?"

"Yes." His direct answer startled me, and his trembling hand reached forward to press back wayward hair stuck haphazardly over my face. "You're so beautiful when you're wet."

"You're insane," I scolded.

"I'm in love."

My mouth came to his, ignorant of the cold rain or the sharp pricks of heavy drops. My lips took control and he moaned into me, letting me lead as his body rested.

"What did you do?" I asked after releasing him. "Are you hurt? You must be hurt."

The rain slowed considerably, passing toward its next victim.

"I'm…a little sore." He rolled his neck and lifted his hands to the back of his head. The front had a welt the size of an egg. I leaned forward again and pressed my lips above his eye.

"What were you doing?" No longer necessary to yell as the rain passed, my voice softened.

"I told you. I was following you."

"Solis," I sighed. "You know you can't."

"Who says?"

"Persephone told me. It isn't the same out here as it is in there. At the estate." My thoughts drifted back to the disappearance of Zeke's property.

"Veva, I come to the world outside the estate all the time. Most of us look human, minus some strange coloring on Triton and Hades. I can walk among you freely."

"Solis, this seems impossible."

"What does?"

"Us."

"Vee, don't say that." But it was true. I'd been stewing over this, us, for the last hour of my drive. Solis and I were not a possibility. If he was something other than human, and I clearly was very human, there wasn't a chance we could be together. Anything between Solis and I was as hopeless as Pea and Hades.

"Vee, you're more like me than you think." His voice lowered. "You're special to me, and your day will come. You'll figure it out. We'll figure it out. Together."

"I can't do this." I sat back on my heels. I didn't believe him. I didn't believe in me.

"Why not?" His forehead pinched, and he winced. His hand came to feel the size of the bump growing over his eye.

"I don't know if I believe all this, although falling from the sky is certainly a grand gesture." I looked up for emphasis at the lightening clouds. My eyes fell back to his. "I just don't see how I could be special in any way. Not me, and I don't know that I want to be. I don't want to hurt you. I don't want to hold you back from who you need to be." My voice faltered as I swiped a hand down his cheek. Leaving him wasn't meant to hurt him. It was meant to free him of me.

"Vee, I explained about Letty."

I pushed back his wet hair and he turned his face into my palm, planting a kiss there. He rested his back against the front of the car and the headlights beamed around us.

"I know, and I overreacted. I always do. But there will be others, and I won't understand. I'll want to, but I can't wrap my head around all you've done and then think you'll settle on only me."

"I'll just keep telling you, I love you. Don't give up on us before we start."

I shook my head. Long tresses dripped water down my already-soaked shirt.

"I'm not giving up. I'm just not giving in. I don't understand any of what I'm learning and I just...I just need time to digest it all." I closed my eyes in frustration.

"Veva, I know it's confusing. You're scared. I'm scared. Hell, we share the same reasons. Abandoned by people who should have loved us implicitly, but we can work. We need to work together. You're the other half of me. I need you." His voice pleaded, and I almost broke. Kneeling on a wet highway, staring into his honey eyes, I almost gave in, but my hesitation was bigger than me. I had to leave him before he'd leave me. One day there would be a different Letty, one he had slept with, one he did foster a child with, and I wouldn't be able to take the heartbreak. As if reading my thoughts, he spoke.

"I can't help my past, but stop doubting it. Doubting me. Trust in us. We can make it." His hands gripped mine together, shaking them as he spoke.

"Can you give me some time? I just need to get away from the estate, get away from all those girls." I smiled weakly, although I found no humor in the harem of women prancing the grounds. I questioned if each one of them had him like me, and I couldn't shake the images haunting my head. Jealousy gnawed at me.

"Sure, Vee." Solis looked off in the distance where the storm carried on. "Take what you need." His shoulders sunk, and his hand covered his face. The defeat in his tone made me question all that I'd said. Did I really want to walk away from him? Did I have the strength to leave? He rolled his body to the side and the motion distracted me.

"Let me help you," I offered with trembling hands. I didn't know how I could lift him, but he pressed his free hand to the pavement and stood easily. Easily in spite of potentially broken ribs.

"Maybe I should look at those." I hesitated, holding my hands out to his mid-chest.

"Why do you…" He took a deep breath, holding in the question: *Why do I care?* "Never mind." He brushed past me, walking off toward the flat expanse of land opposite the car.

"Solis!" I yelled after him. He spun to face me. Sadness stood alive in his expression. He waved silently back at me, and then turned back to the field. In the distance, a lone horse stood, and realization came to me. He followed me. He literally fell out of the sky. For me.

SOLIS

"You're a fool," Heph admonished me as my feet dangled off the rocks we climbed.

"Yep." It was a simple, sweet answer to the stupid, truthful statement and I took another long pull of the sharp alcohol in my flask. My heels kicked at the rock behind my feet and I swallowed hard. Numbing the pain had been my intention since the moment she rejected me. Time. I knew all about time. I'd been alive for thousands of years. I'd had nothing but time as I waited for her. Before. Now, I didn't know how much time I could offer her, knowing she was alive, out there, and I wasn't with her. Time could fuck off, as far as I was concerned. Then I thought of Hades. He'd give anything to stop time as well. My head fell forward, and I exhaled to my chest, my hollow, empty chest.

For a moment, I thought I imagined that night. Veva under me. Veva over me. Veva before me. The night was an endless romp of discovering her body, her sighs and her sounds. I fell into a heavy sleep to wake alone, a single, white, peacock plume on the pillow next to me as the only sign my imagination hadn't conjured the night. My body ached at the loss of her, and yet I sensed her leaving me each time I entered her. Filling her, I begged her to stay. Releasing her, she refused my plea. She would leave me. I wouldn't bother chasing her, or so I thought.

There are other girls, I scolded internally.

They aren't Veva, my conscience answered.

I threw off the covers that morning knowing what I had to do. I had to prove to Veva I meant what I said. Yet, here I sat, watching the early setting sun of August, drinking whiskey with Heph.

"You're the god of the sky and you can't figure out how to woo a girl? Give her sunsets and rainbows, for heaven's sake."

I turned to face my half-brother. In profile, he was frightening, but underneath that exterior, silently hidden, was a thoughtful man.

"Oh yeah, how are things with Lovie?"

"You're an ass when you want to be," he snorted, ripping the bottle from my hands and downing a hearty drink.

"Well?"

"I'm doing what I was told." His eyes stared forward, his gruff voice harsh.

"That's a terrible excuse to marry someone." I tapped the flask on his thick thigh.

"It's better than not marrying the woman I love." I took his meaning and wanted to punch him.

"She doesn't want me."

"You know you don't believe that." He raised the metal container to his lips, shadowed by the heavier growth on his face.

"I don't believe it. You're right." I sat straighter. "And you know what, I am god of the heavens, or one day I will be. I can give her sunsets and rainbows. The question remains, how?" I stared back at the setting sun, remembering Veva's details, comparing it to her pleasure. I wanted to be the only sun that set for her. I also wanted to be the one that rose for her. Suddenly, I had a plan.

VEVA

"What do you mean, I can't get out of this class? I don't even understand how I got in it." I waved the registration ticket at the secretary behind the registrar's desk. Greek Mythology 101. How the hell did I get into such a class as a super senior, studying to be a midwife and counseling? I had clinicals to participate in this year. I didn't need an elective course at the freshman level.

"I'm sorry, Ms. Matron. It says here you're registered, and only the professor can remove you from the course."

"Uhhh…" I exhaled harshly. *What the hell?* "The art building, right? The course is in the art building. Who's the professor? I'll just go speak to him myself."

She clicked and clacked on her keyboard, and I wondered once again why my registration hadn't listed the professor's name. Under the course title sat TBA: to be announced, where the course instructor name typically appeared.

"It says here Cronus. S. Cronus is the professor."

I blinked several times, clearly misunderstanding the name she spoke.

"Solis Cronus?" My teeth clenched as the name hissed from my lips.

"Yes." The slight blush and radiating smile projected at me confirmed my question. His charm preceded him, but not with me. I didn't have to ask her if she'd met him. Her glowing expression proved she had.

"Thank you," I hissed as I removed the registration from the counter and stormed for the art department.

Yanking open the door to the classroom, I proceeded down the sloping aisle between auditorium seat sections. My body vibrated with both anticipation and frustration. My heart raced with excitement. *Had he really followed me?* I hadn't been able to forget the argument that ensued after I watched Solis walk away and Persephone admonished me.

"He just flung himself from the sky for you. How much more of a grand gesture do you need that he loves you?"

"Just what do you think you are doing?" I don't know why I barked at him. My hands twitched to reach for him, and my legs shook, pulsing stronger than a drum between my thighs. Excitement and trepidation collided inside my stomach. I was positive he could see my heart beating, it thudded so hard under my skin.

"Good afternoon, Ms. Matron." He pulled a pair of fake glasses off his beautiful face, and my breath caught. He'd blinded me with his beautiful smile, and I froze, knowing if I came any closer, I'd rush for him. I'd climb him like a mountain range and launch myself over the cliff, begging him to take me.

"Greek Mythology?" I shook the paper in question. "And a professor?" I snorted in disbelief. No one would believe he was a professor. He looked too young. He looked too good. They'd take his class only to stare at him.

"I could have taught sex education." My thighs pressed together.

"Please," I spit. "Remind me why I don't hate you." My eyes narrowed, but his smile widened.

"Okay, fine. I could have taught electrical engineering, but I didn't think you'd believe that one."

I shook my head in disbelief.

"Or meteorology, but that doesn't go with your major."

I glared, crossing my arms.

"Art, but then they'd all want to paint me in the nude." He winked. "Oh wait, you've already done that." He wiggled his eyebrows at me.

"You're infuriating." My arms released, and my foot stomped. Memories flooded me. The hollowness in my chest leapt to life, racing faster than a horse, or a flying hang glider.

"I prefer invigorating," he stated, as if he read my thoughts and remembered the day we flew through the sky.

"Incredible," I hissed.

"That's a good word, too."

"Not good," I tapped my foot. "As in, unbelievable." My arms flapped out at my side and slapped on my thighs.

"As in, how I feel inside you."

My breath caught at the comment. That racing heart jumped a fence and landed with a thud.

"Give me time to prove myself." He walked around the large podium, hosting a laptop and a projector. He took a step toward me, but I crossed my arms again, setting a warning not to come closer, though every fiber of my being vibrated with the need for him to touch me. We stood like polar opposites attracted by the electric energy between us. He tilted his head at my protective stance and leaned against the side of the large desk. Crossing his own arms, he chuckled.

"Pick a number."

"A thousand," I huffed, uncertain at this strange request.

He snorted. "Number of years I plan to spend with you, but too high."

"Thirty," I blurted.

"Hmmm...plausible." His lips twisted and instantly my own recalled the feel: the weight, the pressure, the pleasure they produced. He spoke as if to himself, tapping a finger on his chin. "That's the cycle for the moon. Not bad, but I'm leaving the moon to Leos."

"What?"

"Never mind. How old are you?" His honey eyes mesmerized me.

"Twenty-three."

"Pick something lower than that number."

"Twelve, the age you're acting." I snorted and let my arms fall from their barrier shield.

"Twelve." His finger rose to trace his lips and my mouth watered. Not just a hard swallow, but a full-on desire to drink him in again. His finger tapped his lips, hinting he'd caught me staring, and then his lips curled upward. "How very Grecian of you. I prefer thirteen, but we will do twelve. Twelve days it is."

"Twelve days for what?"

"For me to woo you."

"That's ridiculous. Plus, if you're going with some crazy system of numbers, doesn't twelve months make more sense?"

"Too long. Twelve days. That's all I need. Come on, Veva. Twelve days to prove I'll stick." His eyes melted to that caramel color I couldn't deny. "We don't even have to have a sex."

"Well, what a relief," I said dryly. The very mention of sex had my center drumming up a beat. I was afraid to move, or I'd combust before him. "And on day thirteen?"

"Lucky thirteen starts our life together. No more doubts. No more running."

I stared at him. *Was he kidding me?*

"Think of it like this—what's that holiday so many humans go ga-ga over? Oh, right, Christmas."

"You don't celebrate Christmas?" I cut him off, shaking my head.

"The twelve days of Christmas," he stated ignoring me. "Think of it like the twelve days of Solis." He wiggled his brow.

"I think that might be sacrilegious." My arms folded over my chest again as I glared at him.

"After twelve days, I'm going to be all the religion you need. You're going to worship only me."

+ + +

"His confidence pisses me off," I stated to Persephone as we sat in the back of the auditorium. I hadn't gotten out of the class, which started that same evening. Persephone sat beside me for support. She wasn't mysteriously enrolled in some random course like I was.

"Welcome to day one. Of Greek Mythology 101, that is." His booming voice carried out over the auditorium filled with girls of varying ages, including a few older women I'd seen working on campus.

"I think it's romantic," Persephone whispered to me although we were too far back for anyone to hear us. Belligerent as I could be, I sat with my feet propped up on the seat before me.

"What's romantic about hijacking my classes?" I huffed, although my insides twisted. From the moment I saw him earlier in the day, thoughts of seeing him again consumed me.

"He wants your attention."

"There's such a thing as a phone." My agitation wasn't with my friend, but my sharp tone bit out my frustration. He hadn't called me, but then I admonished myself: *Why would he?* He walked away from me on the side of the highway and that was it. I thought I'd ruined everything by asking for time, but here he stood preaching about Greek Mythology like he wrote the stories himself.

"He fell out of the sky for you, Vee." Persephone's harsh tone surprised me, remind me again of the argument she and I had after I let him walk away.

"You know, if it were me, I'd be walking after him," she had said, reminding me of her delicate emotions. Hades' return left her raw again and I damned him for hurting her.

Suddenly, the image of a rock formation appeared on the screen. My feet fell with a thud to the floor and I sat forward. I recognized the precariously stacked rocks.

"What is this?" His voice boomed and Persephone turned to me.

"I know this one." Her harsh whisper carried out into the large room. She smacked my arm for emphasis and raised her hand.

"Yes, miss…" he looked down at his roster, as if he didn't recognize Pea. "Miss Fields."

"Oh my God," I muttered, and caught his wink in our direction.

"It's a cairn. People make them to mark a space. To say I was here. Or to leave a message to someone. Say, I am thinking of you." Her voice slowed, and her head spun to me.

"Thank you. Correct." He paused. "And Miss Matron, do you notice anything special about this stack?"

The special part was that I made it. I made the structure myself outside his cottage the morning I left. I wanted to make my mark. Say *I was here*, as he taught me, as I hoped he would remember, before he considered bringing other girls to his painting den. I bit back my retort and added something different.

"It's a pile of rocks." A few girls giggled in front of me. "Ouch," I cried out as Persephone pinched me.

"Sometimes we need to look closer. Things aren't always as they seem. Our attitudes cloud our perception." He narrowed his eyes, lowering his glasses slightly. I stared at the image, counting the rocks.

"It has twelve rocks," I sputtered, thinking my answer smart.

"That's right." He turned to face the projected image. "The Greeks believed in balance. Twelve hours marked half of each day. Ante meridian, before midday and post meridian, meaning after midday. Before and after. Opposites making up one whole. Twelve gods and goddesses. Twelve months. Twelve days." He turned to face his captive audience, focusing on a girl in the back, holding her breath. Me.

SOLIS

She'd left the auditorium as soon as class ended, but I had her attention. Day one done, I had eleven more to prove myself. Veva believed I'd cheat on her, still fresh from the disturbing situation with Letty. I could read the doubt in her face, that if it wasn't Letty, there were others who would haunt me. I wanted nothing to cloud her judgment. Leaving the estate and following her to prove myself outside my home was the best idea.

The girls lived in a small apartment just off campus. University life was certainly different with each generation, and I hadn't tried to pretend I was a campus co-ed in a long time. The role of professor seemed more fitting, until the class filled with women. Veva's concern for my intentions vibrated from the back of the room, and several times I lost my focus, knowing she watched me. To be so close and yet so far from her unnerved me. I only had twelve days, but I convinced myself I could persuade her to pick me. Trust would take longer to earn, but Veva had to first decide she wanted me. Wanted us. She still sat in the crossfire of the known and the unknown.

I sat in her bedroom, waiting for her, envisioning what she'd see the second she opened the door to her apartment. Growing anxious as I waited, I stood and crossed to her bedroom door which had a clear shot of the living room.

"I won't even question how you got in here." She paused, letting her eyes drift from mine to her present. "What are all these?" Her softened tone, hardened my lower region. My body recognized the tender side of Veva.

"Memories." I leaned against the door jamb while she walked among the images strung from string and dangling down from the ceiling to decorate her living room. Twelve miniature sketches captured our story.

Rain on a window. Sunset behind rocks. Lightning against the sky.

223

Her eyes shifted to me and then returned to other sights. I knew where she focused next.

Her gorgeous dress the night I threw her in the pool.

Her stunning attire for Zeke's celebratory dinner.

Her sleeping form under a comforter on my cottage floor.

Her thumb traced the edge of the picture and her mouth curled. Her eyes flitted forward.

A peacock plume. A hot air balloon. A cliff near the sky.

Her brows pinched. With happy memories, came the difficult, but I hoped the final three would please her. I held my breath.

A shower head. A warm tub. A giant bed.

"The places we made love?" Her brow pinched.

Made love. That's how I wanted to her view the experience. She wasn't sex. She wasn't a one-night stand. She was love.

"Some of the best memories for me." The weight of Veva's eyes pinned me to the ground. A cyclone of fear twisted through me; I didn't want her to forget. I didn't want her to hate the memory. She stepped past the sketches and strolled to me. That sacrificial lamb sensation washed over me, and I couldn't look away from her as she stalked to me. My arms unfolded and my hands slid into my jeans, hoping to disguise my body's hypersensitivity to her, and hold me still from reaching for her. Standing before me, so close, but not close enough, her breasts brushed my chest. I sighed as she inhaled. The tender swish of fabric ignited the imagination of skin-on-skin.

"Those are the best memories for me, too. Thank you." When it was only Vee and me, I felt invincible. Her tenderness shone bright, and I wanted to lay under her light. I was even further convinced that outside the estate was the place to win her over. Her head leaned forward, and I licked my lips.

"No sex," she whispered. *Was that a hint of disappointment, or did I imagine it?* Her forehead pressed to my chest and my arms wrapped around her. I wanted to breathe her into me and hold her against me. I wanted everything from her, but I had ten more days.

+ + +

"Here." I handed her a silver balloon outside the art building after class on day three.

"What's this?"

"You need to find them all. One of them is not like the others and it marks where you are to stay and wait for me."

"What?" She laughed in that popping bubble way, signaling her pleasure and intrigue at my mysterious trail. "How will I know I've found them all?"

"You just will. I have faith in you, but hurry. The balloons will be harder to find in the dark." She skipped down the art department stairs, her flouncy dress kicking out behind her, and found a second balloon a short distance from the building, tied to a bench. The floating orbs spread further and further apart the more she crossed the campus. At one point, she turned back to see me following her at a distance. The rays of her smile found me, and my body warmed at her excitement.

"Twelve balloons? How fitting." She'd found the final destination and waited outside the observatory. A yellow balloon marked her last stop, and she stood under her bouquet.

"Better than a dozen flowers?"

"Maybe," she teased without conviction in her tone.

"We shouldn't be here," she giggled, as I pressed open the door. Originally locked, I had a special key for entrance, as well as assured privacy. She followed me, her balloons trailing behind her, ribbons tight in her fist.

"It's perfectly okay." The space wasn't large, and I led her to the center of the domed room. A canopy painted in celestial blue with fluffy white and graying clouds covered the curved canvas over our heads.

"It's beautiful," she whispered.

"Yes, it is." She caught me staring at her instead of the heavenly image overhead and I turned away slowly. "The sky is such a mystery. The stories told about the unknown over our heads began because we need explanations for the unknown. Humans want answers." I walked slowly around the large telescope in the center of the room. Veva followed me, still focusing upward. "But not everything in life can be explained with such detail as how the atmosphere formed and protects the earth. Some things are unexplainable." I stopped, resting an elbow on the edge of the base for the giant eye.

"Faith was born because some things are unknown, but we have to believe. No, we *want* to believe certain things exist. Faith in the weather watering a field. Faith in the sun coming back around every day. Faith in a religion. Faith in love." Her head lowered and her brows pinched. She stared at me.

"The unknown. We can't touch it, but we feel it." I tapped my chest.

"We feel it so strongly, it must be real. We trust ourselves that it exists because we feel it inside." My fist beat once. "I think therefore I am." I stepped toward her. "But it's more than that. I feel therefore I exist. Without feeling or emotion, I'm dead. And the things I feel for you, my beautiful girl, prove to me, I'm very much alive."

My face was in front of hers, and my forehead pressed down to meet hers. I closed my eyes, drinking in the ever-so-slight contact. My mouth watered so fiercely. *Just one sip*, I told myself, but it wasn't true. I'd tasted the sweetness of Veva—her very name meant life—and I needed more than one drink to sustain me. My thirst would never be quenched.

"Kiss me," she whispered.

"No sex," I teased.

"Just kiss me," she snipped without snark behind the words.

My mouth met hers with a touch so tender it would make a lesser man cry. Rain kissed, a sprinkle of drops, a misting brush of a breeze. My mouth moved slowly, methodically, whispering over her lips. *I love you*, I said with each delicate dip. *Stay with me*, I implored as I sucked on swollen skin that took its time to response to me. *I want to believe*, cried out from closed lips caressing over mine. No tongue crossed the line, only an admission of attraction contained in a kiss passionately slow but heating up fast. We pulled back in unison, as if we each read the other. Breaking off before the sparks flared, when the gentle candlelight was all we desired.

226

"I'd like to show you something." I crossed the room quickly and flipped several switches. The cylindrical room darkened slowly, and the dome opened overhead. The sky shifted to a navy blue and evening was on its way. I took her balloons and tied them to a railing on the side of the base. Directing her behind the telescope, I positioned it to point out various constellations.

"It's amazing," she sighed. "We try to lie out at night on the farm, just to stare up at the heavens. Then you get attacked by mosquitos." Her bubbly sound filled our private space, and she told me other stories about her farm, the river behind the property, and the brilliant night sky.

"There's something in particular I want to show you." I took control of the telescope, positioning it to the correct coordinates.

"Here." I pressed her in front of me, positioning my arms on either side of her. "Look for the turquoise dot. It should be straight ahead."

"Found it," she giggled and my jeans strained. I inhaled her fresh rain scent and then warned myself to settle. She observed the sky for a moment or two before pulling back from the lens. "It's a beautiful color."

"It is. And it's yours." Reaching into my back pocket, I pulled out a folded paper and handed it to her. She tilted her head, licked her lush lips, and hesitantly unfolded the page.

"I don't understand." Her eyes turned to liquid.

"Stars are suns, millions and billions of miles away. They are an energy source. You're my energy source. My life source. It's written in your name, Veva: life, and now, it's written in the heavens. You have a proper place in the sky."

"You bought me a star?"

I smiled slowly in answer.

"You're the only sun I want to orbit."

She giggled again, but a tear splashed down on the paper. Crushing it to her chest, she chuckled. "Thank you." Her arms enveloped my neck, embracing me. In response, my arms wrapped around her lower back. She *was* my sun and I would circle her for eternity.

VEVA

Day four began with miniature sunflowers in abundance. We hardly had room for them in our apartment, and I was tempted to give some away, but Persephone refused. The scattered arrangements reminded us both of home in the early fall and the bright, feathery pedals around a dark center personified Solis.

If flowers are better than balloons, I give you a dozen dozens, but I'd never take back the kiss.

My lips tingled at the reminder of his tender kiss. Soft and sweet, the heat grew quickly. Reading me, Solis pulled back before I burst into flame or imploded with the crackling energy between us. A gentle rainstorm of desire pattered on my lips when I thought of that kiss, but I was quickly longing for a summer storm.

+ + +

Day five included a late afternoon picnic high on top of a cliff overlooking the valley and the university.

"Why do you seem so down?" Solis asked as he handed me a grape. He lay on his side, legs stretched long, and crossed at the ankles. His lean body perched up by an elbow. He could have been modeling jeans or something, with his rock star good looks. My lips twisted in worry. I didn't know how to tell him what I'd overheard.

"I was at the dean's office this morning." Solis sat up straighter at the statement. "I heard him reprimanding you."

Dean Bonner had given Solis a stern warning.

Student/professor relations are strongly prohibited. I would hate to remove her from the school because of your clouded judgment in morals, the dean growled.

228

"He can't do anything." That's what Solis had said earlier in the day in response to the dean's threat. *You can't do this.*

I can do as I please. What is best for the university. I don't care if your father is a major contributor here. You do not run my university. I do.

"I don't want to lose my place at the university, but I don't want you to go, either." This brought a smile to Solis' lips and he turned to face me. The words were true. It had only been five days, but in truth, he had me within the first five seconds of seeing him. Meddling with my schedule or falling from the sky, Solis went above and beyond what he needed to do to prove we were meant to be. My body reminded me every time he was near how much he was the other half of me, and every time we separated, I didn't feel whole.

"I'm not going anywhere, and neither are you."

"He could fire you."

"He won't."

"He could kick me out."

"He won't do that either." Solis handed me another grape. "I don't want to hide us, but I know we need to be careful for your sake. Humans have different rules about teachers and students." He wiggled an eyebrow at me. "We'll just continue to keep a safe distance, like we have been." I didn't miss the sarcasm in his tone.

"How did he come to question you, anyway?"

"Office cleaners saw us leave the observatory. Told the dean, instead of asking security, who would have covered for us."

I nodded in understanding.

"I didn't know your father was a major contributor."

"Zeke appreciates education. He's fond of learning." Solis looked off in the distance, as if holding off more details. I waited in silence, but he offered no further information, and I wondered if my education was part of Zeke's bountiful generosity.

"Think I'll ever learn a gift?" This question had plagued me ever since I left him on the highway. I meant what I had said. I didn't think I'd develop a gift, or discover one, or whatever was supposed to happen.

My eyes remained focused on a grape rolling between my fingers. It was strange to discuss these things, stranger still to believe in the possibility of them. What if a gift never came to me? Would Solis lose interest in me?

"You have your clinicals now, right? I think you're discovering every day where your talent lies." He swallowed, and I felt his eyes on me, but I refused to look up. "I know what you did with Letty was difficult, but your patience and compassion with her proved you're on your path for discovery, Veva." The mention of Letty made my heart ache. I turned to look out at the valley.

"How is she doing?" I asked softly, frightened of the answer, feeling a pinch at the memory. He had slept with Letty. The thought hadn't fully left my mind. I told myself repeatedly it didn't matter. I understood what all those women saw in Solis, what all those women had received from him. I only wanted what they had shared, I argued with myself, but I was wrong. I wanted something more. I wanted something special for him, and me.

"Don't." The boom in his voice startled me. "Don't think it. Don't go there. It's over. It's history. You and I are the future, not the past, Veva. We are not our parents. We will not be them." His hand reached for mine, but deciding it wasn't enough, he bent to his knees and crawled toward me, towering over me as I fell back on the blanket. He balanced above me, blocking out the sunshine behind him. "No more thinking of past mistakes." His tone softened and he lowered his lips to brush mine. The kiss was tender, like the night at the observatory, and my body jolted with the renewed energy of a revved engine. Electric sparks and tender shocks pulsed throughout my being. I wanted him, and yet we'd made our pact. No sex. His mouth pulled back and my body lay wired. He was the lion, and I, a willing prey to his capture. *Take me*, my core screamed, but I let my head overrule my desire. I would stick to our deal. Kissing wasn't sex, though, and I let his mouth cover mine again.

+ + +

I had my first exams and I needed to study, so I avoided Solis as much as possible on day six. A sweet note filled with singular words found me later that night.

Twelve days, and twelve ways to say how I feel about you.
Love. Hope. Destiny.
Feisty. Complete. Free.
Sunshine. Peacock. Rain.
Forever. Calm. Storm.

I'd fallen asleep in the midst of my books after shoving my laptop to the side of my bed. A strange warmth surrounded me, and I wiggled into the comfort of heat. My body melted along the ridge and I slept peacefully, waking in the same cozy temperature as the night before. Slow to open my eyes to a new day, I squirmed in comfort. Suddenly, the familiar feel of arms wrapped over me and my back molded to a chest forced my lids to spring open.

"Solis," my sleep-laden voice croaked.

"Hmmm, Peacock, I was having the best dream." His hip gyrated forward to meet my behind, which moments before had rubbed against him.

"Solis, you promised." My grumbling tone came out seductive and deep. His responding moan at my ear only intensified the heat surrounding us.

"We sleep, that is all." But his hips jutted forward again, and my backside replied in kind. A sharp hand at my hip stilled me, and a pinch of my skin told me my little tease would lead to no joke in another second.

"We might have said no sex, but I could still please you. I want to please you."

Like a lazy kitten, I arched back, drawing my behind over the hard length of him once again. I played with sunshine, and it burned, but I wanted the heat on my skin. His thick hand slid forward at my invitation and pressed against my lower abdomen. Slipping into my pajama shorts, a long finger stroked over warm skin.

"Peacock." The growling tone of his booming voice sent a shiver down my spine. His entry was swift, and I jolted back, my body responding in a private dance over the length of the finger inside me. My ass rubbed over him and his mutters of encouragement increased.

"Fly for me." Lips lingered at my neck as our bodies synchronized. My thighs clamped and stiffened, holding in the scream as I clenched the edge of the bed, floating as if hang gliding over a valley. As I stilled, his pace continued behind me.

"Fuck, Peacock. The things you do to me." A final thrust and he swore again. "I haven't experienced something like that in a while." He chuckled, and I didn't know if he meant the dry-humping or the orgasm. Afraid to ask, afraid of his answer, I remained still with my back to him. His hand removed from my pajamas and he gently twisted me to face him. Honey colored eyes searched mine.

"I missed you." His warm breath at my ear sent shivers over my skin. "Let me love you." He tugged me closer against him and my body betrayed me. I gave into the comfort and snuggled against his chest, my own arms wrapping around him to press tighter into his embrace.

"I've missed you, too." The truth didn't hurt to speak. A gentle kiss to my shoulder let me know Solis liked what I said and my eyes drifted closed at the start of day seven.

+ + +

Each time Solis drew near me, I thought the electric attraction would spontaneously combust. On day eleven, he seemed edgy and out of sorts. He had been spending each night with me, and I couldn't figure his mood, but it matched the start of a gloomy day. "Let's stay in bed," he mumbled and my desire to act on such a thought propelled me from the sheets. One more day. We could hold out one more day, but the growing anticipation filled me with an achy need.

By day twelve, the romantic gestures and sweet kisses had kindled a fire so fierce, I shook with desire. I awoke to a gentle nudge at my shoulder.

"I have something to show you." I stared up at honey eyes glowing despite the darkness. "Get dressed." His whispered tone and the heavy blackness surrounding me hinted at the early hour.

"What time is it?"

"Maybe four. Hurry." He stepped back from the bed and his smile enticed me to rise. He chuckled and I reached for my hair.

"If you're going to laugh at me, I'll just go back to sleep." I flung myself back to the pillows, but two columns of muscle caged me in. Narrowed eyes peered down at me.

"You are the most beautiful thing I've ever seen. Peacock hair and all." He chuckled again and I spun away from him. The soft caress of a peacock plume brushed over my cheek but I swatted it away. Solis had taken me back to the Peacock Preserve on another day of his countdown. Today, we were out of days. The thought made me spin. The motion surprised him.

"It's day twelve." My throat thickened at the thought.

"It's day twelve." His lips crooked up on one side. "Now get up." The peacock feather drifted over my lips to my neck and dipped down to my chest. My heart leapt at the possibilities of that plume rubbing all over me and what day thirteen might bring. Twelve days of teasing had been torture. My reassurance of his commitment would come from consummating ourselves to one another again. And again. And again.

I sat up at the thought, and he stepped back so I could exit the bed. Dressed in minutes, he guided me out the door to his sporty Camaro and we sped through the darkness to the same cliff where we shared our picnic. Solis sat behind me, holding a blanket wrapped around us as we watched in silence the dawning of a new day. The sun rose with a rich buttercream, spreading out to a bright yellow and cresting the hill in a deep circle of orange. The flaming orb lifted slowly, gracing the world with subtle rays before bursting force in blinding brightness. The experience filled me with hope and a renewed desire for Solis. This wasn't the lazy heat of a setting sun, but the explosive passion of a future. I nestled into Solis as he kissed my neck.

"I have something for you. A request." He removed the blanket holding us hostage and retrieved a folded paper from his jeans. "Read this at noon today. Not a moment before. Promise me." Additional kisses followed the request and with his lips on my eager skin, there was nothing I'd deny him. The time was roughly 6 a.m., though, and noon seemed a lifetime away.

+ + +

As my phone alarm signaled twelve-noon, I ripped open the hand-painted envelope, breaking the seal of a sun caught between setting and rising. It all depended on perspective.

> *Veva, I've given you twelve days, but I'm hopeful thirteen will be the lucky one. Let's begin our life at the stroke of twelve. If you wish to start our future, come to me at midnight, and let us embark on day thirteen together.*

My heart raced with anticipation. Time would not pass fast enough. I clutched the envelope and note to my chest and sent out a silent response. *I will follow you.*

I had no concentration for classes, but hope sprang at the thought of seeing Solis before midnight in our Mythology course. The material fascinated me, as I learned the ins-and-outs of relationships, once foreign and removed from me, now relevant and important to all I wanted to know about Solis. Sitting with a thud in my seat, a large smile crossed my face as I eagerly awaited Solis' arrival near the raised lectern. Instead another man, portly and balding, crossed the stage.

"Good afternoon. I'm Professor Cartwright, the original professor for this course and I've returned from my unforeseeable illness. I appreciate Professor Cronus holding down the fort, or as the Greeks said, the forum. As Professor Cronus left in a rather rushed state, let's have a brief review of all that's been covered to date, shall we?"

I sat up straighter at his words, dread setting in and weighing my body to the auditorium seat. I chewed on my pen, confused at what to think.

Had Solis been fired after all?

Did he really leave?

Has he left me behind?

Panic set in at warp speed. I took a deep breath to calm my racing heart as Persephone sat next to me with a huff.

"I'm so glad I found you." Short of breath, she swallowed hard and brushed back wayward hairs from her forehead.

"What's the matter?"

"Solis called me. He had to leave."

"What's wrong?" My harsh whisper carried, filled with frustration and disbelief that Solis hadn't contacted me himself.

"He tried to call you, but you weren't answering."

"He didn't call." I reached into my bag, scrambling to retrieve my phone. Slowly fumbling with each inconsequential item, I quickly removed the larger items: wallet, pencil bag, sunglasses. No phone.

"I…" I nearly stuck my head in my bag, searching for an item not present. I had no idea where I'd left my phone. I had it before noon, but after checking it nearly every five minutes for an hour, I…I couldn't remember what I did with it so it wouldn't distract me from counting down the hours.

"He had to return to the estate. He said he left you a letter. He hoped you'd understand. He'd understood that his departure made the plans a bit impossible."

"He hoped I'd understand what?"

"He didn't say, just said he had to go."

elda lore

His lack of explanation didn't sit well with me. The abrupt departure without a message sent a shiver of uncertainty through me. I sat back with a soft thump against my auditorium seat.

I would not follow him, I told myself. *I would not go anywhere without an explanation.* But there was no conviction in my self-argument.

"Well, if he couldn't tell you, I doubt he told me in a message. I'm not chasing after him," I huffed with no steam behind me. I didn't doubt he had a reason to return home. I doubted me. Maybe he changed his mind. Maybe he didn't want me. Maybe he realized he couldn't be with me after all.

Persephone's blue eyes softened.

"It's not chasing, Veva. It's following. It's hoping. If I could follow Hades, I'd go in a heartbeat." She smiled sadly. "I'd go in the tick of a second." Her eyes fell to her knees and she picked at lint not present on her jeans.

"That's different, Pea. You and Hades love one another."

"You can't convince me Solis doesn't love you. I won't believe any argument you try to use on me, and it's not just because I'm used to your form of arguing. He fell from the sky. He gave you a star. I saw him worship you. And I saw you shine in his light."

"I…" I didn't know how to respond. *Was she right? Did I shine in his presence?* I did love Solis, wholeheartedly. "I don't have some secret way to argue," I snapped, harsher than I intended and giving confirmation to her comment. I also tried to divert the conversation. Thoughts of Solis loving me, but leaving me, brought liquid to my eyes.

"You do. You like to argue, especially with Solis. It works for the two of you. Storm and sunshine." She could have no idea what her comparison meant to me. To us. It was the very one we used on each another. I stormed around him; he orbited around me. Either way, the concepts were opposite and attracting. Opposition. Two halves making a whole.

By ten o'clock that night, I'd argued myself into my car and hit Highway 99 with the hopes my speed would get me to Solis in time. The

236

cairn on my desk in my apartment sent me a message: thirteen stones. The future awaited. I didn't want to be late.

SOLIS

Midnight drew near and I hadn't been able to reach Veva. My heart filled with trepidation. *What must she think? What did she fear?* I didn't even know if Persephone found Veva, if she knew I couldn't meet her at midnight. Cell phones didn't work on the estate in the typical fashion. Once I crossed into the groves, the phone was useless to me, but I had to get to Heph.

The news of a fight between Heph and War brought out an all-call. Those near enough were forced to return home. I had remained too close, but I wanted to be around Veva. Playing the role of professor at some small valley campus meant nothing to me other than a means to an end: winning back Vee. We were almost there. Day twelve. Midnight. I'd seen it in her eyes even before this day began. She would return to me, and I would follow her. I would remain at the campus and continue the charade until she could discover her talent or graduate with her degree. Whichever came first. Whichever she wanted. As long as I was with her, nothing else mattered to me.

The call home beyond my control, the magnetic cry too fierce to ignore, I returned in fear for my brother. I adored Heph and the added complication of him being Veva's brother endeared him more.

"Are you all right?" I asked, pacing the floor of his room once again. The deep rich blues and cloudy grays sat in contrast to my burly brother. His forehead bled again. Ice still wrapped over his knuckles. His lip swelled below the growing scruff on his face.

"I'm fine." Heph's lie wasn't disguised in his tone.

"How can you be fine? The woman of your dreams just got caught humping another man!" I blurted, my hand slapping down on my thigh. My other hand fisting, twitching to hurt someone on his behalf.

"Thank you. I had forgotten the image of my fiancée's ass in the air and someone pummeling her from behind."

"Not someone," I screeched still enraged and insensitive. "War, that bastard."

Heph's head hung and his brow pinched, forcing a new stream of blood to seep from the gash at his head.

"I'm sorry," I muttered, crossing to his bathroom and returning with a fresh, wet washcloth. He winced as I touched his head. Feeling uncomfortable playing nursemaid to him, I set the cloth on the table beside him.

"I don't think it was meant to be." Heph's gruff tone rasped and shook at the statement. I couldn't continue my tirade. No one thought it was meant to be. Lovie, the beautiful creature of Aphrodite's birth, couldn't possibly love the large oaf of a man like Heph. Not because she was too beautiful, or he was too innocent, but because she was too flirtatious and carefree, while he was reserved, cautious and tender. Heph deserved better than a beauty queen obsessed with another man, which was also Lovie's position. War had her under his mischievous spell. The military hero, he knew how to woo women, and Lovie had been no different. Oil and water those two, and yet who knew better than me that opposites attracted.

"Did you get in touch with her?" Heph broke my thoughts, as if reading my mind filled with Veva.

"I can't reach her from here." My pacing trail returned as I strutted to the window and returned to the door. Like a caged lion, I forged a path over the dark carpet, growing agitated with each about-face.

"I'm sorry you had to return."

I stopped.

"Don't be sorry, Heph. It couldn't be helped." After discovering his fiancé in the compromising position, Heph lost control of his usually reined-in temper. A fight ensued, leaving both sides battered and bruised, but aching more in heart than body. Lovie stormed off in embarrassment. War had to be removed by Zeke. Heph was left in my charge. I couldn't leave him.

"This is your duty," Zeke warned me. I wanted to remind him I wasn't an official Olympian. I didn't sit on some invisible throne like his combination of siblings, friends, and offspring. Not a member of the chosen dozen, I stood outside the circle as number thirteen. The prophesied thirteenth. The one Zeke wished hadn't been born, hadn't been found, and hadn't grown strong. After midnight, the number thirteen would be my lucky number, but not until Veva was in my arms and my bed, proclaiming her love to me. Until that moment, I feared day thirteen, as I feared our lack of communication would keep us apart. My hand shook as it swiped into my hair. My fingers slid to the back of my neck and held my hand there.

"What are you going to do?" I asked Heph, in hopes of distracting myself.

"Obviously, the engagement is off." I didn't disagree with the harshness in his tone. I wished to feel relief for him, but instead my heart pinched. It seemed at any moment I might feel the ache of loss like my large friend. He shook his head, and his eyes drifted shut briefly.

"I guess I'll head to Hestia's as I planned. I could use a break from this estate."

Hestia was the third sister in the small harem of Zeke's obsession with the daughters of Titus. The oldest daughter by a number of years, she lived a reclusive life in the upper northwest, deep in the woods, where she hid secrets and helped protect horrors. Heph found comfort there, as Hestia was the only mother figure he'd known. Her experience with fire aided Heph in teaching himself to craft and sculpt, using flames as the medium to mold his tools and art.

I had no words to respond to his need for escape. I agreed wholeheartedly. A knock came at the door.

"I'm sorry to interrupt." My heart dropped at the presence of Callie, a friend of Mel's and a former one-night stand. Speaking of harems, my blood rain cold, knowing the estate thrived on temptation and I no longer wished to participate. I was better around Veva, and Veva was better off of the estate, without the reminder of the women of my past.

"Hello, Callie." Just saying her name caused a deep flush to the rosy skin of the larger girl. I had nothing against any shape or size of a woman. My own Veva rocked curves, but Callie was not my type. Our union had

240

been one of many mistakes I'd made in the past that I wished to erase from memory. Her smile deepened.

"I just thought you'd want to know…" She let herself in the partially opened door and helped herself to closing it behind her. Her back fell against it, her hands braced behind her rear as if holding the door shut. "I thought you'd like to know a car was discovered off the property."

I spun away from her. Cars were occasionally found outside the grove: broken down, flat tire, out of gas. The humans found their own assistance and their issues did not concern us. I faced Heph and rolled my eyes. His dark circles remained focused on the woman at his door.

"Callie," he muttered under his breath as way of greeting. The strangled tone forced me to look from the fallen face of my brother to the deepening flush of Callie. *What the…?*

"What do you need, Callie?" The innuendo was triple-fold. I wanted to know what the car had to do with us, what she wanted being in Heph's room, and if she needed some personal relief, perhaps she arrived right in time to help my brother forget his wayward fiancée.

"I…" She blinked, as if she'd forgotten I was in the room. Her gaze broke away from the head-hung Heph, and she twisted her cheek away from him, as if he struck her. Facing the wall briefly, Callie spoke with tight lips.

"I thought you might want to know whose car was found and where."

I let out an exasperated sigh, brushing fingers through my wayward hair again. I didn't have time for the games of this girl.

"Heph." The plea in her voice offered a second attempt to gain his attention. It was his turn to face away from her. The avoidance of her proved my brother may have been a bit unfaithful himself, or at least giving promise to another girl before he was betrothed to Lovie.

"Okay, I'll bite. Whose car and where?" My exasperated sigh, I hoped, would remind them both of my presence and get me out of their subtle lover's quarrel.

Her eyes snapped to mine.

"The south entrance."

I nodded, not understanding. It wasn't a common place to enter the estate. Only special invites entered…I stopped all movement. I don't think I even drew a breath.

"The car was a black Jetta," Callie added.

"Veva." I gasped for air, choking deep in my lungs, with hope.

"It was found running. The driver door open. No driver present."

And the oxygen in the universe washed out of me. A violent roar escaped.

VEVA

Without my phone, I navigated by ancient map, a rather huge mistake. I couldn't see anything as I climbed the mountain I knew housed Olympic Oil. My fear was that I wouldn't find the house itself. Confirmation came as the altitude rose and a heavy cloud cover fell. The fog grew thicker and thicker, and under darkness of night, my headlights reflected back at me. Twice I'd thought I'd found the two-tire trail Persephone and I witnessed in the rearview mirror, to find the home or barn at the end of the drive wasn't my destination.

I slowed the car as the hazardous conditions didn't allow more than five miles per hour. In my snail-crawl pace, I found a hint of another trail. Praying third time was the charm, I turned the car onto the narrow pile of earth in the ditch and faced a plethora of olive trees. Hopeful that some mysterious gate of recognition would open and allow me entrance, I pulled forward to be stopped suddenly as if I'd hit an invisible wall. I could see the grove in front of me under the narrow stream of headlights, but my car could not go forward. Setting the gear into reverse, I pulled back and swung out into the street, prepared to push forward again with greater force. Peeking over the back of the driver seat, I slammed on the brakes.

Directly behind my trunk stood a cow.

What the…? I took a deep inhale, as it quickly occurred to me there had been no impact. I hadn't hit the creature, which seemed to stare at me through the rear window. I twisted in the seat, prepping to accelerate, when something else caught my eye in the rearview mirror again. I exhaled the breath I'd been holding and blinked twice. A girl with dark hair and large eyes stood in the middle of the road, dressed in an ankle-length dress of white. Looking ghostly and Grecian, she didn't move, and my hands shook on the steering wheel.

I'm dead, I argued with myself. I hit the cow, didn't even feel it, and I've passed into the afterworld.

Hades? I called out in my head, then shook it as hysterical giggles rippled through me.

I've lost my mind. Slamming the gear into park, I heaved open the door and stepped into the cool, fall mountain air.

"I could have killed you," I yelled, uncertain if it was the mirage of a cow or her I could have hurt. The thought gave me pause. Did I imagine the cow? My head twisted slowly left to right before I took another hesitant step toward this beautiful creature.

"Ionia?" She hadn't spoken but she smiled at my recognition of the girl in silent tears on that first day in the pool house. The girl Solis slept with, and the other girls mocked. She was stunning, with her raven hair and dark eyes. Her body was lithe and she stood picturesque. Artists would kill to paint her. My heart dropped at the thought. Solis might have already created art from her body. With her body.

"You've returned for him, haven't you?" Her melodic voice broke my thoughts as if she could read them.

"I…" I didn't know what to say. I was here for him, but was I too late? And how could I find him if I couldn't get past the olive grove? "I was trying. But it seems I'm not invited." My head hung. Persephone and I had been invited to Olympic Oil this summer and that's how we entered the first time. Each other time we came or went from the estate we were escorted by Solis or another member of the plantation. How silly I was to think I could come here, unannounced, uninvited, and proclaim myself to Solis.

"She'll never let you pass." A nod in the direction of the tire trail forced me to look at the dark grove. A shimmery cloud moved in opposition to the fog surrounding it. The wobbling movement hinted at something other than an olive tree behind the heavy shadow.

"Who?" I asked, still focused on the mirage of fog before me.

"Mel. She knew you'd follow him. He has that appeal, attraction. Once you feel his warmth, you crave more of the heat."

I grimaced at the comparison and hint of experience so many had found in Solis.

"She forced the protection. She's keeping you out."

"Is there no way in?" The plea in my voice surprised me. "He'll think I didn't show. He'll think I didn't follow him." The thought saddened me, even more than I realized. Liquid filled my eyes and I blinked to clear the haze.

"Tell me you love him."

I didn't want to tell this girl before I told Solis, but I blurted my affirmation. "I do."

A sad smile graced her porcelain face. "The first moment he looked at you, I knew you were the one he'd waited for. The one that kept him hesitant. The one that allowed him to play but not commit. Only you," she smiled larger, without pleasure, but imposing no fear. "Only you could make him shine the way he deserved." She held out a hand, but I didn't trust taking the offer.

"I can take you to him."

"How? Why?"

"Because I saw you in that mirror. I saw me in that mirror. The image of someone who wanted to hate him, but couldn't. The image of someone afraid to love him, but could. You would give to him what he deserved." A strangeness came over me as I reached out for her hand. I didn't trust the process, but I needed to have faith in her. Faith that she would guide me to him. Time cut closer to midnight and I didn't want to be late.

"You can lift the cloud."

"I can?"

"Think of it. Imagine it."

I closed my eyes. My teeth clenched and I imagined my hands against the hazy shadow. I felt the force of pressing forward, exerting the effort to push away a seemingly airy presence that appeared solid and unmovable. Sweat dripped off my temple. It wasn't working, and I broke the concentration. The process seemed silly to me.

"Veva, try lifting it with your mind. Don't strain. This isn't physical. Relax. Concentrate. Think of something pleasant and warm that could burn away a cloud." I hadn't realized I'd been tightly squeezing the hand of Ionia. Releasing her delicate fingers, I exhaled, letting my shoulders fall. I closed my eyes again, imagining heat, warmth, and sunshine. I envisioned the sun rising, pressing the cloud upward, breaking it into water crystals, dissolving it into air like particles of sparkling dust. Thoughts of the sun drew images of Solis, and I pictured him walking out of the sunshine, rays of light radiating from behind him as he brushed through the cloud, separating the fog, expelling it with his brightness.

When I opened my eyes, the winding drive to the estate lay before me. Up on a hill, twinkling lights lit the way to the house. I was afraid to look back, afraid the welcoming home would disappear. It would be faster to drive the distance. Returning to my car was a thought, but I feared I'd be outside the barrier, if I crossed into the street. I turned to my side and found Ionia missing.

"Ionia," I called, spinning left then right. The girl had disappeared. Without hesitation, I glanced behind me. My car remained running in the road, but an awareness that I stood within something unknown, something protected, warned me not to risk retrieving my Jetta. My final trek to Solis would have to be on foot. Without a phone, I didn't know the time, and I could only pray I wasn't too late as I began the hike up the darkened path ahead.

SOLIS

"Where is she?" I barked, staring into the empty vehicle. The driver door stood open and the lights within the car projected into the vacant space. Headlights beamed forward, but there was no trace of Veva. I shook with rage, and a clap of thunder smacked the sky.

"If anything has happened to her, I'll rock the heavens," I warned as two minions of my father circled the vehicle. Heph paced a few feet forward, breaking the stream of the headlights.

"I don't see footprints. It's like she vanished."

My heart dropped like a leaden weight to the earth. Other organs pummeled downward as well, including my lungs, which could not contract enough air. My skin prickled with dread.

"She couldn't have vanished. Search for her." I snapped the command and a crack of lightning lit the sky from within the olive grove. I walked behind the car after closing the driver door. Twirling the keys in my hand, I spoke to Veva in my head.

Where did you fly off to, Peacock? Yet another thought came to me. *Why did you follow me here, love?* Snorting and huffing, Thunder stood centurion near the open gate. The entrance hadn't been used since Persephone and Veva's exit for school a few weeks prior. How she found it under the protective ward of Zeke was beyond me, but my girl was observant. I could only hope she was resourceful.

Rain broke the heavens as I mounted Thunder, urging him up the drive. Focused on reaching the main house, I didn't notice the pelts of cold rain jabbing at me like small daggers. Fire fueled my blood and steam rose off exposed skin as each crystal of ice stabbed my heated skin. A sudden crackle of lightning rippled through the sky, and I recognized the energy. Zeke had forced this storm. Although it matched my temper, Olympic Oils stirred with more than just my battle.

VEVA

My scream strangled under the firm hold of a hand at my mouth. Dragged by my hair, I collapsed into the mud, scrambling under my feet for solid earth. My hand clasped a small wrist whose fingers were woven tightly in the tendrils firmly secured on my scalp. Although the palm covering my lips held tight, the distinctly feminine scent alerted me to my captor.

Mel.

My head screamed for her to release me, but my smothered protests were in vain. The darkness of night and the imposing storm hid any effort for sight or sound.

"Give in, you heavy cow," she scolded behind me.

It was only hair, I decided in that moment, and spun under the hold. My head rammed into her lower stomach with force, but tears filled my own eyes at the pain of tearing skin at my scalp. The battering of my head against her caused her to release me, and I stood to face a bent-over Mel, soaked through like the drowning rat she was. My palm made contact with her cheek, and the resounding echo of thunder heightened the intensity of the moment. She stood to face me.

"How dare you?" she screeched, cupping her cheek.

"How dare you?" I snarled in return. "Will you stop at nothing to get what you can't ever have?"

"He loved me." Her rage matched the torrential rain, and the wind was picking up its rabid pace.

"He loves me!" My fiery tone soared into the air, steam following the heavy exhale of my voice.

"You aren't one of us."

"I never want to be. I only want to be me, and that seems good enough for him."

Never had I felt so defensive of myself. Never had I felt empowered that my words rang true. It could all be a lie, but I believed in what I thrust at her in my anger. Solis wanted me, and I wanted him.

248

"You have his father," I added, clarifying her status with Zeke.

"He'll never be the same as the son."

I could imagine this was true. Solis was a Greek god in stature compared to the toned, but aged, body of his father. Solis also didn't thrive on power like Zeke, nor did he procreate excessively to prove his own worth. Solis would never be his father. We would never be our parents, as he promised me.

I motioned to step around her, but she blocked my path. Stepping right, she stopped me again. The only way around Mel appeared to be through her. The fiery energy that hadn't crawled under my skin in weeks prickled and crept through me, fueling my anger. I'd never been a violent person, despite my angry disposition, but Mel fueled my wrath.

"Veva." A thunderous sound stalled my balled fist from lashing out at my target.

"Zeke?" Mel muttered, in a faltering voice.

"We've been searching everywhere for you. What are you doing in the rain?" His voice came behind me, but his visual of Mel could not be obstructed. "Mel?"

Her face froze for a moment before curling into the falsest smile I'd ever seen. Her eyes hollowed, but her teeth bared as her lips spread, and she answered through clenched teeth.

"I was escorting Veva to the house."

The silence following Mel's lie was more deafening than the claps of thunder crashing in the sky. A bolt of lightning struck feet from our sides, and my scream pierced the surrounding trees, drowned out by the brightness of the energy crackling upward.

"Mel, I think we need to get both of you to the house." A large arm came around my waist, providing protection, while a thick hand reached forward for Mel's. Mel swiped at the offering.

"You always choose her side." Mel's tone clawed through the air. A menacing scraping sound lingered, sending a wisp of breath to float in the cold air.

"I'm not taking any side. I just want to get my girls inside."

"I'm not…" I started, but Mel interrupted me. "She's not your girl. She's *his*." The venom in her tone grew bitter. Poison filled the air around us.

"I meant it figuratively. I protect my own."

"You only protect her. Her and her silly blonde friend." Mel mocked.

"I think we need to get inside. Warm you up, and we can chat."

"I don't want to chat. I'm tired of your talk. You promised me things. You told me you'd show me. You'd give your power to me." Mel stomped her foot like an errant child.

"Mel, I've already told you, I can't share with you."

"Solis did."

Collectively, my breath and Zeke's hitched. My mind raced instantly with questions. Had Solis shown Mel his back? Had he told her what he could do? Cursing my ignorance, I scolded myself: *of course he had. He slept with her, too.* I weakened under Zeke's hold. My knees gave out a little and I crumbled, but his tight embrace held me upward.

"And when exactly did my son show off his strength to you?"

"At the Olympiad. He tossed the bolt. Nothing happened to me."

I recalled watching in horror and wonder as Solis tore the bolt from his back, tossed it through the air with expertise, and then stalked toward me like he planned to own every inch of me. He jostled me away from his brother, Leos, with less finesse, and we ended up in the shower by the pool house. I nearly smiled at the memory.

"My son is different. His power is still growing. If I share what I have with you, it will destroy you. I care too much about you to see that happen."

"Care about me? You care about me? How pathetic a response! How funny, when in bed, you *love* me."

I did not want to hear this, I screamed in my head. Another strike of lightning inched closer to where we stood, protected only by a small line of cypress evergreens.

"Maybe we could take this inside?" I shouted over the rain and the threat of more thunder. The rumbles raced within seconds of each other.

"Maybe you should shut up," Mel snapped, glaring at me.

"Maybe you should disappear." A booming familiar voice spoke, and my heart leapt, but a bolt of lightning struck so close it cracked the earth between Mel and me. Clumps of dirt sprang upward as the light chased the current to the sky. Instantly, I closed my eyes and turned into Zeke. The heat from the bolt toasted my skin, sizzling me dry from the cold, pelting rain. Within seconds, the light passed, the warmth seeped away, and I shook uncontrollably. Mel was gone, and in her place stood Solis.

SOLIS

Seeing Veva curled into my father nearly crushed me, but the insults Mel flung at Veva broke me. I'd had enough of her whining, her power climbing, and her conniving ways. Exposing Mel to my lightning bolt was dangerous for Veva. If she didn't possess a trace of goddess in her, the bolt could blind her, or disintegrate her with its energy. How I knew it wouldn't happen was when she touched me in the shower by the pool house. The current lingered, and Veva's loving kisses and tender massage would have drawn sparks of residual energy to her, if she didn't have a history buried inside her, waiting to be released, waiting to be discovered, waiting to be exposed, by me.

"Veva?" My tone pleaded with her to look at me. Her head buried into my father's side concerned me. Perhaps the bolt had been too much, too close. Had I blinded her, in my anger?

Slowly, her head rose, and she drew back from Zeke. He muttered something to her and kissed her forehead. Releasing his arm from around her waist, she spun to face me. She blinked repeatedly, as if ridding the light from her eyes.

"Solis?" Her voice choked. Her body trembled. I didn't think she'd make the distance across the grass to me. I stepped forward, and she took a step toward me at the same time. With another step, she leapt for me, and I caught her around the waist, her face buried in my neck as her legs wrapped around my hips. Her quaking body shook against mine.

"Shh, Veva. I've got you. I've always got you." My hands caressed up and down her back for a moment.

"I'm late," she muttered into my neck.

"You're here." I kissed her hair. "And that's all that matters."

Her legs dropped, and I scooped her up, cradling her against my chest. Her cheek hadn't left my neck.

"Tell me you're real," she mumbled before kissing me under my ear. "Tell me I'm not imagining everything."

252

"I have no idea what you've seen, but I'm very real. You're really in my arms, and I'm about to prove how real the rest of me is." I didn't release her as I strutted through the main foyer, over the tiled sun, and straight out the backdoor. I circled the pool and broke a new path to my cottage. I didn't stop to set her down but walked us into the shower. Still holding her against me, I fumbled with the dials, releasing a new rain shower, this one warm and inviting.

Placing her feet on the tile floor, her body shook as the heated spray covered her clothed body.

"We need to get you out of these cold clothes."

She nodded numbly, her teeth chattering. I worried she'd suffered shock like she had before. She would unravel before me, and run for the hills, cursing her return. Which reminded me that Veva had found her way here.

"How did you get here?"

"Photographic memory," she stuttered as the chill seeped out of her and the steam rose around us. I worked with shaky fingers, unbuttoning her transparent blouse. The tremble came from nerves. I'd already told myself I'd do nothing with her, but warm her, hold her, but as her skin pinked and her shivers subsided, a new energy sputtered to life between us.

"Why were you here?"

"You were here," her voice trembled, and I slipped the wet shirt over her head. Her arms crossed instinctively, attempting to cover her saturated bra, but my fingers at her wrist lowered her shield. I'd already seen what peeked through the wet material. I'd already tasted the heat of her skin and the spark of those nipples. My dick leapt to life. My heart thudded in my chest.

"You followed me?" My voice shook, the words falling low, rasping from my lips.

"I followed you. Will you follow me?"

"Wherever you go, Veva. I will follow you."

"Can you follow my lips?" A tiny smile curled her mouth. She pecked at my chest. Then I bent at the knees and kissed over her racing heart. My fingers fumbled with the button at her waist.

Her mouth covered my right nipple, and she sucked at it, lingering to ripen the peak.

I bent forward at the waist to meet her right nipple and nip at the point protruding through the wet, silky material.

"You have too much clothing on for me to follow you properly."

"Take it off of me." Her gentle command snapped tenderly, and I followed her demand. Slipping the wet covering over her, my breath caught at the sight.

"Veva," I growled. "You're so stunning." I corrected my attempt to follow her lead and sucked at her right breast. The nipple drew tight in my warm mouth, and my tongue flicked over the hardened nub. My fingers multitasked as they worked the zipper of her jeans. I pulled back, awaiting another command.

She dropped to her knees and slipped down my jeans in one motion. She didn't even respond to the lack of underwear, but licked at the tip of my length. Her mouth opened, and drew me in, and my knees nearly buckled. My hands reached for the tile wall, bracing me as her lips assaulted me in the most heavenly way. I bucked as she took me deep. Within moments, I was too close. While I'd dreamed of this type of release from her, I had other plans first. I lifted her to stand.

"I wasn't finished," she snarled, no sting to her words.

"I'm not either." Falling to my own knees, I removed her jeans and underwear in one swift tug. She stepped out of the heavy, wet denim and stood before me in all her glory.

"I love you, Veva." I praised her. Without waiting for a response, I worshipped her, feasting at her core. Her back fell against the tile as I knelt at my favorite altar and offered up tongue and lips and fingers.

"Solis, I'm going to fall." Her breath caught as her hips rocked subtly with my homage.

"Never," I muttered. I'd never let her fall, only fly. The intensity of that promise increased, and she sang out my name in response to my offering.

The shower stall wasn't enough. I needed more of her. Turning off the warm spray, I wrapped her in a lush towel and walked her out of the small bathroom.

"You have a bed?" She hadn't seen the new addition to the cottage when I carried her in.

"Space for a queen," I said, sweeping my hand forward. The queen-sized, four poster bed was dressed in silvery grays with dashes of bright orange, fluorescent yellow and my favorite shades of blue in the dozens of pillows at the headboard.

"Is that my painting?" Behind the bed, the original image created by Veva, left behind when she departed, hung as a backdrop to the new arrangement. I continued to draw her closer to the new structure, lifting her to crawl to the center of our haven. Her hand swiped over the silky covering.

"It's like being in a cloud." Gauzy material in a silvery tone draped like a canopy and hung around the four posts, giving the corners an airy feeling and the enclosure some privacy.

"I told you. I want to make love to you in the sky. This will have to be close enough." My mouth came to hers, reestablishing the hours lost since I'd seen her.

"It's officially day thirteen," Veva said, breaking away from me.

"My lucky number," I chuckled before taking those peachy lips again.

"I'm sorry, again, that I was late." She spoke between kisses. "There was a cloud. And a cow. And…"

"A cow?" I chuckled.

"It's a long story. I can tell it to you later?" Her lids lowered, but her lips curled. My mouth found hers one final time. Later was good for me. In fact, our time was as infinite as the stars in heaven. A thousand days. A thousand years, as long as she loved me. We picked up where we left off in the shower. Hands roamed. Pleasures discovered, but I wasn't complete until I entered her and we were one.

"I love you, Sunshine," she purred, as we moved, dancing the slow rhythm of rolling clouds over a summer sky.

"I love you." My life was complete, as now I had one bed, one roof, and one woman under me, who claimed my destiny.

Epilogue

Solis stood behind me on the plateau as we overlooked another spectacular sunset. The days grew shorter as August turned to September. He meant what he promised, he followed me. The living arrangement would have been awkward had Persephone not agreed to let Solis move us to a house near campus. I didn't want to live another day without him, but I couldn't leave Pea. Not yet. Her room was on the first floor, giving us the privacy of the second.

In the quiet of the cool evening air, I recalled a few nights prior when Solis removed the rock necklace from me and slipped it over his head instead.

"Hey," I snapped. Naked and poised between my thighs, the heart shaped stone lay against his sculpted tan chest. I imagined he could feel the lingering warmth, radiating from me, in the heat of the rock against his skin. Covering it with his palm, he leaned forward to kiss me. The pendant fell between my breasts as his lips lingered on mine. The stone tickled, and I giggled into his mouth. Drawing back a short distance, he reached for the heart and began to draw over me, delicately tracing swirls over my skin. He started on the flat of my chest and worked up the range of my breasts, dipping into the valley between and continuing his manuscript over me. He brushed down to my waist, then rushed up to my throat.

"You know I love your neck." He bent to kiss me there.

"You love all of me," I teased.

"That I do," he whispered, letting the rock dangle from his neck as he pressed upward and slipped into me. My breath hitched as it always did, stealing the oxygen from me as he entered me. I didn't need it where he'd take me: higher and higher until I flew. Solis loved to race, and

some nights we fought a battle until the end, but that night, we floated, soaring together.

"Do you remember the other night?" His mouth sucked at my exposed neck as he broke into my very same thought.

"Yes."

"Did you like my painting?"

Confusion hit me. Maybe we weren't thinking of the same night.

"The one I drew on you." He reached forward and removed the leather strap inside my shirt, dragging the heavy rock to tease up my skin before releasing from the neck of my T-shirt. The motion confirmed his thought was the same as me.

"I wasn't exactly clear what you drew. I was distracted by the naked artist doing the painting," I teased. He nipped at my neck again, and I shivered with pleasure, rubbing my hand over the arm wrapped around me. Heat radiated from his tanned skin despite the growing chill.

"I sketched out stormy clouds and steamy sunsets. A lightning bolt down the center to claim you as mine." His voice deepened, and my head tilted so I could see him behind me. We'd both wrestled with doubts, at first. Solis didn't know what he'd do in the human world, but Zeke allowed him to continue learning the mechanics of a multi-million-dollar olive oil company. I struggled to face each one of Solis' past lovers, but his continual reassurance that the future held only me helped.

"I also asked you a question in my scrolling." His throat rolled as he swallowed and I watched him toy with the rock in his hand.

"Really, what was that?" His eyes shifted to mine, that honey color melting to caramel before me.

"I wondered if you'd wear another rock from me." He gave a little tug on the pendant, giving the strap a gentle pull on my neck. His curling lips teased me.

"If you found me another heart shaped rock, I'll have Heph make me more jewelry."

Solis nodded and I worried that thoughts of our brother would take over the moment. Heph had left for Hestia's, as he said, shortly after the broken engagement. I didn't want to ruin the sunset with our mutual concern for the tender spirit of our gentle giant.

"Well…oh, look."

In a move that replicated the same one he used the first time he took me rock climbing, he dipped us toward the gravelly covering, his arm wrapped around my waist, holding me to him, so I wouldn't fall as he promised me. Standing upright almost as quickly as we bent to the side, Solis' hand cupped something inside. Releasing my waist, he used his free hand to open my palm, supporting mine with his.

"Would you wear this rock from me?"

Thick fingers placed a gold ring in the center of my hand, graced with a heart-shaped diamond.

"Solis?" My voice squeaked, tender and uncertain what he was asking me.

"Would you wear this rock from me?" He spun me to face him, but my eyes hadn't left the gem sparkling up at me, reflecting the light from the setting sun. On further inspection, I noticed the diamond reflected hues of gold and pale yellow. A smaller set of silvery diamonds outlined the large center.

"It's a yellow diamond, rarer than rare, and rivaled only by the sun." His thick finger swirled over the jewel as he explained. "The outside are diamond chips, giving off that cast of silvery gray. Sunshine in a cloudy day." His voice lowered as he explained and my eyes finally fluttered up to his.

"Veva, I don't want to spend another gray day without you. It won't always be sunshine, but I promise not to rain every day. I promise more steamy sunsets and romantic rising suns and making love in the clouds, if you'll only promise to take the chance with me. Veva, will you marry me?"

Stunned, a moment passed before I answered. I didn't feel the tears raining down my cheeks because the love inside me heated their chill away.

"Persuade me," I teased, curling up one side of my lips.

"Vee," his voice dropped as a hand swiped through his blond hair, but I stepped closer to him, forcing contact from my breasts against his chest. I slipped the ring on my third finger and lay my hand flat on his firm pecs.

"Vee?" he questioned, but his eyes didn't leave my answer.

"Yes, Sunshine. Yes, yes, yes. Now kiss me."

ACKNOWLEDGEMENTS

No imaginary tale is complete without the reality of those how help make it something magical. In many ways, it starts with you – the reader, willing to take a chance as an author writes in another genre, and than loves my characters as much as me. You have made my fantasy a reality each time you select one of my books, so thank you. A cairn to the moon to thank you.

Additional queens of making fantasy a reality include, Amy Queau of QDesign, for another enticing cover as well as Kiezha Smith Ferrell from Librum Artis Editoral Services. Another shout out from the mountain tops to Michelle Mankin, author, for her eye for magical twists and Karen Fischer for her eye at finding everything I miss.

A cairn to the sun and back for Sylvia Schneider, friend, PA, book-share extraordinaire. Thank you for taking this twist in my author journey, and making it an amazing climb.

To the hundreds of BLOGGERS who took a chance on *Hades*, and took another chance with *Solis*. Thank you for loving my fictional gods as much as me.

Finally, HUGE sunshine rays of credit to MD2, my fantasy girl, who talked me through several scenes and added a few details I hadn't even imagined: heart shaped rocks, rock climbing, photography, and strikes of lightning. You are quite the plotting partner! BUT love to all my rocks: Mr. Dunbar, MD1, MD2, JR, and A. Who knew a bike ride around Mackinaw Island could inspire quite a story?

elda lore

CONNECT WITH

elda lore

Stalk me: www.facebook.com/eldaloreauthor

Search me: www.eldalore.wordpress.com

Read me:

https://www.goodreads.com/author/show/15614540.Elda_Lore

Follow L.B. Dunbar

Search me: www.lbdunbar.com

Pin me: www.pinterest.com/lbdunbar/

Read me: www.goodreads.com/author/show/8195738.L_B_Dunbar

Follow me: https://app.mailerlite.com/webforms/landing/j7j2s0

Hang with me: www.facebook.com/groups/LovingLB/

Tweet me: @lbdunbarwrites

Insta- me: @lbdunbarwrites

WHAT'S NEXT FOR THE MODERN DESCENDANTS?
HEPH

Blurb:

Phyre has a haunting past. The girl without a last name and fire in her hands burns with a history of destruction to save herself. Solace is finally found in the cozy comfort of Hestia's Home, a place for women who need hiding. Just like her five surrogate sisters-in-solitude, Phyre yearns to extinguish memories and rekindle her spirit. Her plan blazes forward until *he* arrives.

Hephaestus Cronus considers himself an ugly man. A near-death accident left him disabled but not without heart. His gratitude lies with the protection of his foster mother, Hestia. Running from a failed relationship, Heph only desires the familiar fires of the hearth at her home. Burned from the heartache, Heph never expected to spark a new flame in the rose-bud-cherry-haired girl missing a name.

This modern tale of *Hephaestus*, the metal working god, rights the wrong of a crippled man failed at love. Here the flaming passion he deserved as an under-recognized god is written in a new fashion with the fiery spirit of a woman who ignites true love between these twin flames.

~~~

Heph (Chapter 1)

"What the hell?"

I spoke aloud to myself as the tire thud-thud-thud, forcing me to a halt on the two-tire path in the woods. It was hard enough to find the entrance to Hestia's property. Turn right at the large boulder, head south three miles. Search for the gravel road. At the curved tree, enter a barely visible trail leading into the thick forest.

The evening light of the northwest made it harder to see in the first place under thick coverage of the trees. A puncture to the tire would result in finding the rest of the drive-in darkness.

A puncture, as that's what had to have caused the flat.

The first arrow whizzed past the windshield at enough speed I questioned the object. I dismissed it for a low hanging twig. The second one was unmistakably recognized. The long shaft with a narrow head hit the driver side window and repelled backward. My 2016 Camaro was no match for a flimsy piece of wood, but when something hit the tire, I rethunk my thought.

I stalled the car and exit to find a thin shaft sticking out of my front tire. A tender tug with my thick hands and the stick came clean, but the damage was done.

"Kids," I cursed, believing wayward children scrambled through the forest as their playground. A sharp poke to my back made me think otherwise.

"Turn around. Slowly." The voice was distinctly female. Feminine and sweet, but sharp like the point of the arrowhead and quivering like the release from a bow. Whoever she was, she wanted to sound tough. Turning as she directed, I came chest to face with a minion of a woman. Her head hardly reached my shoulders, her frame almost as slim as the arrow pointed at my lower region.

"Don't move."

Considering where she had her weapon aimed, I didn't plan to cross her, although the differences in our stature was almost comical. I stood over six-four and twice her width, maybe three times. A large man by nature, my only curse was a limp from a false leg hidden under my jeans.

My hands lifted slowly in surrender and her eyes traveled the expanse of me. Under a cap that covered her hair and a scarf over her mouth, the next thing to pierce me were eyes the cobalt blue of rare sea glass. Smoky, but brilliant, my breath caught in my chest and I choked on the very air I needed to breathe. Her eyes opened wider as she stared aback at me and a moment passed where I felt as if she recognized me. My heart thumped in my chest, like an eager pet happy at the return of its master. In that thirty seconds, I sensed this woman owned me and I was thrilled to have her home. But her eyes squinted and the recognition passed.

"oh rrrr ew?" she muttered through the scarf. Still froze in the awkward position of her arrow at my zipper and my hands in the air, I didn't fully understand her. My hand lowered, thinking only to remove the scarf from her cheeks, but she flinched sharply to her right, and it gave me the entrance I needed. Snap went the arrow aimed at my dick. Holding up the two halves, sliced by my finger like a broken pencil, she blinked at me. My heart fell to my feet like Icarus falling from the sky. A thud even echoed back to me. I'd frightened her and it showed in those smoky blue eyes. Instantly, she straightened and took a large step back. Using the bow as her next weapon, she leveled the tip to my chest.

"Stay back," she snapped, removing the light lavendar colored yarn covering her mouth and revealing lips in a deep, magenta-purple color. My mouth watered, thirsty for a sample of such a rich color, curious if they taste as juicy as a plume.

"Look," I spoke, my gruff voice rippling around us in the enclosure of tightly packed trees. "You're the one who shot my car, so don't suddenly look afraid of me."

"I'm not frightened."

The harsh sound of her voice even excited me. *Stop it, Heph*, I cursed myself. *I wasn't interested*, I argued. I'd been burned enough by women. Even a quickie in the back of my car wouldn't satisfy me. I was here to forget women, not forge my way through another them. *Oh, the irony, of where I was headed.*

"Look, maybe I can help you. Are you lost?" I turned my head left and right, knowing where the narrow path in the growing evening could lead. No other inhabitants lived near Hestia's Home. That was its purpose: to be hidden and harbor those it housed.

"Do you know Hestia?" I questioned with a tilt of my head. It was the only answer to wandering the woods so close to her home.

"Do you?" she snarked, and I had to smile a little. She reminded me of my sister, Veva. Fiesty and terse, Veva could sting.

"I do."

"How?"

"How do you?"

Her eyes pinched again, the expression telling me, no, *warning me*, it was none of my business. Taking another quick scan of our surroundings, the darkness grew deeper under our covering. I wouldn't be able to see to fix the flat unless my huntress helped me.

"Maybe you could help me with the tire?"

"Maybe you could just follow me?"

My eyebrows rose in surprise until I realized she meant, I could lead, as her prisoner, and she poked my back with her damn bow. The crunch of heavy leaves and snapping twigs under foot gave warning to any wildlife. A giant and his capturing mouse proceeded through the jungle-green foliage of the wooded northwest. Although, not all the leaves remained green as fall settled in slowly and the colors changed subtly to yellows and oranges and browns.

If I stalled to look with my wandering gaze, a sharp pinch to my lower back reminded me of my warden. Unafraid of her, I dredged forward knowing I'd have to return in the morning to retrieve my vehicle and hope all the parts remained after my tyrant issued me over to Hestia.

In front of us, the house appeared as if from nowhere, plopped down in a large, circular ring of cypress and pine, serving as centurions of protection. The white house stood two stories high with a plethora of windows on each floor and a large covered porch on the front. A huge barn to the side, several feet from the home housed the small factory where Hestia taught her trade, and where I'd learned to control fire myself as a child. A billowy cloud of white puffed out the large chimney which meant the fires inside were hot. The house had the same effect only small plumes rose from the three stalks, smaller in wispy trails as they reached for the sky.

The air was chilly this far north and I was thankful for my lined flannel shirt and cap. The warmth inside the house before me enticed me further. A prodding at my back reminded me to keep walking. When I turned for the side door, I surprised the peanut behind me, but she'd soon learn I was as familiar with this home as her. Opening the door, helping myself to enter, I found Hestia in a position I often would: stoking the fires in an old-fashion hearth, complete with copper pots on one side and a large black kettle on the other. The stomp of my feet signaled for her attention and she turned quickly. Her blazing smile welcomed me, and for the first time in months, I relaxed.

"Hephaestus, my darling," she addressed me as she approached, her tiny frame opening her arms to take me in although I was twice the size of her. White-blonde-haired, and weathered skin, she wasn't old, although comparatively to her siblings, she was older. The oldest of the three daughters of Titus: Hestia, Hera and Demi, she lived hidden here versus the family farm in Nebraska.

"You're so late." She pulled back from our embrace, holding onto my thick forearms.

"I was detained." I looked over my shoulder and found I blocked the view of my captor. Stepping left, the minion stood exposed and a bit perplexed by the warm greeting.

"I seem to be captive to this one." I nodded in the direction of the muse still covered by scarf, hat and fingerless gloves. Removing those first, delicate fingers wiggled with relief. The ends of her nails were short with the look of grease under them. Next came her scarf, wound triple around her neck, revealing skin, pale as a china doll. Finally, her cap slipped off her head and a tumble of rose bud cherry colored hair fell past her shoulders. My heart leapt at the color that matched her lips and my chest rose and fell as I took in short breaths of air. Her blue eyes sparkled in the reflection of the flaming hearth, and I suddenly wanted to lay her down in front of it, mapping out each inch of white skin and slipping fingers through that vibrant color teeming off her head.

"I see you've met," Hestia said, breaking my stare. "She's a little spitfire, isn't she?" Hestia chuckled as her hand slipped over my elbow and her head rest on my bicep.

"A little spark of something," I replied roughly, my lips twisting at the strange attraction after my sudden break-up. It had to be lover's remorse. The need to replenish the loss. I shook off the burning sense of recognition again. The feeling that I knew her and she knew me.

"My name is Phyre. And I'm the whole flame."

CONTEMPORARY ROMANCES

L.B. Dunbar

The Sensations Collection
Small town, sweet and sexy stories of family and love.
Sound Advice
Taste Test
Fragrance Free
Touch Screen
Sight Words

The Legendary Rock Star Series
Rock star mayhem in the tradition of King Arthur.
A classic tale with a modern twist of romance and suspense.
The Legend of Arturo King
The Story of Lansing Lotte
The Quest of Perkins Vale
The Truth of Tristan Lyons
The Trials of Guinevere DeGrance

Paradise Stories
MMA chaos of biblical proportion between two brothers and
the fight for love.
Paradise Tempted: The Beginning
Paradise Fought: Abel
Paradise Found: Cain

Stand Alone
A rom-com story for the over forty.

The Sex Education of M.E.

ABOUT THE AUTHOR

Meet elda lore, the alter ego of the contemporary romance author, L.B. Dunbar. As elda lore, the classic world of mythology is captured and retold in modern tales, rekindling stories of endless love. Her enjoyment of fantastical romance began the moment the Beast gave Beauty a library. Continue to join her on her journey through paranormal romance where love is timeless.

20052435R00161

Printed in Great Britain
by Amazon